WHITE PETALS

For Charla
For the readers & dreamers
For Emmelines everywhere

Maria Grace was born in Caerphilly, South Wales. She studied Creative & Professional Writing at university, and graduated with first-class honours. She enjoys walks on the beach, afternoon tea, reading good books and watching bad telly. She now lives in Pontypridd with her daughter, her partner and her shih-tzu Bella. *White Petals* is her debut novel. *www.mariagrace.co.uk*

Publisher's note:
The illustrations at the beginning of each chapter are all drawn by artists aged 11-18 who entered our *White Petals* competition. The winners are listed at the back of the book. A huge thanks to them and to all the excellent young artists who entered the competition.

WHITE PETALS
MARIA GRACE

Firefly

First published in 2015
by Firefly Press
25 Gabalfa Road, Llandaff North, Cardiff, CF14 2JJ
www.fireflypress.co.uk
Text © Maria Grace 2015
Illustrations © the illustrators 2015

A CIP catalogue record of this book is available from the British Library.

Print ISBN 9781910080245
epub ISBN 9781910080252

This book was published with support from the Welsh Books Council.

The author wishes to acknowledge the award of a Writer's Bursary from
Literature Wales for the purpose of completing this novel.

Cover image and design by Isabella Ashford

Typeset by Elaine Sharples

Printed and bound by Bell and Bain Ltd, Glasgow

ONE

I walked up the garden path, stepping over the bits of broken glass on the ground. Like them, I felt shattered. But I realised I wasn't scared. When the thing you fear most happens, you can actually be quite brave. The worst was over now.

She was safe. We were safe. That's all that mattered. I could hear the sirens in the background, fading out into the crisp October air.

My social worker, Mel, put my bag in the boot of her car and turned to Grandma Coalman. 'Are you sure you're going to be OK, Anna?' she asked.

'I'll be *fine!*' Grandma Coalman answered in her too-high voice, which meant that she really wasn't fine at all. 'I would just like the girls to stay with me, that's all. I don't see what the problem is.'

'Anna, we've been over this,' said Mel. 'If it was my choice, of course I would let them stay with you. But it's not my choice. We have to stick to the rules, and the rules say that three people can't stay in a bungalow with just one bedroom.'

'*Balls* to the rules!' Grandma Coalman stamped her foot and tears started to roll down her face. 'They are *my* grandchildren! If their mother isn't going to be here, then I should be. If my son was alive, this wouldn't be happening. He was their father and he would never allow it.'

Mel put her arm around her, and for a second Grandma Coalman submitted to the comfort. 'I just feel so *helpless.*'

'I know,' Mel consoled. 'But I swear to you, Anna, I will make sure the girls are looked after. And I will bring them to see you every week, without fail. Just give them a couple of days to settle in, and then I'll get them to ring you, OK?'

Grandma Coalman nodded her head sadly.

I looked across at my little sister, Freya. Her foster family were helping to get her bags in their car, ready for the move. I knew that she would be OK because she'd been visiting Bill and Nora's house for a long time now – it was like a second home to her. She'd been there every month since my dad died. And she had Lola – Bill and Nora's foster-daughter – to play with while she was there.

I was too old to go with her, apparently. Respite was mainly for the little ones, Mel said. And besides, they only had enough room for two kids. I understood, but I wished they'd had room for me too.

'Em!' Freya ran to me, excited. 'Bill and Nora said that I can Skype you tomorrow! So it will be like we're in the same room!'

'Cool!' I did my best fake smile.

'How long will we be away from each other this time?' asked Freya. 'Will it be like a holiday again or will it be longer?'

'I think it's going to be a bit longer this time, Freya,' I replied. 'But that's OK, isn't it? It will give us a chance to get the house all fixed up for us to move back in again. Like new.'

'Yeah, I s'pose.' Freya looked at the mess around us. 'What happened, Em? You can tell me. I'm not a *baby*, you know!'

'I know that! You're almost as tall as me!' I measured her against me as I shrunk myself to be as short as I could get. She stood on tippy toes to reach my height.

'Well, tell me what happened then.'

'Oi!' Grandma Coalman saved me from the interrogation. '*I* told you what happened, Missy!'

Freya laughed out loud. '*Gram!* That story isn't true.'

'It is!' Grandma Coalman protested. 'Ask Bill and Nora. They'll tell you.'

3

Freya looked over to Bill and Nora, and they both nodded in solidarity with Grandma Coalman. Then she looked at Mel, who also nodded. Finally, she looked at me. I dutifully nodded to show that I too believed the story. Even though I knew it wasn't right.

Freya turned to Lola. 'Lola, do you want to know happened to my house?' she asked.

'What?' Lola looked wide-eyed at Freya, waiting for the revelation.

'Grandma Coalman says that a *lion* escaped from the zoo!' Freya snarled for dramatic effect as she spoke. 'My mum was cooking beef for dinner, and because the lion was hungry, it could smell the beef from fifty miles away! So it made its way here – to my house.'

Lola gasped in shock, loving the danger.

'And *then…*' Freya paced slowly, milking every word. 'The lion *JUMPED* through our front window, ran all the way through the house and broke *EVERYTHING!*'

'That must be why there's glass on your garden path!' shouted Lola, pointing at the broken glass from the front-room window.

Freya nodded proudly at the evidence. 'And then my mum *wrestled* the lion to the ground, like *Tarzan of the Jungle*. She managed to tie its paws together until the RSPCA came to take it back to the zoo, but now she's had to go into hospital for a little while so the doctors can make sure she's OK. It's not every day that you wrestle a *lion*, you know.'

'WOW!' Lola clapped her hands together for Freya's mum – the hero.

Freya beamed with pride.

Lola's eyebrows lowered as she thought carefully and asked, 'What happened to the beef?'

Freya and Lola both looked to Grandma Coalman.

'Unfortunately, your mum wasn't able to save the beef,' Grandma Coalman said in her most sympathetic voice. 'But it's OK. It's on offer for half-price at Tesco, so I'll just buy some more.'

Bill and Nora got the girls into the car and Freya wound down the back window to say goodbye. I leant inside and kissed her forehead, promising I'd speak to her on Skype the following day.

I waved to my little sister as the car drove away, and as it disappeared out of sight, the entire contents of my stomach felt like they were going to come out of my mouth or out of my backside. *That's* how stressed I was.

I walked around the side of the garden and closed my eyes.

When I opened them, I was faced again with the carnage my mother had so kindly left behind today. As I tried to absorb everything that had happened, I caught sight of our old rose bush in the corner of the garden, looking as pitiful as I felt.

It used to grow the most amazing white roses I had ever seen. But since Dad passed away, not even the tiniest buds had graced its branches. What was once a burst of white petals, was now just ... *thorns.*

'Right then, kiddo.' Mel opened her car door for me. 'Are you ready to go?'

I hugged Grandma Coalman tightly. I could feel her shaking a little, and guilt brought tears to my eyes.

Hold it together, Em. Don't let her see you upset. She has enough on her plate as it is.

'Ring me tomorrow, OK?' Grandma Coalman held my face and kissed my cheeks.

'OK,' I replied.

'I'm so sorry that I can't keep you both with me,' Grandma Coalman said, 'but Mel says that the bungalow isn't big enough, and that I'm too *old.*'

'Anna!' Mel shouted. 'I did not say that you were too old!'

'That's what you *meant.*' Grandma Coalman scowled at Mel.

'I'll be fine, Gram,' I reassured her. 'Honestly!'

I sat in the back seat of the car. Mel got in and switched on the engine.

Grandma Coalman started to wave goodbye, but something to the left caught her eye and her face hardened.

I turned to see what she was looking at.

Stood on the pavement were Zoe-two-doors-up and her niece, Stacey Lock.

They both smirked at me and Grandma Coalman. They were clearly pleased with the chaos of the afternoon. It would give them something to tweet about.

Great. The last thing I needed was Stacey Lock knowing my business. She wasn't exactly the kind of person who kept things to herself, and she always relished the chance to embarrass me in any way. The entire school would know by the time we went back after half-term.

A sudden sharp pain attacked my eardrum. I cupped my hand over my ear to try and soothe it, but it was really strong. A loud ringing noise filled my ear, high-pitched and piercing. It felt like someone was blowing a whistle inside my mind.

'Aaarghhh!'

Mel quickly stopped the engine. 'Em! Are you OK?'

Grandma Coalman yanked the car door open. 'What's the matter, love?'

'It's just my ear,' I replied, wincing. 'It'll ease up in a couple of minutes.'

Grandma Coalman looked over to where Zoe-two-doors-up and Stacey Lock were standing with smug grins on their faces. 'Funny how your ear plays up whenever that girl shows her face, isn't it?'

'It's probably just a coincidence,' said Mel, laughing.

Grandma Coalman and I exchanged a knowing glance. She raised her eyebrows. 'If there's anything that this family understands, it's that there is no such thing as coincidence.' She cast a watchful eye in Stacey Lock's direction. 'I think you might be allergic.'

'To what?' I asked.

'*Trouble.*' She closed the car door again and waved goodbye to us for the final time that day.

I looked through the back window and caught a glimpse of Stacey Lock laughing out loud as we drove away.

TWO

When we were nearly there, the car passed a little park with a rose bush by the gate. White roses blossomed eagerly, jumping out from the leaves to greet me.

I stared at them, hardly able to believe my eyes. I knew those beautiful white roses, though I hadn't seen them in a long time. The rose bush was *identical* to the one that used to grow in our garden.

Goosebumps covered my arms. A quick shiver went right through me – like walking into the sea and letting the water hit your belly for the first time. I folded my arms and wished I had my lucky cardigan to keep me warm. But it was in my suitcase, so I'd have to wait. I loved that cardigan. It was the first item of clothing I had bought completely by myself: a declaration of independence. I had bought it to go and see Ed Sheeran last year, and during the concert he reached out from the stage and actually *touched* my cardigan as he sang. I won't lie to you – I nearly fainted.

I snapped back into the moment. *Focus, Em.*

I didn't understand. How could I be seeing those roses again? Logically, it just wasn't possible. But this little voice inside me – so faint, I could feel it more than hear it – told me that they were the white roses from my garden.

What did it mean? Was I seeing things now? When Nana Rose was alive, she always said that I was like her and Mum. They both had second sight, in different ways. But I didn't have anything like that. So why did I feel there was something strange going on? I had a sense of déjà vu and it made me restless. The roses were some kind of sign. A sign of what, I wasn't sure.

My tummy flipped over and an involuntary burp came out of my mouth. I took a deep breath and tried to settle myself.

I leant my head against the car window and watched trickles of rain run down the glass. This day was a load of pants.

I wasn't sure how far away we were from my house, but I knew it was quite near because we'd only been half an hour on the M4.

'You OK back there?' Mel asked from the driver's seat.

'*Super,*' I replied sarcastically.

'I know you're angry,' said Mel. 'But you'll be OK, I promise. You're a tough cookie, Em. And this place isn't bad. It's actually quite nice. Definitely one of the more pleasant places I've worked with.'

Mel was alright … for a social worker. She always wore hippie clothes – which was shaming – but other than that, she was almost cool. But the woman never shut up! She was like a *machine*. I sometimes wondered which one of us was the social worker and which of us was the kid, because it was supposed to be me talking and her listening, but it was usually the other way round. I didn't mind, though. If she was bumping her gums about her boyfriend problems, instead of me bumping mine about my home problems, then that was fine by me. Well, when I say 'home problems', what I mean is *Mum*.

A regular contributor to the Child Protection Register, Mum wasn't just a risk to me and Freya, she was a risk to the whole of society.

There's me – fourteen years old, sitting in the back of my social worker's car, on my way to Alcatraz or somewhere.

My little sister Freya, was once again in temporary foster care at Bill and Nora's house.

Poor Grandma Coalman was probably having a double stroke all down her right side from the stress.

And where was Mum during all this?

The friggin' nuthouse, that's where.

11

Mel must have clocked my face in her mirror, because she asked me again if I was OK.

I said yes, and nodded. My voice sort of croaked a bit, like I was going to cry or something. I daren't look up, just in case I caught her eye, because then I probably would cry and I'd feel stupid.

So I just kept my eyes on the window as we drove up the hill and turned into the car park of the children's home.

THREE

The home was a bit of a dump. It had a stale feel to it, like a dirty office building. The same carpet ran all the way through. Every wall was cream – magnolia, Mum would say – but with dirty handprints and a yellow tinge. Like spit.

The place just *smacked* of disadvantage.

Mel went into some kind of office with a woman called Sue, who looked about sixty with short grey hair. They said they had 'some things to go over'. I reckoned that whatever they had to 'go over' probably involved me, so why was I not invited into the office too? Adults could be real plebs when they wanted to be.

I sat at a table in the dining area, with my suitcase next to me, gripping it like it was the only thing I owned. Well, it was, I suppose. At least while I was staying here anyway.

I had a room of my own at home, with a laptop and a telly. I had a mini chandelier in the centre of my ceiling, with little crystals that cast rainbow shadows over my bedroom walls. The colours could cheer you up even on the most rubbish of days. But for now, all that was mine lay inside my suitcase, and my white knuckles showed how much I treasured it.

Oh, no. Did I remember to pack my lucky cardigan? Yes... Yes, I *definitely* packed it.

The place wasn't like I imagined a children's home to be. I'd pictured hundreds of wild kids running around, screaming and smoking joints. But in real life, it was very quiet. I wondered where everyone was.

When Mel and Sue came out of the office, Sue told me that the other kids had been on a camping trip and were due back that evening. She offered to show me to my room, so we all walked through the corridors and up the stairs to a spacious room with two single beds. One of the beds had a mini-skirt and a hot-water bottle on it, so it obviously belonged to someone else.

'That's Karra's bed,' said Sue. She adjusted Karra's bedcovers to tidy them. 'You'll be sharing a room with her. She's got a mouth like a sewer, but a heart of gold!'

I smiled politely as Sue crossed the room to the second bed and said, 'And this bed here is yours.' She fussed with my bedcovers the same way that she'd fussed with Karra's, and the fairness of it brought a lump of relief to my throat.

Sue left the room to go back downstairs. I put my case on the bed and sighed.

I was in a children's home.

How did this happen?

Mel looked around the room and raised her eyebrows enthusiastically. 'Oooh! This is nice!' She tried to make light of the situation, but I could spot a lie a mile away, and she knew it.

'Are you *serious*?' I stared at her for a second, an unexpected wave of anger surging through me. You don't bring someone to a place like this when they haven't even done anything wrong, and then have the cheek to pretend it's *nice*.

Degrading, I think it's called. My best friend Megan threw that word around a lot in school. The three words she'd used the most this term were 'degrading', 'empowered' and 'dichotomy'. She was a feminist, see.

Mel's smile quickly faded and she shuffled awkwardly from foot to foot. I felt guilty because I knew that it wasn't Mel's fault that I was here, but pride was a hard pie to swallow and I couldn't bring myself to apologise for snapping.

We went back downstairs and Sue moved to the kitchen so I could have ten minutes with Mel before we said goodbye to each other.

Mel put on her coat on and turned to face me. 'How are you doing, Em?'

'I'm OK,' I replied. I felt really bad for giving her the evil eye upstairs and I wanted to say sorry, but I didn't have the guts. Something about the way she looked at me made me choke up a bit, and for the first time that day, I really felt like crying.

'Come here.' She opened her arms to hug me. 'Bring it in!'

I buried my head in her coat. 'I'm sorry for being nasty to you,' I said. 'I didn't mean it.'

'There's no need to apologise,' she consoled. 'I wasn't offended. I understand that you're not really angry at me, you're angry at the *situation*. It's been an emotional day for you. Under the circumstances, I think you've coped with everything very well.'

Sue called from the serving hatch in the kitchen. 'Emmeline, I'm just making you a bit of food. Mel says that you haven't had your tea. Are you OK with fish fingers?'

'Yes, thank you!' I called back.

'I'll get out of your way and leave you to settle in,' said Mel. She picked up her bag, gave me a kiss on the cheek and shouted goodbye to Sue as she left.

I watched her from the window. She got in her car and waved to me as she pulled off. Once I was sure Sue was in the kitchen, I took one deep breath to stop me from crying, and this desperate little sound came out – from somewhere inside me, where I was just a tiny version of myself, invisible.

Sue called me over for my tea. I pulled myself together, walked to the table and sat quietly to eat.

She started chatting to me as I chewed some chips. She said that she knew it must be difficult for me, being in a strange place, with strange people, but if I wanted to talk to her or anyone else, then there was always a member of staff available. She told me that I could call her *Auntie Sue*. That's what all the kids called her, apparently.

Freaks.

I called my Auntie Sally 'Auntie Sally' because, even though she's not actually related to me, she's known me since I was little. She used to babysit me and my sister. Everyone has some kind of auntie or uncle who's not really an auntie or an uncle. But this wasn't like that. I didn't even know this woman. Not being funny or anything, the lady seemed alright, but I really wasn't comfortable calling her *Auntie Sue*. But I suppose if everyone else called her that, then I'd better get used to it.

I tried to relax and eat my fish fingers.

I could hear her speaking on the phone in the office.

'Emmeline Rose,' she said to the person on the other end. 'No, not Emily; Emme*line*. No, you're saying it *wrong*, Jim, you stupid man! It's Em-eh-*leeeen*.'

I laughed at the defensive rise in her voice, and even though I didn't really mind when people got my name wrong, I was grateful that she cared enough to correct the person on the phone. It reminded me of something a crazy aunt would do, and when I realised this, I decided that it wasn't so bad if I had to call her Auntie Sue.

I finished my food and put the empty plate in the kitchen, unsure whether I should wash it or not. That's what I would usually do at home, but I wasn't in my own home now, was I? I decided to swill it under the taps and leave it on the side by the dishwasher. I left the kitchen and took myself back into the living area, pacing back and forth nervously.

I sat on the peachy-coloured sofa, watching telly on the edge of my seat. Sue – sorry, *Auntie* Sue – must be a fan of baking programmes, because she was watching a marathon of them.

'I love a bit of Victoria Sponge!' Auntie Sue's voice came back into the room. 'You should have seen the one they made earlier. *Gooorgeous,* it was!'

I tried to watch the programme with her, but I couldn't concentrate. Imagine going to visit someone's house, and you've never met them before in your life. You feel like you have to be on your absolute best behaviour or when you get home, your mum will ground you for a *month.* Then take that feeling, multiply it by about twenty-seven, and you're somewhere close to how I felt, sitting on that sofa. The only difference was that I had no mother there to ground me.

Every now and again, my eyes would flicker at the window – the tiniest sound would send my guts into overdrive.

I'd never met anyone that lived in a children's home before. What if I didn't like them? What if they didn't like me? I hated all this. I didn't want to meet all these new people. I just wanted to go home to my own room and forget that any of this ever happened.

The waiting was the worst. Every time a car went past the place, my heart would go like the clappers.

'Are you OK, Emmeline?' asked Auntie Sue.

I nodded, avoiding eye contact. I was frightened that even a grain of sympathy would break the dam. I felt so uncomfortable. Initially, I'd been glad that none of the other kids were there, but now I felt sick with nerves. I just wanted them to arrive so I could get it over and done with.

I could feel her looking at me. I shifted awkwardly on the sofa. She reached her arm across and just patted my shoulder to comfort me.

'It's just so *quiet*,' I said.

Auntie Sue laughed. 'Not for long, love. I'd make the most of it if I were you.'

As if on cue, a conked-out old minibus drove slowly into the street and pulled into the car park.

'Here they come!' Auntie Sue got up from her seat and winked at me. 'Brace yourself, kiddo!'

FOUR

What did she mean, brace myself? Now I really felt sick.

I kept still on the sofa, watching through the window from a stomach-churning distance. Even from here I could hear the minibus was filled with noise. I could see bodies jumping over the seats and pushing each other around.

'TYLER!' A giant Santa-man stepped out of the minibus. 'I'm telling you now, LEAVE IT THERE! Stop arguing with me and shut *up*!'

'But, Jim!' A little boy tumbled out of the bus after him. 'He's lying! I didn't do anything!'

I watched them walk down the path to the front door. The man was carrying a fishing rod and wearing a poncho, and the little boy had blond hair and a fishing net. He looked about seven.

The others all pushed through the corridors and started dumping their bags on the floor and arguing with each other. There was a bit of a scrap as they piled on the sofas, fighting over the remote control.

The little boy looked at me. 'Who's the girl?' he asked, turning to the staff.

'I don't know, Tyler,' replied Auntie Sue. 'I asked what her name was, but it seems she's an elective mute, because she obviously can't speak for herself, can she?' She rolled her eyes to signal for someone to talk to me.

'What's your name, girl?' Tyler stood right in my face, eyes wide with curiosity. I could smell chocolate on him.

'Emmeline,' I answered.

'Emma*what*?'

'*Emmeline*.' I was used to this. 'Like Emily, but with an 'n' at the end ... Emmeleeen.'

He looked at me blankly, with his mouth slightly open.

I picked at the skin around my fingernails. 'Just call me Em.'

'Emily...' he said. 'Em ... Emily with an N ... Emma*leeeeeen*...' He dismissed me with a wave of his hand. 'I can't be doing with all that. I'm confused now.'

The giant man laughed out loud. 'HA! HA! HAAAAA!' He threw his head back and roared. '*Buuuriful!* He's a *buuuriful* boy, aren't you?' He ruffled Tyler's blond hair. 'Don't mind our Tyler. He's a bit hyper today. We popped into Big Tesco on the way back. He gets excited when we go in there, because of all the stuff.'

'Oh, Jim…' Auntie Sue looked sternly at the man. 'Not *again*.'

He looked guilty and apologised under his breath.

'You *know* we can't take him to Big Tesco!' Auntie Sue rubbed her forehead with the stress, and then explained to me. 'Tyler can't do Big Tesco,' she said. 'It sends him demented.'

I tried to look like I understood what she was talking about.

Auntie Sue clapped her hands together to get everyone's attention. 'EVERYONE!' she shouted, but nobody listened.

'YOU LOT!' she shouted louder, but still no one took any notice.

She was just about to shout for a third time, when the giant man put his thumb and middle finger together in a circle, put them in his mouth and let out an almighty whistle.

Everybody stopped and stood to attention.

'Thanks, Jim.' Auntie Sue smiled at the man. 'Everyone, I want to introduce the newest member of the household.' Auntie Sue gestured to me. 'This is Emmeline Rose, and she will be staying with us for a little while.'

'Alright?' A boy with a baseball cap nodded at me. He was about sixteen years old and had his tracksuit bottoms tucked into his socks.

'Alright,' I replied, and nodded back.

23

'My name's Beano.' He smiled. 'Pleased to meet your acquaintance.'

'Stop flirting, Beano.' A red-headed girl frowned at him from across the room.

'Jealous?' Beano smirked at the girl and winked mischievously.

'Oh, get over yourself, will you?' The girl rolled her eyes and walked over to me.

My mouth went a little dry.

'Take no notice of that dickhead.' She nodded her head in Beano's direction. 'I'm Karra, by the way.'

Before I had the chance to reply, a muddy sock hit the back of her head. She started freaking out and ran after Beano, vowing to get her revenge.

There were some mumbles of acknowledgement from the others and I smiled politely at them. Everyone carried on with what they were doing and I sat on the sofa, digesting it all.

The giant man came over and reached out his hand for me to shake. 'Hello, Emmeline. My name is Jimmy. You can call me Big Jim. Everybody else does. It's a pleasure to meet you, love.'

I shook his hand easily, already fond of the Big Friendly Giant. He excused himself, saying he had some reports to fill out in the office, so he would see me later.

'How did the fishing trip go?' Auntie Sue walked with him towards the office. 'Did you catch many fish?'

'I won't lie to you, Sue. It didn't go well.' Big Jim looked solemn. 'I can't help but feel that if I had a longer, stiffer rod, I'd be a better fisherman.'

'Yes,' Auntie Sue smirked. 'That's what they all say.'

'What do you mean?' Big Jim looked at her, confused.

'Never mind,' she said, and chuckled to herself.

I watched the other kids – my brain processing their looks, voices, and personalities. And I felt, as I watched these strangers, as if I was a character from a very different sort of book to them. There was something untamed and rugged about them – something free. I knew that I probably seemed polished and temperate by comparison.

There was a short, cute girl called Charlie. She looked younger than the other girls – maybe twelve years old?

A girl called Quinn wore a lot of lipgloss and kept blowing bubbles with her chewing gum. It looked like strawberry flavour.

And then there was a stocky girl called Bett, who I guessed had a learning disability of some sort, but I wasn't sure what. Bett wore a bright orange tracksuit with neon yellow trainers, and her hair was bunched up in a messy ponytail. She looked like she could gladly take on all the Six Nations rugby teams at once and teach them a lesson. She called everyone by their full name – first *and* surname. She was friendly, but clearly temperamental. Auntie Sue told me that Bett's key worker – the woman who mainly looked after her in the home – was called Gladys Friday.

This was important for me to know, because Gladys Friday must *always* be referred to by her full and proper name. Nobody was allowed to address the woman by only her first name because if you did, then Bett, who had a real disdain for sloppiness, would go ab-so-lutely *mental*.

I was trying to retain all this information to help get me through the next few hours. I knew that if I wanted to survive, I would need to stay fit and alert.

'*You.*' Karra acknowledged me again. She had a real edge to her, but I felt I could sense loyalty in her brilliant blue eyes. 'Auntie Sue says that you're sharing a room with me. You best not have sat on my bed.'

I shook my head and smiled slightly, desperate not to show any fear – I knew if I did, she'd have me for breakfast. She held my gaze for just a second longer than was comfortable. When she was satisfied I wasn't quite prey, but sure that I was no match for her either, she said, 'Well, come on then. Are you coming upstairs or what?'

We made our way through the living room and as I followed her, I threw up a little bit in my mouth. You know, the mini-sick? I think it was nerves. I could feel it swishing around the back of my throat, hot and full of acid.

When we reached the corridor, I heard Tyler shouting from the living room. 'Emmeleeeen!' he called after me.

I turned around and reluctantly swallowed the sick.

He looked over the sofa and grinned at me. 'Toast and tea is at nine. I'll save you a seat.'

FIVE

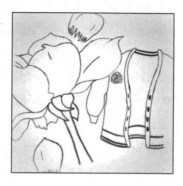

I hadn't been upstairs ten minutes before the clothes raid began.

Two girls stood at the end of my bed, rummaging through my suitcase like they were in a Top Shop sale.

'*Oh-my-life!* Can I borrow this?' Quinn held up a blue cardigan with a white velvet rose on the front. My lucky cardigan! I knew I'd packed it!

She folded it over her arm and sprayed my perfume on her neck.

'Bugger off!' Karra shouted, and I winced as she grabbed the cardigan. 'I want that to go with my skinny jeans when we meet the boys tonight! There's another one there – have that one instead.'

Quinn huffed and carried on searching through my things for something else she fancied wearing. They both spotted my pink top at the same time, and Quinn seized it before Karra had a chance.

'*Give it.*' Karra gave Quinn a look of warning.

'I'll swap you for that blue cardigan.' Quinn held the top out of Karra's reach.

'Deal!' The two girls exchanged garments.

Charlie, the little blonde girl, sat quietly on the edge of my bed, smiling at me sympathetically.

I wanted to tell them to leave off my stuff, but I didn't have the guts. I watched as they tackled each other over my lucky cardigan, and my heart skipped a beat every time it was thrown or grabbed. The white rose was so delicate, and it had little specks of glitter on it. It was my favourite cardigan in the world. Ed Sheeran had *touched* that cardigan, for goodness sakes! I washed it in the bath because I was too frightened to let it go in the washing machine, in case it got ruined.

'Quinn!' Karra's voice was full of command. 'Get off! You're like a scavenger. Give the girl some space. We don't want to make a bad impression on her first day here.'

All four girls walked to the opposite side of the room, sat on Karra's bed and looked at me as if they were interviewing me for a job.

'So, what are you here for, Em?' asked Karra.

'Just some trouble with my mum,' I answered.

'Do you mean your *mam*?' asked Quinn.

"That's what I said,' I replied.

'No, you didn't.' Quinn looked at me as if I was stupid. 'You said, your *mum*.'

'What's the difference?' I asked.

'People from England say *Mum*,' answered Karra. 'And people from Wales say *Mam*. It's a fact.'

'I don't think that's an *actual* fact,' I said.

'Yes, it is,' Karra declared. 'Check it on Google, if you don't believe me. I'm not thick, you know!'

I coughed nervously.

'So, you're having problems with your mam, are you?' Little Charlie asked, picking up the conversation again.

'Yes.' I nodded.

'*Ahhh*,' they all empathised in unison.

Quinn looked me straight in the face and asked, 'Is she a junkie?'

'Nooo!' I answered, caught off guard.

'Is she a boozer?' she pushed further.

'No.' I could only remember a few times in my life that my mum had properly been drunk.

'A slag?'

'No.'

'She beating you up?' Quinn looked hopeful.

I shook my head.

'Well, what the *Donald Duck* are you here for then?' She stood up, miffed at the insufficient amount of gossip.

'Her old man's a wife beater, probably,' said Karra. 'Given your old girl a pasting, has he? *Typical*, that is.'

'My dad would never do that to anyone,' I answered sharply. 'He's a good dad… *Was* a good dad. Not now – he's dead now. But when he wasn't dead, he was a good dad.'

Discomfort rose between us. I had to break the uneasy silence. 'I mean, he's a crap one now, of course. He's never here for a start.' The bad joke instantly made me feel guilty, but the girls laughed.

'So why are you here then?' Quinn asked. 'You must be here for *something*. They don't just chuck random kids into children's homes, you know. My mother was smacking up about five times a day before they brought me here.'

I stared at her, shocked. Was she telling the truth? Or joking?

'Well,' she said, 'it was probably more than that really, but I'm not allowed to see my files until I'm eighteen. So I don't really know how bad she was. But you know what I mean – they don't just bring you here for nothing.'

'Yeah,' Karra agreed with her. 'Specially not now, what with the depression and everything; they can't afford it.'

'The recession,' the girls corrected Karra, and they rolled their eyes like this was an everyday thing.

'Worrevs,' Karra said. 'You know what I mean, you bunch of tits.'

'Oi! Now that's enough, Karra-Jayne-Lewis,' Bett told her off. 'I've heard enough swearing from you today, thank you very much. I won't have it. There's no need. And if Emmeline Rose doesn't want to talk about why she's here, then that's up to her.'

Quinn frowned at Bett. 'Oh, shut up, Betty Morris. Nobody asked you.'

'No! *You* shut up, Quinn Davies.' Bett folded her arms. 'She's not trying to bully you into telling her *your* life story, is she? Because it's private, see. I mean, you wouldn't like it if she knew that your mother was a slag, would you, Quinn Davies?'

Karra snorted under her nose.

Little Charlie moved to the top of the bed where she was safe as she tried not to laugh.

Quinn's mouth fell open. '*What* did you just say?' She narrowed her eyes at Bett.

Karra had thrown herself backwards on the bed by this point, laughing hysterically. Little Charlie had buried her face in the pillow.

'I *said…*' Bett moved closer to Quinn so they were stood face to face as she spoke. 'Your. Mother.' She emphasised the words. 'Is. A. Slag.'

'You best take that back, Betty Morris,' Quinn threatened, and even I was trying to hide my smile by now.

They glared at each other.

Karra laughed out loud. 'Girls! Come on! We've got a visitor. Behave yourselves. Can't you two just get along for one day?'

An hour later, the girls were lying around, listening to music and painting their toenails with my new cherry-red polish. They'd introduced themselves properly, talking over each other as they defined themselves by three different categories: what their criminal convictions were, how many boys they'd boffed, and what they wanted to be when they grew up.

Karra was sixteen years old, had one ASBO and one GBH charge. That's Grievous Bodily Harm, she said. I didn't know this. The closest I'd been to a police encounter was watching *CSI* on a Tuesday night.

She'd boffed two boys and had one pregnancy scare, but then she'd had the implant afterwards so it didn't matter now, apparently. She wanted to be a teacher but couldn't because of the ASBO, so was thinking of going to college to be a beautician instead. The other girls said this was a shame because they all agreed that it would be lush to have a teacher like Karra – you'd be able to do whatever you wanted in class!

Quinn was fifteen, and she had one record of TWOC – Taking Without Owner's Consent. She'd stolen Auntie Sue's car the year before, after an argument with Bett. She said she just needed to get away for a bit, so she drove to Carmarthen for the day and ate chips on the beach at

Llansteffan. The police picked her up, halfway down the M4 on the way back to the children's home. Although she was gutted to be arrested, she was flattered that the police thought she was a very conscientious driver, considering she'd never had any driving lessons. She was quite proud that she was the only person in the home to be an official *twocker*, which was the police's term for car thieves. Because there was no damage to the car, she'd got off with a community service order, cleaning up dog mess in the park. Quinn said it wasn't so bad in the end – she'd met a nice boy there, and he now bought her curry and chips from the chip shop down the road every Friday night.

She eventually wanted to be a nurse, and she had also boffed two boys, but made them both wait six weeks on account of not wanting to turn out a slag like her mother.

Little Charlie didn't have any criminal convictions, and she hadn't boffed any boys because she had only just turned thirteen and wasn't fussed by neither men nor trouble. The Mormons from the church down the road had recently convinced her to join them every Sunday, and even though she wasn't fussed by them either, she still went for the free tea and biscuits. She wanted to be a social worker when she grew up, because she said she wanted to show the social workers what they were all doing wrong.

And then there was Bett. The eldest of them all at almost seventeen years old, she hadn't boffed any boys, and she'd had one charge of ABH – Actual Bodily Harm. But Quinn had later dropped the charges when she'd had a chance to calm down. When she was older, Bett wanted to be a librarian or a bodyguard for her key worker, Gladys Friday.

I watched Bett trying to paint her right toes with her left hand, frowning because she couldn't reach. Quinn leant over, took the brush out of Bett's hand and painted the last two toenails for her.

I got up from the bed and looked around the room. It wasn't so bad, really. I wondered if the staff would let me paint it. Or maybe I could put some posters up. I walked over to the window. In the right-hand corner of the window, on the outside, was a spider's web. No spider, just the web. I remembered someone telling me ages ago that spider's webs were a good omen, and even though I hated spiders, I hoped this was true.

I looked a bit further into the distance and I could see the park at the bottom of the hill. The rose bush stood tall, and the white roses shone like lucky pennies in the sunlight.

In the background, Quinn and Karra started to argue over my lucky cardigan again. I could hear them, but I was mesmerised by the white petals calling me from the park. Something about them brought real comfort to me.

'EM!' Karra's voice made me jump.

I turned around quickly.

'Do you want to come out with us tonight?' Karra asked.

I was being invited out with them – that meant they must like me. But it had been such a long day and I was completely exhausted.

'No, thanks.' I shook my head. 'I'm shattered. I think I'll stay here to have a bath and unpack properly.'

'Suit yourself,' she replied.

Off they went, calling each other names as they quarrelled their way out of the room.

'Girls, can you do me a favour, please?' I called. All four of them turned round to look at me. I flushed with embarrassment. 'Can you just make sure that you don't rip the cardigan? It's my favourite.'

I knew it was childish, but I'd loved that cardigan since the first day I saw it, and I'd saved my pocket money for, like, a month to buy it. The fact that Ed Sheeran had touched it was just a bonus.

They all looked at me like I was off my tree. To them, it was just a cardigan. I caught Quinn's eye, and I felt myself go even redder because I knew I was blushing.

I looked away, trying to stay cool.

'*Come on*, Quinn!' shouted Karra. 'I haven't got all day. Let's go!'

Quinn looked a little guilty, taking the cardigan with her, as they rushed from the room to get ready.

When they left, I breathed in the foreignness of everything. The space was vast, and I felt insignificant standing in the middle of it. A small shiver ran through me, and I felt cold and alone. I desperately wanted my lucky cardigan, not just to keep me warm, but to keep me calm. It was a bit like a security blanket, and being without it was overwhelming.

I sat on my bed for a few minutes and blew out hot air to stop my eyes stinging. Why was I getting so upset over a stupid flipping cardigan? I knew I was being irrational, but I just couldn't help it. It was *my* cardigan; my lucky cardigan that I had bought completely by myself. *Ed Sheeran* had touched it!

Just then, as my cheeks puffed out like a teary blowfish, Quinn walked back in.

I froze.

She looked at me.

I tried to smile, but I could feel my lip wobbling as I struggled to stop the tears running down my face. I probably looked a right knob.

Without saying a word, she nodded to me and folded my lucky blue cardigan with the white velvet rose on. She laid it delicately on the edge of my bed, and left the room.

SIX

It was nine o'clock. I'd unpacked my case properly and laid out my half of the room as comfortably as I could, trying to make it a bit more like home.

In the bath, I'd forced myself to try and forget about the day; let it all sink down the plughole with some raspberry bubbles that Auntie Sue had given me.

I remembered Tyler telling me that toast and tea was at nine, so I put on my pyjamas and went downstairs.

As promised, Tyler was sitting there with an empty seat next to him. There was an A4 piece of paper folded in half on top of the table, with 'REZERVD' written on it in black marker. He smiled widely and patted the empty seat for me to sit down.

In the middle of the table was a big tray with a mountain of toast stacked up on it.

Karra and Quinn had gone out, so there were just five kids for supper, and three members of staff – Auntie Sue, Big Jim and a short lady with brown hair and a friendly face. She smiled and came over to greet me.

'I'm glad it's Friday!' she declared. 'And you?'

I didn't really know how to respond. I mean, it had been a pretty rough day, but I suppose that Friday was usually a good day. And the woman seemed enthusiastic about the weekend, so I didn't want to dampen her spirits.

'*Yes…*' I replied a little warily. 'Yes, I'm glad it's Friday, too. It's nice to have the weekend to chill out.'

She laughed heartily and gave me a hug. 'I like your sense of humour, kid! But seriously, what's your name?'

Bett was sitting at the table. She started chuckling through a mouthful of toast. 'No, Emmeline Rose! She's telling you her name – Gladys Friday!'

Oh. Nice one, Em. *Fool.*

'Gladys Friday, this is the new girl, Emmeline Rose.' Bett licked some butter off her thumb as she continued the introduction. 'Emmeline Rose, this here is Gladys Friday,' she said, beaming with pride. 'Gladys Friday is *my* key worker.'

'It's lovely to meet you,' I said and smiled at her.

I reached across for a piece of toast and Beano looked at my pyjamas, amused.

'Nice PJs.' He smirked.

'*I* think they're nice.' Tyler shrugged.

'Yeah, but they're not exactly *sexy*, are they?' Beano laughed, nodding at the little sheep on them.

'*I* think they're sexy,' Tyler said, with strawberry jam dripping down his chin.

'Thank you, Tyler.' I smiled at him, and then gave Beano the evil eye.

'So what's a girl like you doing in a place like this?' Beano asked.

'What do you mean, *a girl like me*?' I frowned.

'Well, you're not like the other girls here, are you?' he explained. 'You're posh, you are. You shouldn't be here – you make the place look messy.'

I felt the colour rising in my cheeks.

'Don't you listen to him, Emmeline,' said Gladys Friday. 'He's just annoyed because he's skint and single. He wanted to go out with Karra and Quinn earlier, but they told him to get lost. He's got a little soft spot for our Karra, haven't you, Beano?'

They all laughed and Big Jim gave Beano a playful dig in the ribs.

After supper, I sat in the reading corner, flicking through a magazine and listening to the staff gossip about last week's lottery winners, and what they were going to spend their own winnings on when they eventually won the syndicate.

I had made a disastrous error during supper, so I thought it best to keep a low profile until Bett had forgiven me.

I had called Gladys Friday by her first name only. The whole room fell silent and I stopped mid-chew. Bett, sitting opposite, looked at me like I'd just asked her to drink my dirty bathwater. I quickly apologised and promised to address Gladys Friday properly from now on. It had been half an hour ago, so I hoped that Bett was now in a better mood.

I walked over to the peachy-coloured sofa.

Bett studied my face. 'Are you sorry, Emmeline Rose?'

'I am, yes,' I apologised.

'Well, I suppose you're still getting used to everyone's names,' Bett reasoned. 'But don't let it happen again, OK? Gladys Friday doesn't like to be called … *Gladys*.' She winced as she said it. 'Her *real* name is Gladys Friday!'

'I understand,' I replied. 'I'll be more careful in future.'

This seemed to be sufficient enough, so Bett invited me to watch a quiz show with her, Little Charlie and Beano. Tyler sat on the floor, playing *Guess Who* by himself.

Beano was trying to show off by answering the quiz questions, but he was being brutally beaten by Bett. I soon got into the competition, trying to answer as many of the questions as I could to gain extra points for the girls. But Beano was too quick for me. He'd answered most of the questions before they'd even been read out.

The commercial break came, and I was glad of the opportunity to rest my brain for three minutes.

'OK, Posh?' Beano smirked at me.

'Why do you keep calling me that?' I was annoyed. 'What makes me *posh*?'

'Well, you got, like, shiny hair and stuff, haven't you?' he pointed out. 'And you don't smoke or nothing, either.'

'Just because I don't smoke doesn't mean that I'm *posh*. It just means I don't smoke, that's all,' I said. 'But thank you for the hair compliment.'

'I knew it!' He grinned. 'I saw you giving me the glad-eye earlier. You *fancy* me, don't you?'

Auntie Sue shouted over. 'Beano! Shut up, will you? It's bad enough when you're drooling over Karra every five minutes, without you sexually harassing Emmeline, too.'

'Harassing!' Beano shrieked. 'I think you'll find it's the other way round, thank you very much. Karra can't get enough of me. She's *gagging* for it, Auntie Sue. She's just playing hard to get!'

'Of course she is, Beano.' Auntie Sue smiled sarcastically. 'And I suppose you don't fancy Karra at all.'

'Yeah, course I do,' Beano said. 'I'd smash the pasty off her. But what I'm saying is that she wants to smash me, too. She's just stubborn, that's all. You know what they say about ginger girls…'

'What's that?' Auntie Sue asked.

'Redheads burn the hottest.' He winked and Auntie Sue rolled her eyes.

'HA! HA! HAAAA!' Big Jim laughed loudly. 'Oh, Beano! You are shameless! You just say what you want – please or offend. It's a *buuuriful* thing!'

Auntie Sue and Gladys Friday glared at Big Jim, and he laughed even more. 'HA! HA! HAAA!' He threw his head back. 'At least the boy is honest!'

The commercial break ended and the battle continued. We all fought to get the answers right. If it wasn't for Bett's ridiculously accurate general knowledge, Beano would have really stumped us. How did he know all the answers? I didn't get it. He didn't seem that clever.

The staff were sitting around the table, watching us and sipping their tea.

The show was just about to finish, and the host asked the final two questions. *'What is the most common element on Earth?'* he said in his game-show voice. The audience was quiet, tense.

'I know this! I know this!' Little Charlie shouted as she shot her hand up to answer. 'I think it might be salt or something... Yes! Yes, it's salt. SALT!'

'Shut it, Charlie!' Beano snapped.

'What's the matter, Beano?' Gladys Friday called to him from across the room. 'Don't you know the answer to this one?'

'Stay out of it, WOMAN!' Beano shouted, chuckling at something I didn't know.

Gladys Friday looked particularly pleased with herself. 'Why so touchy, Beano?' she asked. 'Does your infinite wisdom not know the answer to these last couple of questions?' She grinned. 'Could it be that when you watched this show last night, you missed the final few minutes because you were too busy peeing all over the toilet seat, as usual?'

What did she mean? Had he already watched the show? But that meant...

Beano covered his face to hide his smirk.

He was cheating all along!

'It's Hydrogen,' Bett said matter-of-factly. 'The most common element on Earth is Hydrogen.'

'And the answer is C – HYDROGEN,' the host declared.

Whoops and cheers came from the staff and Bett grinned proudly while Little Charlie folded her arms in a sulk.

I couldn't help but giggle as everyone teased Beano.

'I don't know what you're laughing at, Posh,' he said. 'You didn't answer the question, she did.'

'SHE is the cat's mother,' Gladys Friday stated, in the way that only women of a certain age do.

'Excuse me, Beano Pritchard,' Bett added, 'it doesn't matter who answered the question. Fact is, the girls got it right. And if you're so concerned about beating Emmeline

Rose, then make it final on the next question: you against her. The loser makes tea for everyone.'

'OK, Posh!' Beano winked at me. 'Prepare to take your little sheep pyjamas to the kitchen and make eight cups of tea, because you-are-going-*DOWN*.'

I had to focus.

'Which nation gave women the right to vote first?' the TV host called out.

Bett was sitting on her hands with her mouth squeezed together like she was going to burst.

'Britain!' Beano shouted triumphantly. 'Screw you, Posh!'

'New Zealand,' I answered, hoping that I was right. I remembered learning this in school.

The light showed up on the TV screen, highlighting the answer.

'NEW ZEALAND is the correct answer!' the host announced.

A collective roar of laughter filled the room.

'Screw YOU, Beano Pritchard! Screw YOU!' Bett jumped up and down with delight, pointing at Beano.

He laughed and high-fived Bett. 'Well played, girls.' He shrugged in defeat. 'You win. I lose.'

'And how do those words taste, coming out of your mouth, Beano?' Gladys Friday teased.

'Like vinegar,' said Beano.

'That's funny,' she replied. 'Because I thought they tasted like eight cups of tea.'

SEVEN

At bedtime, the room seemed oddly quiet without the girls there. It made me think of my sister, because this was how our house felt every time she was away at Bill and Nora's.

I tried to sleep, but it was weird being in a new room. I kept expecting Mum to walk in, complaining that she couldn't sleep and asking if I would make her some hot chocolate.

You know how you spend all your life wanting to get away from your parents, because you feel like you're in jail? Well, here it was: *freedom*.

I had no idea how freedom felt. I'd grown up in a house where I had to be in before it was dark otherwise Mum would go hunting around the whole town, knocking on doors in her best fur coat, armed with a pack of twenty and her life story, convinced that something terrible had happened to me. It was easier to stay in.

I remembered my friends calling for me on Halloween the year before to go out egging, all dressed up as vampires and witches. It was only an hour or so after I got home from school, but I wasn't allowed to go with them because it was getting dark and my mother hadn't seen me all day.

'Why don't you come in, kids?' She looked at my mates, standing awkwardly in their costumes, with their bags of flour and cartons of eggs hidden behind their backs. 'Me and Emmeline can make you something to eat – some ham sandwiches and crisps. I think I've even got some cheese and pineapple there. You could stay here tonight. We can play ducking apples!'

She got so excited that she started fumbling around the kitchen for apples and a bowl, giggling to herself.

My mates made their excuses and started backing out of the hallway, trying to escape the pleading look on my mother's face.

'Don't go!' She took a drag of her cigarette, her eyes wide with nerves. 'Stay! It'll be *fun*. Emmeline will love it, won't you, Em? She won't moan about staying in if you're here. I haven't seen her all day. I've been lonely…'

Oh, Lord.

'She's usually here to keep me company and keep the place ticking!' she said with a mock-sergeant-major-type

voice and saluted to nobody in particular. 'Please stay…
Please?'

They didn't stay.

The humiliation was enough to drive a girl to scraping
herself with a compass to try and self-harm. Year eight had
started that off in school, and the trend had taken off like a
rocket. You couldn't get a cubicle to pee in when you went
to the bogs because there were so many girls in them, sitting
on the toilet, scraping emo cuts into their arms. It was
messed *up*.

I only did it once. I realised straight away that cutting
was pretty lame, so I never did it a second time. Funny
thing was, it didn't faze anyone in the slightest. The
blood, I mean. Nobody gave a toss. The only time it
occurred to us that it was actually really weird was when
one of the dinnerladies walked into the toilets and saw
this mass of tear-and-blood-stained schoolgirls sitting
on the cold tiles, watching each other's arms bleed, with
manky compasses lying all over the floor. I thought the
poor cow was going to have a heart attack. She started
crying and shouting for help, screaming, 'They're slitting
their wrists! They're killing their selves! The girls! The
GIRLS!'

Drama queen.

No one was killing themselves. We were just bonding.

Anyway, here I was now … in a children's home. I realised
that when the girls had invited me out with them earlier, I

hadn't said no because I was tired – I'd said no because I was scared.

I was scared because I'd never been able to just *go out* like that.

I was scared because it had been drummed into me and Freya that it was better to stay in, to stay with Mum. Like subliminal little messages downloading into our minds, telling us to copy and paste the actions we observed, we had turned into these nervous little wrecks, like *her*. And now that she was gone, I was like one of those puppies that get so anxious and excited at the same time, they end up wetting themselves.

It was all too much.

You spend your time wishing for freedom and planning your escape from the place where you grow up, and then overnight, you get what you want.

Be careful what you wish for.

The thought made me want to vomit.

I had so much freedom all of a sudden, I felt suffocated. I had to fight for the air in my lungs. I thought I was going to pass out, so I stood on the bedroom windowsill and opened the window to let some air into the room, so I could breathe.

Eventually I got back into bed. There was no chance of sleep. I hadn't slowed down for long enough all day to let the pounding settle, to process everything that had happened. Lying in my new bed, in my new room, in the dark, I tried to take it all in. I had to do it slowly. Like an air freshener you buy for the car; you have to open it up a little bit at a time or the smell will make you feel sick.

I just didn't understand. What was Mum thinking? What happened?

A memory of the paramedics came into my head, followed by an image of the needle. The way they jammed it into her leg ... so fast, so harsh. I could almost hear it scrape her bone. My brain winced at the thought of it.

I thought of poor Grandma Coalman, sat at home in her little one-bedroom bungalow, worrying that we weren't allowed to stay with her because she didn't have the space. She had tried to work something out with Social Services, but I knew that she didn't have any choice – we had to go into temporary care. I would ring her tomorrow to check if she was OK. Times like this, she really could have done with Dad and Nana Rose around for support. I was really annoyed with them both for popping off and leaving us. Dead people were so *selfish*.

All those years, Nana Rose told us about her clairvoyance. She was what our family called a Seer. She could see visions of the past and from the future. Yeah, well she didn't 'see' all this coming, did she? And if she did, she certainly hadn't warned us about any of it before she died.

There was no use being bitter. I would just have to try and make sure that Grandma Coalman and Freya were coping as best they could. I didn't know how I was going to manage it, but I had to do whatever I could to keep our family strong.

I thought about Freya. She was probably tucked up in bed by now. I was glad that she was staying at Bill and Nora's house instead of here. Mel said that they usually tried to keep brothers and sisters together when something like this happens, but she had no choice but to separate us because Bill and Nora didn't have the room for both of us. I preferred Freya to be there, though – there was no point in two of us being stuck in a children's home, was there? But now that I couldn't see her, I desperately wanted to.

And then finally, I thought of my mother. I thought of her face as she left; all doped up on that stuff they gave her. I thought of the blood. And I thought again of the needle. I'd held her hand as they wheeled her to the ambulance. I had tried not to cry as she slurred that I'd left the dishes and she was worried in case we had visitors.

Lunatic.

I squeezed my eyes shut and rested my forehead against the palms of my hands, trying to breathe out the frustration. My foot kept moving up and down, up and down. Angry tears ran down my cheeks, hot and salty with guilt and rage. Why did I let her do this to me? This was NOT MY FAULT.

Why did I feel like I was responsible for all her cock-ups? Like I was supposed to somehow orchestrate it so that she would stay sane?

I hadn't done anything wrong, yet here I was … *lost.*

I didn't deserve this. I was no angel, I knew that. But I also knew that once you got past my mouth, I was alright, you know?

The wave of emotions hit me like a crowbar, and a little voice inside my mind tried to soothe me.

Calm down, Em.

I told the voice to bugger off, because it was disturbing my wallowing self-pity, and then I felt guilty for being mean to myself. So I sobbed by the bucketload for twenty minutes straight. It was quite impressive.

Mum had looked so frightened. I remembered them racing towards her, and she'd looked at me with panic in her eyes. The way a child looks to their mother to save them when they're in danger.

But I didn't save her, did I? I just let them take her.

My stomach hurt. I remembered Megan's auntie having a baby a couple of years ago. The only thing that baby did was scream. It was at such a high octave that the dogs outside would go nuts. Megan's auntie said that the baby had 'colic', which apparently is the worst stomach pain in the world for them. That's why she made that weird screaming noise all the time.

I wondered if adults could have colic, too. Not that I was a full-on adult yet, but my boobs were growing at a spectacular rate, and I'd gone from a B cup to a C cup in the last six months, so I was almost there.

I managed to silence the nasty little sounds escaping from my mouth as I sobbed, and I squeezed my stomach to stop the pain, but when I did that, I couldn't breathe properly, so eventually I just hugged myself and that seemed to do the trick. I sat on the bed with my head resting on my hunched-up knees, and my arms wrapped around them, trying to keep them together. If I could keep my knees together for five whole minutes, then the pain would go away. I just knew it.

And then that little voice – again so faint that I could hardly hear it – started to 'Shhh' me.

The sound was so familiar it could have been my own mother.

It occurred to me it could be Nana Rose. When she was alive, she had the same kind of voice as Mum.

In the midst of my snot-ridden heaves, I spoke out loud, 'Hello, Nana Rose. It's Emmeline, here. How are you?'

I felt silly, talking to an empty room.

'I'm really sorry to bother you, but I was wondering if you could do me a favour, please?'

I looked around for some kind of response.

'I've got this pain … right here.' I pointed to my belly. 'And it won't get lost. I know you're probably busy up there, but could you do something to help?'

Silence.

I may as well have been speaking to thin air. Well, I was.

I sat there for a few seconds, waiting for something that I couldn't quite put my finger on. But nothing came.

The room was completely still.

What was I doing? What was I expecting? A voice? A person? Did I really think that my dead nan was going to speak to me?

'This is *stupid*,' I said.

I got up from the bed, angry with myself. I wiped my face, but the tears still came and this frustrated me even more because I couldn't control it.

I felt like screaming! I just wanted it to STOP!

Like a faulty radio signal, there was a sudden ringing noise in my one ear.

I shook the noise out with my finger. It came back straight away, and I banged my ear to try and get rid of it.

It was so piercing that everything seemed distorted for a moment – like my head had been banged between a pair of music cymbals. I couldn't focus on anything else. It made me feel dizzy, so I sat back down and breathed slowly.

Breathe in...

Breathe out...

Breathe in...

Breathe out...

And then it happened.

I was aware of something, but I wasn't sure what. I sat there, quiet. A sob shook my shoulders. My senses seemed to be on overdrive and the hairs on my arms stood to attention. I wasn't scared exactly, just … alert. I reached for my lucky cardigan and put it on, glad of the familiar feel of the cotton wrapped around my shoulders.

The ringing had died down now, and there was this buzzing around me, but it was silent at the same time. There was no actual noise, just the feeling of it.

In made-up stories, this would be the part where a beautiful white light shines through the window. But no. What happened next was *so* much cooler.

I just stopped crying.

Completely stopped.

Just like that.

I couldn't understand how I had gone from sobbing so hard to being perfectly calm in about forty-three seconds. It was *amazing*.

Something caught my eye. I looked up and saw the spider's web on the corner of the window frame. It sparkled in the rain like it was covered in little diamonds. I felt drawn to the window, something calling me to look outside.

I walked over and looked out to the park at the bottom of the hill. I could see the rose bush, illuminated by the street lamps. The roses shone in the dark and I could almost feel the warmth and comfort of their white velvety petals – as if they were making a special blanket just for me.

I suddenly felt really tired. I got back into bed and pulled the duvet tight under my chin.

And finally I was able to sleep.

EIGHT

I jumped awake, startled.

For a moment, I forgot where I was.

You know when you're dead scared at the thought of waking up one night to find someone standing over you, watching? Like in a horror film or something? Well, *this was it.*

A tall figure stood at the foot of my bed.

Oddly, though, when it happens in real life, it's not as bad as you expect. It feels a bit like a dream. You don't scream or anything, you just lie there.

And then it spoke.

'Well, don't just lie there like a wet fish – *say* something!'

Ahhh, Karra.

She moved, and I could just make out her long red hair

in a streak of light that snuck through the bedroom window.

'What are you doing standing at the bottom of my bed like that, you psycho?' I asked, my heart pounding in my chest.

'Shhh!' she hissed. 'Keep your voice down. I've only just got in. S'posed to be back at ten, wasn't I?'

She switched on the lamp by the side of her bed, and I squinted at her wobbling around, trying to get her pyjama bottoms on.

'*Oh-my-life!*' She looked at me with wide eyes. 'What's happened to you? Your eyes are swollen like a monkey's backside! Have you been eating crab sticks? My cousin is allergic to crab sticks, and every time she eats them, her eyes swell up like balloons.'

I got my little mirror from the bedside table. She was right; I looked dreadful.

'Ohhh,' I groaned. 'I look like a right minger.'

'Big time,' she agreed. 'Been crying or something, have you?'

I didn't meet her eye as I shook my head. 'Just tired, I expect.'

'Fair do's.' Karra nodded. I think she'd sussed me out, but she didn't push it any further.

She switched off her lamp and we lay in the dark, talking about the lads that she'd been out with that night. University students, apparently. She said that one of them told her that he'd got eight A* GCSE grades, and three B grades for his A levels, before starting his degree. Pretty impressive. That reminded me: I was back to school after half-term, and I'd be choosing my options this year, ready for my GCSEs. What if I was still here for my GCSE year? No, that was almost two years away. I'd be long gone by then, back at home, like none of this ever happened. I tried to convince myself that everything would be fine, but panic started to rise in my chest. There was no way I'd be able to study for my GCSEs in this place! How would I get the grades I needed if I didn't have anywhere quiet to study?

I could see it in my mind, now. My GCSE results paper would say: 'Emmeline Rose has failed her GCSEs with 'U' in every subject.'

U.

Un-fluffing-classified.

All my life, I had daydreamed about being a teacher, being a writer, being a stylist, being an actor, being an inventor, being *everything*. If I got rubbish GCSE results, it would seriously cook my swede. I'd hate it.

'Do you reckon I'll ever be able to get into The University?' Karra interrupted my thoughts.

'What do you mean, *The* University?' I was puzzled.

She laughed at me. 'What do you mean, *what do I mean*?'

'Well, you said it like there was a particular university

that you want to go to,' I replied. 'Which one is it?'

She switched the lamp back on and frowned at me in confusion. '*The One.*'

'Yes, but which one?' I asked.

'There's only one university, you moron! The big one, innit? In *London*. Everyone knows that. There's only one that you *can* go to … *The University*.'

'No, Karra.' I didn't want to offend her. 'There are lots of different universities. You can choose which one you go to. There's not just one university, one big building that takes on all the students in the world. There are loads of universities – there has to be, or there wouldn't be enough room for everyone.'

She was trying to suss out whether I was joking or not.

'And where exactly are all these universities?' she asked, half-mocking.

'Well, some people might go to Cardiff. Some people might go to Bristol, London or Manchester. Or perhaps they want to go to university in Ireland or Scotland. And some people might go to Spain or America, or somewhere like that. It depends where you want to study and do your degree.'

She thought about this.

'So everyone doesn't just go to one massive building in the middle of London that looks like a castle?' She sounded disappointed.

'No.' I shook my head.

'Well, tit me up with a packet of cheese and onion crisps!' She laughed out loud. 'I didn't know that!'

It turned out that Karra wasn't very scary at all. She was actually quite nice. She told me that she had been in and out of care since she was about six years old, because her mother was an alcoholic and her father was a heroin addict. They had spent years together, with her father knocking her mother about, and both of them giving the kids a few nasty digs along the way, before Karra and her brothers were taken into care. They had moved around a lot since then. They hardly saw each other because they were all in different foster homes or children's homes and never got the chance to spend any time together. Her mother was still an alcoholic, but her father was clean now because he had spent the last five years in jail after doing an armed robbery on a corner shop.

I cringed at some of the things she told me. She was very open about it all, and as I listened, I remembered Quinn easily mouthing off about her own mother's drug addiction earlier that day. I realised that being in care for so long had made these stories normal. Like *EastEnders*.

I felt ashamed. This girl lying in the bed next to mine, who'd had a pretty sick upbringing, was sharing terrible stories of her life with me even though she had never met me before today. Yet there I was, lying in the bed next to hers, desperately hoping that she wouldn't ask me any questions about my own life. I couldn't decide which one of us was mad – me or her? Was she abnormal to be that open with a complete stranger, or was I abnormal to be so closed-off? Either way, I felt sad for us both. No fourteen and sixteen-year-old girls should be lying in any bed, talking or not talking about these things.

Karra switched the lamp off again for us to go to sleep.

'Do you miss your family?' I whispered in the dark. I thought of Mum, Grandma Coalman and Freya.

'Not much to miss, really. Do you miss yours?' she whispered back.

I nodded my head, not able to speak for a second. I think Karra sensed my answer.

'You can cry if you want to,' she said. 'I won't tell anyone. I'm not a grass.'

I couldn't see her face in the dark, so I couldn't tell if she was looking at me or not.

'I'm OK.' I shrugged.

'I can't really remember much about when I first came into one of these places,' she said. 'But I do remember that every time I went to a new one, I would bawl my eyes out for about three days straight. The staff would give me lollipops to shut me up. By the time I'd moved to the fourth or fifth place, I'd wised up to the lollipop thing, so

I would cry my eyes out even if I wasn't upset. Free lollipops, see.'

We laughed quietly.

'But since I got older,' she continued, 'if I ever want to cry – which I never do, because I'm pretty solid like that – then I only ever cry at night. Nobody knows about it then.'

I couldn't really imagine Karra crying.

'Anyway, I know the ultimate cure for sadness,' she declared proudly.

'What's that?' I smiled.

'A hot-water bottle,' she replied. 'Auntie Sue bought mine for Christmas a couple of years ago, and I swear it's my favourite thing in the *world*. Whenever I feel upset or when I'm not well, I just fill it up and it always makes me feel better. I take it to bed every night.'

The street lights outside shone in through the curtains. Our eyes had adjusted to the darkness, and the room was bathed in a subtle glow.

'Have you got it now?' I propped myself up on the pillow.

'Yeah. I filled it up before I came in here.' She folded her arms around the hot-water bottle.

'Can I see it?'

'Course you can. Be careful, though – it's sacred.'

I looked at the pink hot-water bottle, and remembered seeing it earlier that day when Auntie Sue had first shown me and Mel to my room.

I wished I had one of my own. I passed it back to Karra and she held it preciously, like a baby.

'I'm the same with my lucky cardigan,' I said.

'Your what?' Karra looked confused.

'You know the blue cardigan that you and Quinn were arguing over today? The one with the little white rose on it?'

'Oh, yeah. I know.' Karra nodded. 'Quinn wanted to give it back to you, because you said it was your favourite. She's alright like that. Why is it a lucky cardigan?'

I beamed with pride. 'Ed Sheeran touched it.'

Karra's eyes widened. 'Are you *kidding* me?'

I shook my head.

'You're telling the truth?'

I nodded and smiled.

'*Oh-My-Donald-Duck!*' Karra looked at me in awe. 'You are a lucky girl, Emmeline.'

We both lay back down, ready for sleep.

'How did you get back in tonight?' I asked. 'I thought they locked the doors at half-ten.'

'The pool room,' she said. 'It's got a dodgy lock, so if you stick a bit of wire in it, the door unlocks automatically. We all do it. But the staff don't know about it, so don't say anything. Sometimes we get caught coming in late, but they haven't got a clue how we manage to sneak in. They've been trying to work it out for months – it's hilarious!'

'What happens if you come in late?' I asked. 'Do you get punished?'

Karra shook her head. 'They can't do nothing to us, can they? They're not our parents, at the end of the day. They try to punish us, but they can't force us to listen.'

'*Class.*' I grinned.

'Yeah, but you've got to be careful,' she said. 'If they find out you've come in late, they might stop your pocket money. And where can you go if you ain't got no money?'

'Good point,' I agreed.

'Exactly!' She was full of conviction. 'They're clever, them staff – they're not as stupid as they look. So you have to play them at their own game. Screw the system, and all that! Burn your bra, or whatever it is that Auntie Sue always bangs on about. She's one of them rug-munchers, you know.'

'Auntie Sue is gay?' I asked.

'Naaah, not gay.' She shook her head, trying to think. 'The other one … what's it called? A feminist.'

'Ah, right.' I nodded. 'My best friend Megan is one of those.'

'Is she?' Karra sounded impressed. 'She must be smart then, innit? I wouldn't mind being a feminist one day – when I get enough qualifications.'

'I don't think you need qualifications to be a feminist,' I said.

'Yeah, you probably do,' she replied matter-of-factly.

We soon settled into a tired silence, and I turned over to fall asleep.

'You won't tell the staff about that dodgy lock in the pool room, will you?' Karra asked.

'Of course I won't! What do you think I am?' I was insulted.

'Just checking,' she said, and then yawned.

'That is pretty clever,' I whispered. 'Tricking them like that.'

'Clever enough to get into university?' Karra asked.

'*Definitely.*' I smiled and closed my eyes.

'Em?' she whispered in the dark.

'Yeah?'

'Do you think that at one time there was just the one university? You know – *The University*? Or do you think there were always loads of universities, and I'm just thick?' Her voice seemed suddenly fragile.

'I think that originally, there was probably just the one university, like you said – *The University*,' I replied. 'I mean, they had to start somewhere, surely? And they probably didn't have enough room for everyone, so they had to build another one, and then another one, and that's how there are so many universities now. They all came from that one, big university.'

She sighed happily, satisfied with the answer.

'Cheers,' she said. 'Here you go. You can lend this for tonight.'

There was a thump as something heavy landed on my bed.

I felt the warmth through my duvet.

'Thank you,' I said.

I hugged the hot-water bottle to my chest.

'You're welcome,' replied Karra. 'Goodnight, Em.'

NINE

Breakfast time.

People were scrambling over each other to get to the plates heaped with slices of warm toast, dripping in butter. Every plate was loaded with sausages, tomatoes, beans and scrambled eggs.

I rushed down the stairs, Karra knocking me out of the way.

'Nothing personal,' she said, as she power-walked past me and slammed me into the wall.

I pulled myself together and picked up my pace to get into the living room – the smell of freshly cooked bacon making me drool like a dog.

I didn't know where to sit. Was everyone assigned a place at one of the three tables, or did you just sit wherever you wanted? As I stood on the sidelines, trying to work out what I was supposed to do next, the room was filled by a huge thundering noise, like a stampede.

'Bett...' the three tables seemed to say at once. And with that, Bett crashed through the door like a semi-pro wrestler in a pink and black velour tracksuit.

'MOVE, TYLER SMITH!' she boomed as she charged past me with 'MISS SEXY' written in neon pink over the back of her big backside. She skidded onto a chair at the middle table, and Tyler scooted quickly out of the way, moving two chairs across.

'Sit with us, Emmeline Rose!' Bett grinned goofily and patted the empty space between her and Tyler. I went to the middle table and Tyler and Bett looked very pleased with themselves as I took my seat. But I didn't have much chance to get comfortable because Quinn and Karra had other ideas.

'What do you think you're doing, Bett?' Quinn challenged her.

'SHUT UP, QUINN DAVIES!' Bett shouted through a mouthful of sausage and egg.

'YOU SHUT UP, BETTY MORRIS!' Quinn slammed down her fork in temper.

I watched Bett, who was sat next to me, looking directly at Quinn and opening her mouth as wide as possible to show her the contents of her mushed-up breakfast.

'I don't know what you're playing at, Bett. Emmeline's

sitting on top table with us.' Quinn pulled out an empty chair next to her.

Karra gave me a look of warning, making it clear that she expected me to move. I smiled apologetically at Bett and Tyler, and went to join the top table with the rest of the girls.

Bett got up from her seat and followed.

'I don't think so, Bett.' Quinn waved her finger. 'You know you don't sit on top table … *ever*. You sit on your own table, there, with the rest of the rejects. Now don't be difficult with me today, alright? Because I warn you, I'm not in the mood.'

'What will you do, Quinn Davies?' Bett frowned. 'Kill me with your little finger there? You'd better watch I don't bite the thing off … because I *will*.'

'Now now, girls!' Gladys Friday called from the serving hatch. 'Let's not start today! Bett, go back to your table! And Quinn, stop throwing your weight around! If I have to sort you two out again today, so help me God, I'll batter the pair of you!'

'That's child abuse, that is.' Quinn pointed at a poster that was pinned to the wall of the dining room. It was titled '*WHAT IS CHILD ABUSE?*' and was illustrated with lots of different pictures.

'See, Gladys Friday…' Quinn pinned her finger to the poster. 'It says so right here: "*HITTING OR HURTING A CHILD – OFTEN TO RELIEVE YOUR OWN FRUSTRATION*".'

'Yes, Quinn, I can see that.' Gladys Friday rolled her eyes. 'But I didn't hit you or hurt you, did I?'

'But you *threatened* to, Gladys Friday. It's the same thing, innit?' Quinn pointed to a different section of the poster and said, 'That would count as "*VERBALLY ABUSING A CHILD*". Right next to "*EXPOSING A CHILD TO PORNOGRAPHIC ACTS OR LITERATURE*".'

'For goodness' sake, Quinn! Sit down!' Gladys Friday stomped around the kitchen.

We all tucked into our breakfasts. I don't know what I was expecting. Hot mush? Cold mush? Scenes from *Annie*? I was pleasantly surprised that in real life it couldn't have been more different. The eggs were scrambled to perfection, the sausages were the ideal juiciness, and the bacon was soft and crispy at the same time.

I'd made mine and Freya's breakfasts quite often for the past two years, since my dad died, so I'd had some experience in rustling up something nice to eat. The first few months after he passed away, Mum didn't really get out of bed much. And when she did, she would just sit by the window, staring out at the garden for hours, as if she was waiting for something.

Grandma Coalman and Nana Rose would come down and do the washing and cook our tea, and they would clean the house every week. I'd watch them do it and I took mental notes on separating the whites and the darks, and how to empty the vacuum cleaner or make sure the gas cooker was turned off. I soon joined in with the housework and cooking. I enjoyed the responsibility, and it took my mind off Dad not being around. It was the same for Grandma Coalman, I suppose. I mean, he was our dad, but he was her son. Thirty-seven hours she was in labour with him, she said.

Nana Rose didn't take very well to Dad. When Mum and Dad got married, Dad wanted Mum to change her surname to his. But she was depressed at the thought of having a name like Coalman instead of a glamorous surname like Rose. So she refused to change it. This pleased Nana Rose and she told him so. She said that no daughter of hers was going to change her name to something as plain as Coalman, and that Mum should have married her first boyfriend, Kevin Monroe. That way, at least my mother would have some association with Marilyn.

Although they never really got on, I think Nana Rose missed Dad when he was gone. Every day, she would take a cup of tea up to my mother in the morning, trying to wake her, and tell her that Freya and I were going to school. And when we came home, we'd all take her up another cup of tea, hoping that she would have moved from the bedroom window. She might even have got dressed! But we would usually find her either still in bed or just staring into the garden again.

Sometimes Mum would get out of bed and come downstairs, but it was all too much for her – like she would get angry at the *house*. And she would get so stressed when we talked to her. Just our presence was annoying.

When Nana Rose and Grandma Coalman went home in the evenings, Mum would go back to bed and leave me and Freya in the living room to watch films and eat the sweets she'd bought for us. Guilt sweets, I reckon. And in the mornings I would make Freya breakfast to keep her distracted until Nana Rose or Grandma Coalman came back.

I thought how my little sister would have loved this Saturday breakfast I was eating. And when I thought it, I suddenly felt full.

I was grateful for the distraction of these fascinating strangers. I looked around the crowded room at the three tables full of messy faces and loud voices. I found myself giggling at the banter, enjoying the easy way they all seemed to fit together like some quirky, dysfunctional jigsaw puzzle.

Bett had gone back to her own table, and she and Quinn sat parallel to each other, arguing as they ate their breakfast. Karra was munching mass quantities of bacon, shouting at the two girls through a mouthful of baked beans.

'GIRLS!' she spluttered. 'CHILL OUT, will you? Just

wise UP!' She accidentally spat food onto the table. She picked it up and put it back in her mouth.

Gladys Friday leant through the serving hatch, her chin resting on her hand, thoughtfully. She watched us all for a moment, and then turned her focus to Karra.

'I thought you turned vegetarian.' She nodded at Karra's plate.

'Except for bacon and sausage-in-batter,' replied Karra.

'I see.' Gladys Friday smiled at Karra as she watched her tuck into some more bacon.

Karra put some extra food on both of our plates. 'Come on, Em,' she said. 'You've hardly touched your breakfast. I've got no time for fussy eaters – they get on my nerves.'

Gladys Friday winked at me from the serving hatch.

I smiled.

My appetite was starting to come back.

TEN

The days went by.

I felt strangely detached from my own home, like it was a dream that I'd once had. I was floating around, quietly observing everything from a different dimension. My head felt like cotton wool – which wouldn't have been so bad if I didn't *hate* cotton wool. Every time I thought of it, I imagined it in my mouth, grinding against my teeth, making that horrible squeaky sound.

I spoke to Freya and Grandma Coalman every day. Freya seemed to be coping brilliantly. Bill and Nora said that she had settled in really well and 'had formed an even better connection' with their Lola since they'd been around each other full-time. They said that it was like having a little sister for Lola. That stung me a little.

Grandma Coalman was getting through, but I think things had taken their toll on her. I tried to reassure her that Freya and I were OK, but naturally she worried. There was also the stress of Mum's health playing on our minds. We weren't allowed to visit her in the hospital yet, so Grandma Coalman would ring the ward each day and speak with Mum's name nurse to see how she was doing. Grandma Coalman was getting the house fixed up while Mum was away. She said it was the only thing she could do that gave her a sense of control, and if she didn't have the house to work on, she would have crumbled by now.

I was pleased that Freya had adapted so well. I wished that I could settle in the same way, but my body resisted my new life. I was on edge. I was constantly tired, but could hardly sleep. I was always hungry, but couldn't stomach much food. My brain was filled with chatter all day long, and I'd forgotten what it felt like to be still.

I tried to make my room more homely. I stuck up a few posters to brighten the place up a bit. Maybe I could decorate my bed with cushions, like they do in those American films. They always have big houses with cosy rooms in American films, don't they? I went around the whole building looking for nice, cosy cushions that would make my bed American, but I only managed to find three that were good enough.

The staff must have sensed my restlessness, because Auntie Sue and Gladys Friday said I was like a dog trying to settle in its bed; twisting in circles, pawing at the material, huffing and puffing until it was just right. I tried to keep busy and not worry about my family, but every time I stopped for long enough, my thoughts would drift back to Mum. Even though I knew she was safe in hospital, I was haunted by visions of her alone in a room, crying for me and Freya.

On top of that, the half-term holiday was coming to an end and I was starting back to school on Monday.

What if everyone was funny with me because I was in a children's home? Obviously I'd told Megan. I knew that she wouldn't tell anyone because she was my best friend. But a few other people from school would definitely have found out about it, because they lived in my street and one of the poxy neighbours would have told them.

Zoe-two-doors-up was probably standing by her window, waiting for someone to invite in for a cup of tea and biscuits, so she could share all the gossip.

Nosy cow.

And whatever Zoe-two-doors knew, Stacy would know – and would tell everyone.

Zoe-two-doors-up was the bitch of the street. If there was any trouble, she'd usually be sniffing around somewhere. And for some reason she always felt the need to belittle my mother whenever she saw her. I couldn't remember a time when she had ever been genuinely nice to Mum.

One time, Zoe-two-doors-up was coming out of the house to go jogging with a couple of the other neighbours. Mum, Freya and I were just getting out of our car with the shopping.

Zoe and her sidekicks were in their designer leggings and power-walking trainers. Mum was wearing a denim skirt and Ugg boots, with a pair of giant sunglasses over her nose. Zoe smirked at her friends and they all smiled falsely to my mother, with spiteful gleams in their eyes.

'Hi, Tess!' Zoe sang as she barged past us and almost knocked the shopping from Mum's hands.

'Jog on, Zoe-e-e-e!' my mother sang back in her merriest voice as she balanced the shopping bags and held both of her arms out wide, sticking up a middle finger from each hand. They glared at her. Mum grinned back at them, her middle fingers hanging in the air. They disappeared down the road, huffing and puffing, but never once said anything back. It was *epic*.

Mum might be a nutter, but there was no denying she had guts. I liked that.

Mum was a bit like a cat. She was a loner. She was streetwise. She said what she meant, and there was no pretence about her. She was a bit rough around the edges, but there was something captivating about her; like an actress who knew she was better than her part. She had big, emerald-green eyes that could see right through you. She got them from my Nana Rose. Except Nana Rose's eyes were more intense, because she was a Seer. And get this – Nana Rose had an extra eye.

I'm *serious*.

You couldn't see it, but I believed her when she told me about it. She called it her third eye, and said it was right in the middle of her forehead. You know how some people have a third nipple? Well, kind of like that, I suppose.

I never understood what it meant exactly, but I knew that everyone had one, just not everyone used it. Nana Rose said that if you concentrated enough, you'd be able to see things differently – clearer than usual.

I wasn't sure whether I had a third eye myself, but I sometimes felt that I knew things about people. Take Stacey Lock, for example. She was the niece of Zoe-two-doors-up, and the family resemblance was obvious – physical appearance and personality. Stacey had always been a bit of a bully, but nobody seemed to click onto this until secondary school, except me.

In the last year of junior school, when my dad was ill, I would sometimes hear Stacey talking to people, and she would be smiling kindly at them. But when she stopped talking, I would hear her speak again – except I would hear it in my *head*. And she would usually be saying something nasty. This one time, she told her best friend that she looked gorgeous, even though the girl had snot hanging from her nostril. When everyone was laughing, Stacey apologised and said that she hadn't noticed. But I heard her voice laughing in my mind, and saying, 'Well, you should have checked yourself before you left the house, you minger.'

I talked to Dad about it before he died. I told him how uneasy she made me feel, even though I couldn't understand why. I said I didn't trust her, and that when she spoke, I would get a running commentary in my mind of what she really meant.

Dad looked at me as if he was trying to work out a quiz or something, and then he made us a cup of hot chocolate so we could have a chat about it.

'Em...' He sat opposite me at the kitchen table. 'Sometimes, we get what we call "gut feelings". Most people get those gut feelings, but dismiss them because they listen to their heads instead.' He looked thoughtful. 'But very often, our gut feelings are the right ones. We should give them more of a chance, really.'

He blew on his hot chocolate.

'Your mum and Nana Rose...' He trailed off for a moment. 'Don't ask me *how* they do it, but there are many things that they seem to know, which just can't be explained. Some people, like me and Grandma Coalman, can't really tap into this mumbo-jumbo stuff. But other people, like your mother and Nana Rose ... well, they *can.*'

He looked mystified by his own words.

'There have been lots of extraordinary things that have

happened with your mum,' he said. 'But one time *really* sticks out. I'll never forget it.'

I hugged my hot chocolate to me and my eyes widened, excited at the prospect of a good story.

'One day,' he started, 'we were out for dinner in this little Italian restaurant called Bella's. Lovely place, it was. Real posh grub.' He raised his eyebrows and rubbed his thumb and middle finger together to show that it was expensive. I nodded, impressed that my father could afford to eat in an Italian restaurant.

'We were the only customers in there and it was the perfect setting for a nice, romantic night. But your mum, well, she was a bit funny all the way through the meal – pushing her food around her plate and looking distracted. I asked if she was alright, and she said that she wasn't feeling too well, and would I mind if she popped to the ladies room?'

He took a sip of his hot chocolate and continued. 'So she went to the toilet and I ate the rest of her food because she had steak. None of that rump stuff either. It was fillet. And you can't let a good fillet steak go to waste, can you?'

I shook my head.

'Anyway, when she came back, she still seemed a bit *off,* so I called for the bill.' He settled into his seat.

'The waitress came to our table and asked if everything was alright with the meal. Then, out of nowhere, your mum looked up, put her hand on the woman's stomach and said, *"You're having a little girl."* I'm not kidding you, Em, I could have died of embarrassment!'

I started laughing at the look on his face.

'And with that, the woman starts *crying*. So I'm sat there like a lemon, giving your mother the evil eye because she's just made a stranger cry. And if that wasn't bad enough, the woman then says that she is *not* pregnant and in fact she and her husband couldn't have any children!'

I put my hand to my mouth in shock.

'Exactly!' He mirrored my reaction. 'You can imagine my face when she told us that! Then your mother explained that she had a gift – one that ran through the line of women in her family. It may sound a little odd, but your mum could feel that the woman was pregnant. She said that she could *sense* her symptoms.'

'That's weird.' I shivered. 'What happened then?'

'Well, the woman was superstitious, and she believed that meeting your mother was a sign. So we exchanged telephone numbers and the woman promised to keep in touch and let us know if anything came of it.'

'And did it?' I asked.

He nodded. 'Two weeks later, we got a call from the woman, telling us that she'd just found out she was five weeks pregnant.'

'GO, MUM!' I clapped my hands together.

'Nine months later,' he smiled, 'they invited us back to the restaurant for dinner. They were celebrating the birth of their beautiful baby daughter. I've never questioned your mother's intuition since then. I'm not saying that I understand it, because I don't. But I know that whatever it is and wherever it comes from, it is a gift.'

He gazed at his hot chocolate. 'So if I've learned anything from being around your pain-in-the-arse mother for so long, it's that if you get a gut feeling about something, you should listen to it.'

'So what has this got to do with Stacey Lock?' I asked. 'Are you saying that I shouldn't hang around with her?'

'I'm not telling you to stop hanging around with Stacey,' he replied. 'I'm just saying to be careful, that's all. If you know she's not a very nice girl, you need to trust your gut feeling.'

'But I don't know.' I was frustrated. 'That's what I'm saying, Dad! I don't know that she's not a very nice girl. I just think that she's not. What if these things I hear are just my imagination?'

'Well...' said Dad. 'Maybe while everyone else is listening to Stacey Lock's words, you are listening to something different.'

'What am I listening to?' I asked.

'You're listening to her heart.'

Thinking of that conversation reminded me of the day I came to the children's home, and the way Stacey Lock and Zoe-two-doors-up were laughing as Mel's car drove me away from my home. I hoped that I wouldn't have to deal with Stacey when I went back to school. I tried to convince myself that she probably had better things to bother with, but there was a nagging feeling inside that told me different. I wasn't sure why, but for some reason, that family really seemed to have it in for us.

ELEVEN

I tried to put school and Stacey out of my mind, but it was the last day of the half-term holiday and it was difficult to ignore the fact that, whether I liked it or not, I would be starting school again the following day.

Mel had organised for me and Freya to go out for a meal with Grandma Coalman as a treat, and I was glad of the chance to meet up with my family and make the most of my last day off.

'What are you having, Em?' Grandma Coalman studied the menu with her glasses perched on the end of her nose.

'I'm not sure,' I replied. 'The gammon looks good, doesn't it?'

'Gammon!' Grandma Coalman smiled widely, getting excited at the picture of the big gammon steak with the peas on the side, and ring of pineapple on top. When she smiled, you could see where she'd missed her lips when she'd put on her lipstick, because there were tiny bits of red on her front teeth, like she'd coloured outside the lines of a picture.

Mel and Freya were looking at the menu, trying to decide between spaghetti bolognaise or chicken burger and chips.

'I'm going with bolognaise,' said Mel, slapping her menu down on the table.

Freya scrunched up her nose in disgust. She was going through a phase where whatever you said to her, she'd insist on the opposite, just to prove a point. So Grandma Coalman, Mel and I knew that she would go for the chicken burger, but we couldn't say that, otherwise she'd take longer to choose, to make sure that she didn't have what we expected her to have.

'Emmeline.' Grandma Coalman looked serious. 'If you're having the gammon, then make sure you ask for pineapple and egg, otherwise it doesn't taste right.'

'Who says?' Freya challenged – any excuse for confrontation.

'Me,' said Grandma Coalman. 'Now, shut up and order your food.'

Freya frowned at the menu. 'I'll have the chicken burger.'

'Surprise, surprise!' Grandma Coalman looked smug.

'What's that supposed to mean, Gram?' Freya moved her head from side to side.

'Nothing, love.'

Grandma Coalman and Freya had a funny relationship. They were always sniping at each other, but if anyone else said anything about them, they would be there in a flash with their sleeves rolled up, ready to fight to protect the family.

'I don't want the chicken burger now,' Freya sulked.

'Well, you're having the chicken burger, whether you like it or not!' Grandma Coalman looked at Freya, eyes wide with warning.

'You can't *make* me. What if I refuse to eat it?'

'Then you'll starve. Now cut the attitude and zip the lip, *OK*?' Grandma Coalman had the final say, and the lasagna to go with it.

Grandma Coalman was Dad's mother. If you had known my dad, then you would never have guessed that they were related. Dad was quiet and gentle. Grandma Coalman was a gobby cow.

If you had known my Nana Rose when she was alive, you would know straight away that she was my mother's mother. Not only did they look the same, but they were both off their trolleys. But if you had put Dad next to Grandma Coalman when he was alive, it would have just been like he was standing next to a stranger. They didn't look alike, they didn't sound alike, and they certainly didn't act alike. They were like chalk and cheese. But my goodness, did she love him.

When Dad died, Grandma Coalman was crushed. But she kept busy and got on with it. Her and Nana Rose came and looked after us while Mum lay in bed, crying all the time. Sometimes, I would sit by my bedroom window and watch Grandma Coalman and Nana Rose pegging out the washing together in the back garden. I liked it that they were friends. When Nana Rose died, Grandma Coalman had lost both her son and her best friend in a year. She seemed lonelier than ever, but she carried on taking care of us and always made sure we were washed, fed and that we cleaned our teeth. I probably didn't say it enough, but I thought she was a phenomenal woman.

We all sat around the table, eating mountains of chocolate brownie and ice cream. Mel asked us how I was getting on at the home and how Freya was getting on at Bill and Nora's. I knew Grandma Coalman still felt guilty that she couldn't take care of us, but she had made it her mission to get our house fixed and looking lovely for when we could go home again. Mum had destroyed a lot. Grandma Coalman was having it decorated. She said she was 'project-managing' the whole thing.

'So, what game do you want to lose at when we visit you next week, old lady?' Freya asked Grandma Coalman. 'Pictionary, Hungry Hippos or Scrabble?'

'I'll thank you not to call me *Old Lady*.' Grandma Coalman frowned at her. 'A woman in her seventies is not old by today's standards. And I'll go for Hungry Hippos, I think.'

Grandma Coalman winked at me. I laughed, because I knew that Grandma Coalman hated Hungry Hippos. She would much rather play Scrabble, that was her favourite. But if she had said that she wanted to play Scrabble, then Freya would go for one of the other games. Grandma Coalman was good at tactics.

Freya groaned. 'Why do you want to play Hungry Hippos, Gram?' She threw her head back. 'I thought you'd choose Scrabble – you usually like that.'

'I can't be bothered with Scrabble.' Grandma Coalman waved her hand. 'I'm bored with it, because I always win.'

'You do NOT always win!' Freya shouted and folded her arms. 'Sometimes me and Emmeline win! Don't we, Em?' She frowned. 'I'm good at Scrabble, thank you very much. I'm an excellent speller.'

'How do you know that you're an excellent speller?' Grandma Coalman teased.

'My teacher did spelling tests with me all last year, and I got nine out of ten almost all of the time.'

'Why *nine*?' Grandma Coalman asked.

'What do you mean?'

'Why did you get nine out of ten? Why not ten out of ten?'

'I don't know.' Freya shrugged. 'I just never got the full ten out of ten. There was always that one word that I couldn't remember how to spell.'

'What word?' Grandma Coalman was suspicious.

'I don't know, Gram! How am I supposed to remember what word it was?'

Grandma Coalman frowned as she licked the last bit of ice cream off her spoon. 'What's your teacher's name?' she asked.

'Mrs Griffiths,' replied Freya. 'Why?'

'I think Mrs Griffiths has a superiority problem.' Grandma Coalman scowled.

'What's a superiority problem?'

'It means that she always has to be the best,' replied Grandma Coalman. 'She probably puts a trick word in your spelling tests, so you'd never get it right. Because she needs the kids to know who's boss. *Bloody teachers*. Control freaks, the lot of them!'

'Calm down, Columbo,' said Mel. 'I don't think anyone's trying to trick the kids.'

Grandma Coalman waved her hand at Mel to shoo her away.

'Freya, Spell *Chicken Burger* for me,' said Grandma Coalman.

'C-H-I-K—' Freya thought carefully. 'No, wait!' She took a couple of seconds to work it out. 'I've got it now: C-H-I-C-K-E-N B-U-R-G-E-R!'

Grandma Coalman studied her for a moment. 'Are you sure there's a 'K' in the word *Chicken*?' she asked.

Freya nodded her head.

'Well done!' Grandma Coalman turned serious again. 'If I can't fool you...' She tapped her head in a secret-code kind of way. 'Then your teachers can't fool you either.'

'The teachers are not trying to fool the kids, Anna!' Mel put her hands over her face and shook her head with frustration.

'Oh, shut up, Mel! You don't *know* that.' Grandma Coalman scolded her. 'You get on my nerves, you do. Bloody social workers. Waste of time, the lot of you. Worse than the poxy teachers.'

Mel rolled her eyes and got up from the table. 'Come on, let's go. I need to take the girls back so they can get their things ready for school tomorrow.'

'Oh, yes!' Grandma Coalman looked concerned. 'How are you feeling about going back to school, Em? Are you anxious at all?'

'A little,' I answered.

'You should be,' she said. 'I expect they'll all be talking about what happened.'

'Cheers, Gram.' I sulked as I got up from my chair. Trust Grandma Coalman to point out the obvious.

She stood up and rummaged through her handbag before pulling out a packet of tablets and handing them to me.

'What are these for?' I asked.

'In case you get the runs,' she replied.

Great.

TWELVE

'Alright, Nerd?' Karra sat at the table and grabbed a piece of toast from my plate.

'Karra!' Auntie Sue told her off through the serving hatch. 'I'll make you some toast in a minute. Don't pinch Emmeline's – she's going to school this morning, and she needs a good breakfast.'

'Just make the toast, Auntie Sue.' Karra rolled her eyes, and then turned back to me. 'You're wearing the lucky cardigan. Are you nervous about going back to school?'

I looked down at my cardigan and fidgeted with the white velvet rose on the front. 'A bit.' My stomach did a watery grumble.

'Yeah, well, if you get any trouble, just give us a ring and we'll make our way down there and sort them out for you.'

Karra looked at me without a hint of a joke in her expression.

I chuckled.

'Not being funny or anything, Em, but you need to toughen up a bit if you're planning to stay here long term,' said Karra. 'It's dog-ee-dog in these places, babe. You have to learn to handle yourself.'

'What do you mean, dog-*ee*-dog?' I asked.

'What do you mean, *what do I mean*?' She looked at me as if I was stupid.

'You said it was "dog-*ee*-dog". I haven't heard that before.'

'That's because you're not from the streets, like me,' she said proudly. 'You posh girls probably say something different. It means that you've got to look after yourself: survival of the fittest.'

'Ahhh!' It made sense now. 'You mean dog-*eat*-dog.'

'What?' She laughed. 'That don't make no sense, Em. Why would a dog eat another dog?'

'Well, they wouldn't really eat each other. But it's like a dog fight. Brutal. So it's a dog-*eat*-dog kind of world.'

She considered this for a moment, resting her chin on her hand. 'I always wondered about that saying.'

'Karra, are you leading Emmeline astray?' Auntie Sue passed a plate of toast through the serving hatch.

'Sod off, Auntie Sue.' Karra took the plate of toast, and sat back down.

'You kiss your mother with that mouth, Karra Lewis?' Auntie Sue brought a cup of tea to the table and sat with us.

'She's had worse, believe me,' said Karra.

'Honestly, Karra.' Auntie Sue shook her head. 'You're such a pretty girl, and then you open your mouth and it's like…' She made a vomit action.

Karra laughed and Auntie Sue winked at her.

'Anyway, what are you doing out of bed this early in the morning, Missy?' asked Auntie Sue. 'You never usually get up at this time.'

'Seeing Emmeline off,' Karra said, as she stifled a yawn.

'That's nice.' Auntie Sue sipped her tea.

Karra narrowed her eyes. 'Just because I wanted to make sure that Emmeline was OK for her first day back at school, you think I'm going soft. I just wanted to be a good friend, that's all. And I *do* get up this early sometimes!'

'When?' Auntie Sue asked.

'Christmas,' Karra replied.

We heard a beeping noise from outside.

Auntie Sue clapped her hands together. 'Come on, Em! That's your taxi! You don't want to be late for your first day back!'

I got up from my chair and put on my coat.

'You have some crumbs around your mouth.' Karra pointed and did a circling motion around her own mouth with her index finger.

'Cheers.' I wiped my lips with my sleeve.

The back door opened, and in walked an older jolly man, wearing a brown jumper. 'HELLOOO!' His voice travelled through the kitchen into the dining room.

'Hello, Clive!' Auntie Sue called to the man. 'How are you, love? It's been a while!'

'Well, none of them will go to bloody school, Auntie Sue!' He chuckled and nodded in Karra's direction.

'Alright, Clive?' Karra picked up a piece of toast. 'Work drying up, is it?'

'Hello, Karra!' Clive smiled. 'When I got a call from the office saying that I had a school run from here, I thought your injunction might have been lifted.'

'No chance, Clive.' Karra chewed her toast. 'I can't be arsed to go back anyway – teachers just don't *get me*, you know?'

Clive nodded sympathetically.

'Clive, this is Emmeline.' Auntie Sue gestured towards me. 'Emmeline will be your new school passenger for a little while.'

'Pleased to meet you, pet!' Jolly Clive smiled warmly. I could tell he was a nice man.

I grabbed my school bag and headed for the kitchen door, turning back to give Karra a wave.

'Bye, Nerd!' She waved back.

'Bye, Chav!' I shouted, and we both grinned at each other.

'Have a good day, Em,' said Auntie Sue. 'If you go to school for the whole week, then we'll go to the cinema on Friday as a reward.'

A reward for what? Just for going to school? They must have been used to everyone refusing to go to school if they did a reward scheme for those who do go.

'The *cinema*,' Karra called after me, 'is a place where people go when they have a *life*.'

'And *school*,' I replied, 'is a place where people go when they have a *brain*.'

She laughed and waved her middle finger at me.

I said goodbye and followed Jolly Clive through the kitchen. I heard Karra and Auntie Sue speaking as I walked away.

'Special treatment, that is.' Karra frowned at Auntie Sue. 'You only reward the smart ones. The rest of us have to suffer because we're thick.'

Auntie Sue folded her arms. 'That's not true, Karra, and you know it's not true. We don't give special treatment to anybody; we just reward good effort, that's all. And what do you think you're playing at, calling yourself thick?'

Karra shrugged.

'If you went to school, then you'd be able to go the cinema as well. Why don't you go back, love? Give it another go?'

'Oh, shut up, Auntie Sue!' Karra got up from the table. 'What's the point? Work my guts out for six hours a day, just to get a *'D'* in everything? *No, thank you!* And I don't want to go to the *stupid* cinema either, so just give it a rest, will you?'

Karra stormed off, and Auntie Sue sighed heavily as she loaded the dishwasher.

I closed the back door gently behind me, and walked to the car.

Why was Karra always so hard on herself? And what was this issue she had about being thick? I mean, she was no Albert Einstein, but she wasn't stupid or anything.

We drove out of the car park and down the hill.

'Are you nervous, pet?' Jolly Clive asked.

My stomach churned. I didn't know how I was going to face everyone.

We got to the bottom of the hill and the white rose bush sparkled by the park gate. The roses had grown since the last time I'd seen them. A bit like me, I suppose. Like they were growing with me. There was just *something* about that rose bush that made me feel safe. I smiled at them, and my stomach settled.

'I'm not too bad, Clive,' I said. 'I think I'll be alright.'

THIRTEEN

The registration bell rang.

'*Oh-my-days!*' Megan put her hands across her face, dramatically. 'I still can't believe you're in an *orphanage*! When you told me in half-term, I was just stunned. Not being funny or anything, Em, but your mum is off her tree.'

'It's not an orphanage, Megan.' I rolled my eyes at her. 'You make it sound like I'm in *Oliver Twist*.'

Her brown hair looked dishevelled. 'What happened to you?' I asked. 'Why is your hair such a mess?'

'Ollie destroyed it on the bus,' she sulked. 'I don't want to talk about it.'

She huffed as she struggled to navigate a hair-bobble around her ponytail, and walk safely at the same time.

Megan had been my best friend since we were toddlers, and I'd never known her to be able to do two things at once. She seemed to miss out on the all-important multi-tasking gene that girls apparently had. A simple task like tying her hair back into a ponytail and walking at the same time could cause her, me or somebody else serious injury. My favourite time was a couple of years back, when she tried to sit on a swing and eat an ice cream simultaneously. I wasn't allowed to talk about that one.

Ollie Hart came running towards us with a sparkle in his eyes. 'Hello, my turd-friends! How are we, today?' He ruffled mine and Megan's hair and grinned like a naughty little boy.

'Ollie!' Megan told him off. 'Do you have any idea how long it takes to get my hair looking good in the mornings?'

'Nope!' he replied. 'Mine takes me five minutes, so I can't fathom how girls take so long. I mean, your hair is up in a ponytail, Megan. How long can a ponytail take?'

Megan gasped, insulted. 'For your information, this ponytail is a work of art. You already ruined it once today, and now you've ruined it again! You have *zero* respect for a good hairstyle!'

Ollie winked at us both.

We had known Ollie Hart since we were little. We all went to playschool together. He was a bit of eye-candy for the school, but we didn't find him attractive like the other girls did, because we'd seen him pee in the sandpit when we were seven. You can't fancy someone after that – it's just *wrong*.

'Em, I'm sorry to hear about your mother,' he said. 'If there's anything I can do to help, just let me know.'

'Cheers,' I thanked him. 'I appreciate that.'

The three of us walked to registration class, chatting about what we'd been up to in the school holiday. I let them know what had happened with Mum. I knew there would be different versions of the story circulating the school, so I wanted my friends to have the facts. At least if they knew the truth, they could help to set the record straight if other people got a little too creative with the rumours.

I was feeling anxious as we approached registration. Everyone seemed to whisper as they passed me, and I dreaded to think of what was being said.

We got to the classroom door, and I hesitated.

'Are you OK, Em?' asked Megan.

I nodded and closed my eyes to let the jittery feeling pass.

'Hey.' Ollie looked into my eyes, trying to keep me focused. 'Don't worry about what other people think. I want you to count to three, take a deep breath, and then walk in there like you own the place.'

'Come on, Em,' said Megan. 'You can do it.'

'*One…*' Ollie started counting.

'*Two…*' Megan counted with him.

'*Three*,' I said, and then took a deep breath as I entered the classroom.

By lunchtime, *everyone* knew about my situation. Apparently, it had been the main topic of conversation over the school holiday. I would have known that if I'd had my phone, but Mum had smashed it up on the day she was taken into hospital. In a way, I thought it was for the best because I'd have been going out of my mind if people were messaging me all half-term to ask what had happened. I doubt I would have come back to school if I'd known how popular I had become in the space of two weeks. Funny how people want to be your friend when you have a bit of drama going on in your life, isn't it.

Some were more polite than others, skirting around the issue instead of directly bringing it up. Others were like interrogators, in my face the whole time, asking me loads of questions. What was it like? Were there many kids in the home? Were they rough? Were they junkies? Was I scared? What happened to my mum? Was it true that she tried to kill herself?

One of the neighbours had told Cherise Daniels that my mother had been taken to the nuthouse because she set the whole street on fire by posting petrol bombs through everyone's letterboxes.

Whaaat?

I tried to keep my cool. 'Nobody set anything on fire or petrol-bombed anyone's house,' I said. 'Get a grip, will you? My mother's not an arsonist.'

This went on for a little while before word got around that the truth wasn't as theatrical as everyone had hoped, and then it all died down a bit.

Megan loved the whole thing. In her mind, she was like my press agent and bodyguard rolled into one. She would say things like, 'Back off, people! I said, No Comment!'

I was grateful to have a best friend like Megan. My mother always said that friends are like boobs: some are big, some are small, some are real and some are fake. And there was no doubt in my mind that Megan was a real one. Friend, that is. Not boob.

Ollie was a good friend as well. And at times like this, he was particularly useful because he could warn off the boys if they started annoying me, but he could also charm the girls into talking about a different subject if they got too nosy.

Megan and Ollie stayed with me throughout lunchtime, helping to divert attention from the disaster that was my life. Although there was a lot of speculation and gossip, most of the day passed without too much hassle.

Result.

Last class: Double Science.

Megan hovered over the Bunsen burner, peering at the equipment through her safety goggles. She connected the Bunsen to the gas tap and I watched her slowly open the air hole on the burner, concentration forcing her tongue out as the flame turned from yellow to blue. She was probably the only one in class who insisted on wearing the goggles. Everyone else knew that style and popularity was much more important than health and safety, so if you were going to wear them, you had to wear them on top of your head.

'It'll be your own fault when you burn your face off,' she warned me as she adjusted the tripod.

'Shut up, Megan,' I said. 'Nobody wears the goggles – they're stupid.'

She lifted her head from the Bunsen burner to look at me. 'Stupid?' She stared at me through the goggles, and her magnified eyes looked like they belonged to a giant bug. I tried not to laugh. 'You're the stupid one, Em!' I could see that she was offended by my lack of respect for proper procedure. 'One day, a pair of these might save your life. And they're not goggles, they're safety glasses.'

'Sorry.' I pulled the safety goggles down over my eyes to keep her happy.

'Apology accepted,' she said. 'Now pass me that spatula.'

She bent down to continue her experiment; mixing some sulphuric acid with something else in the beaker.

The second half of the lesson was spent writing about the experiment. Ollie was in a different set from us for English and Science, and it could get a bit boring in the lessons without him. We sat by the wooden table with our exercise books out, counting the minutes until the bell rang for us to go home. We did our work, whispering under our breath to pass the time. We eventually got tired and rested our heads on the desk.

When the bell finally rang, we jumped out of our semi-slumber and gathered up our books and pencil cases into our bags. I dropped my book because I was still a bit woozy. I bent over to get it and when I stood up again, there was a tall, menacing figure towering over me.

Stacey Lock.

Great. This is all I need.

She stood in front of me like a prison guard who wouldn't let me pass. Her two clones stood at each side, with their lopsided smirks struggling to break through the five inches of cheap foundation that plastered their faces.

My left ear started ringing.

Damn it. Not again!

I pushed my earlobe to try and get rid of the noise, but it wouldn't shift.

Stacey was saying something to me, but I couldn't hear her with the high-pitched sound.

'Are you even listening to me, Emmeline?' Stacey looked offended.

'Yes!' I half shouted, nervous and confused, trying to focus. 'Sorry! I think I must have bumped my head on the desk or something… I went a bit funny there, for a moment.'

She studied me, eyes narrowed. 'I said,' she emphasised her point, 'that I heard about your mum. You know, about her losing the plot and petrol-bombing the neighbours.'

'She didn't…' I tried to speak, but she interrupted me.

'Whatever.' She rolled her eyes as if I was a waste of her time. 'I don't really care. So what's it like in the children's home? Can you only shower on Sundays?'

'No. I can shower whenever I like,' I answered.

What a stupid question! The girl watched too much telly.

'Lies,' she said. 'I bet you're a real smelly bitch now that you live there. You should be careful, Em. I watched a programme on the telly about those places, and the care workers were messing around with the girls in the nights. Maybe you'll get a visit from a *special friend* when you go to sleep.'

The three girls sniggered.

'Unless, of course…' She leaned forward like she was sharing a secret. 'You already *have* had a visit.'

She looked at The Clones for a round of applause, and they laughed on cue.

'Actually,' said Megan, 'it's very nice there. She even has her own *en suite* bathroom. I've seen it. And the staff are *super* cool. She's allowed out until whatever time she wants, and she gets to go to the cinema just for going to school. So I don't know what programme you've been watching, Stacey, but it's obviously a load of rubbish.'

They gawked at Megan.

I was so proud, I could have burst. She was lying through her teeth, of course. *En suite bathroom?* Yeah, right! But the look on Stacey's face was priceless.

'And my mum didn't petrol-bomb the neighbours,' I said. 'I don't know where that rumour came from, but whoever started it is a liar.'

Stacey looked annoyed. 'My Auntie Zoe told me, actually.' She scowled. 'She is one of your neighbours, remember? I went to her house on the day that your mother cracked up, and Auntie Zoe said that your mum is a psychopath who was running around, screaming that your *dead father* was trying to ring her, but she wouldn't answer the phone because she thought the police were monitoring her calls.'

Oh balls.

'My mother is not a psychopath,' I said. 'Your Auntie Zoe is just a trouble-making tart!' I tried to control the shaking in my voice.

'What did you say?'

Just then, a teacher walked in and shouted at us to get out in the yard because the bell had gone ages ago.

Stacey glared at me. *'You wait,'* she said. Then she turned around and walked out of the class.

In the safety of the open yard, I allowed myself to breathe with relief.

'That girl makes me *ill*,' Megan said, pale-faced.

'I know. And what was all that about before she left? *"You wait."* What's that supposed to mean?'

'When did she say that?' Panic filled Megan's eyes.

'Just before she left the class. I mean, what kind of threat is that? She makes me nervous.' I shivered.

'I never heard her say that.' Megan spotted her bus and started running so she didn't miss it. 'Gotta go! See you tomorrow!'

I waved goodbye and walked to my taxi at the end of the street. I got in and Jolly Clive handed me a packet of crisps and a bottle of pop.

'How was your first day, pet? Did everything go alright?' He smiled at me.

And for some reason, I burst into tears.

FOURTEEN

'Ohhh!' Bett looked traumatised. 'Emmeline Rose! What's the matter? Your face is red! Have you been crying?'

I walked from the taxi to the smoking area where Bett was kicking a football at the wall while Karra smoked a cigarette.

I had travelled the last half of the journey with the window open; hanging my head out of it like a Jack Russell, trying to get some air on my face to cool me down. But the red rash still spread across my forehead and my nose was still twice its average size. Why is crying so unflattering? I remembered watching one of Grandma Coalman's films when I was little, and there was a woman on it crying. She had this elegant, little white handkerchief, and she dabbed her eyes with it, real feminine-like. She was just perfect.

Like a fallen flower. And I remember thinking that when I was older, that's how I would look when I cried.

Fat chance. When I cried now, I looked like a tomato-faced reject, with black streaks running down my blotchy face. It wasn't supposed to be like this.

Poor Bett just stood there in her pink tracksuit, clutching her football with tears in her eyes. I'd learned, since I'd settled into the children's home, that Bett had the gentlest of hearts. She wasn't one to mess with, mind. Even the boys were scared of her. But she was as sensitive as she was solid.

'I'm OK, Bett.' I tried to smile to reassure her. 'Just a weird first day back at school, that's all.'

Bett nodded her head, agreeing with me, even though she wasn't really sure what I meant.

Karra flicked her cigarette across the garden with her middle finger and thumb. 'What happened?' she asked, blowing the last bit of smoke from her mouth.

'It was just really intrusive,' I replied.

'Speak English.' Karra frowned.

'The rumours were rampant around the place.' I cringed. 'They even thought that my mother had *petrol-bombed* the street!'

Karra giggled.

'IT'S NOT FUNNY, KARRA!' I shouted at her, and she burst out laughing.

'I'M SORRY!' she shouted back. 'But *petrol bombs,*

Em… That's *class*! I mean, if you're going to make up a rumour, you may as well be inventive with it!'

Bett started chuckling, her sea-lion laugh echoing under the smoking shelter as she grinned at me. That sent Karra off again. She was laughing so much now that she was tuttying down on the floor, squatting, holding her belly and shouting, 'I'm gonna piss myself! I'm gonna *piss myself!*'

She ran to the toilet, because she really had started to wet herself a little bit and was worried that you could see it through her jeans. Bett and I followed her inside, ready for tea.

'Cabbage! Oh, I *hate* cabbage!' Tyler slumped into his chair at the dinner table.

'It's good for you, Tyler,' said Gladys Friday. She put a big tray of veg in the middle of the table.

'Yeah, Tyler!' Quinn shouted across the tables to him. 'It's good for you! It helps you to see in the dark.'

'That's carrots, you pleb.' Karra rolled her eyes at Quinn, and scooped some potatoes onto her plate.

'Yeah, Quinn!' Tyler shouted from his table. 'Even I know that! And I'm only seven. Cabbage makes you grow big and strong, carrots make you see in the dark, and swede makes you brainy.'

'Who told you swede makes you brainy?' asked Quinn.

'It's obvious, innit?' Tyler tapped his head. 'Swede is good for your *swede*!'

'I eat lots of swede and I'm brainy,' said Bett, scooping a load of it onto her plate.

'Who asked you?' Quinn scowled at Bett.

'SHUT UP, QUINN DAVIES!' Bett shouted from the middle table.

'YOU SHUT UP, BETTY MORRIS!' Quinn bellowed back.

Karra held up her fork – which had a potato stuck to the top of it – and glared at the pair of them. 'I'm not being funny, girls… But if you two don't give it a rest, I'm going to shove this potato so far up your bum, there'll be fries coming out of your mouth! I *mean* it. I've had enough of you. It's cooking my swede!'

Tyler chuckled again at the metaphor as he put some orange swede into his mouth.

The girls started talking about some boy that Karra had met. His name was Lucas. He was from the next town over, but bothered around here because the parks were better.

'Is he a good snogger?' Little Charlie leaned across the table to Karra.

'*Stonking.*' Karra grinned, happy that she was the only one getting snogged at all.

'The chip-shop girls reckon he's been messing around with that Sticky Vicky,' said Quinn. 'They said that she's met his mother and everything. Just be careful, Karra. Don't let him mug you off.'

'He has not been messing around with Sticky Vicky,' Karra argued. 'He told me last night. He got with her one time, that's all. And he was hammered, so it don't count. But now she won't leave him alone – she's a stalker. She only met his mother because she turned up at his house without him knowing.'

'Nooo!' The girls echoed together.

'Yeah!' Karra nodded dramatically and ate some Yorkshire pudding. 'He's deleted her from his friends list and blocked her from his followers, but she's even got her mates to add him so she can keep an eye on what he's up to!'

'I reckon most girls do that.' Quinn picked at some carrots. 'They only look at their boyfriends' profiles so they can look for pictures of their ex-girlfriends and see if they're prettier than them.'

'Yeah, but he's not even her boyfriend, though.' Karra waved her fork around. 'So she's got no right!'

Beano looked across the tables at Karra, straining to hear what was going on. 'What are you girls chatting about?' he called out.

Quinn swallowed her food and spoke. 'We were just talking about Karra's new boyfriend.'

Karra looked embarrassed.

'Who's that?' Beano tried to look like he didn't care.

Quinn and Little Charlie both spoke at the same time, excited at the opportunity for more gossip.

'Lucas. You might know him – he used to bother with Peter-One-Ball,' Little Charlie shouted down to the bottom table.

'But now he bothers with the gyppos up the caravan site,' Quinn joined in.

Bett looked over from her table. 'It's against the law to say "gyppos". They're called *Travellers*. Have some respect, Quinn Davies!'

'Shut up, Betty Morris.' Quinn looked back to Beano.

Beano leaned back in his chair, nonchalantly. 'I know Lucas,' he said. 'He's been boffing Sticky Vicky for the past month. Peter-One-Ball was talking about it the other day.'

'He is *not* boffing Sticky Vicky!' Karra shouted at him.

'That's not what I heard.' Beano looked smug. 'The chip-shop girls reckon she's met his mother.'

Quinn jumped up triumphantly. 'TOLD YOU!' She looked at Karra like she'd just beaten her in a competition.

'The chip-shop girls are liars!' Karra stabbed her meat and started cutting it aggressively with her knife and fork. 'She met his mother because she's a *psycho* who turned up at his house *uninvited*. If he's been going out with her, then why has he blocked her from all of his profiles and deleted her from his Facebook friends?'

'Good point.' Beano nodded. 'What about you? Is he in a relationship with you on Facebook?'

'Not yet, but we've only just started seeing each other,' replied Karra.

'Well, I'm not being funny or anything,' said Beano, 'but if it's not on Facebook, then it's not a real relationship. *Everyone* knows that.'

Karra sulked as she rammed a piece of broccoli into her mouth and gave Beano stinkers across the tables.

Little Charlie looked thoughtful. 'I wonder why they call him Peter-One-Ball,' she said.

Beano chuckled. 'He broke into an old man's garden a few years ago, and let's just say that the owner had a very good guard dog!'

Little Charlie's mouth fell open when she realised what Beano meant.

'That's karma for you!' Beano laughed out loud from his table. 'It'll teach him to have a bit more respect for his elders in the future!'

The girls finished their food and left the table to go and watch telly. I stayed to eat the last of my vegetables.

The middle table played 'I-spy.' Tyler and Bett made the perfect team. Because Tyler was so young, anything he spied was usually easy for Bett to guess. And Bett took everything in the world literally, so anything she spied would be something that she had directly looked at. Tyler would only have to follow her eyes to guess the answer. She would look straight at the cabbage, and say, 'I spy with my little eye, something beginning with C.'

It was a win-win situation, really.

On the bottom table, Beano was telling Big Jim that a girl at his work placement had been giving him the glad-eye for the past couple of weeks, and he was wondering whether to ask her out for a McDonald's or not. Play hard to get, Big Jim told him. You don't go buying a Big Mac for just anyone.

I smiled at the bizarre conversations going on around me. I was glad that after a difficult first day at school, I could come back to an environment where nobody cared whether or not my mother had petrol-bombed the street. And I realised that even if school was a little stressful, I could come here to a place of refuge. The children's home was fast becoming more of a home to me than my actual home.

I joined the others at the sofa. It was Tyler's turn to pick, and everyone moaned as they sat watching cartoons. I never admitted it, but I quite liked cartoons. Me and Freya would sit for hours watching them. Even as I got older and wanted to watch my own programmes, we usually ended up watching hers. Mum said it was the only way to keep her quiet. She said that when you have kids, you spend the first year teaching them to walk and talk. And then you spend the rest of their life telling them to shut up and sit down. She said that cartoons were the tiny bit of respite in between. I just thought that they were cool.

I still hadn't visited Mum. Freya and I weren't allowed to go until the doctors thought she was ready to see us. That made me laugh – until *she* was ready to see *us*. The cheek of it. Mel said that she would let me know when it was OK. It upset me a bit when I thought about her stuck in hospital, with nobody to talk to. But I knew that she needed to get well again. And she needed to stay well this time.

I didn't like to think of it because if I did, I had to think about what would happen when she got out. I knew in my heart that I'd had enough. I didn't want to go back now. But if I didn't go home, she would be there by herself, unless Grandma Coalman moved in with her. But poor Grandma Coalman was in her seventies; how was she supposed to take care of a mental patient like Mum? She didn't need that at her age. She needed peace and quiet, an easy life. It's what we all needed.

I could hear a familiar song playing in the background. I looked up, and realised that we were watching the same cartoon as I usually watched at home with Freya and Mum. I wondered if there was any chance they might be watching it at the same time as me. I hoped that, even though we were in different buildings, in different areas, maybe there was some kind of connection between us, sizzling between the energy waves of the televisions we were watching.

And like in the cartoons, maybe one day there would be a happy ending.

FIFTEEN

Me, Megan and Ollie were sitting on the steps round the back of C-block, enjoying what was left of lunchtime.

We had a maths test after dinner, so we were trying to keep our minds off it by playing the Virgin-Waddle game.

'I'm not doing it!' I protested.

'Oh, *come on*, Em!' Megan whined. 'I just did it, so now you have to do it. Otherwise it's not fair!'

The Virgin-Waddle game is the most embarrassing game ever invented. You have to walk up and down in front of everyone, and they can tell by the way you walk – the way your bum wiggles – whether you're a virgin or not.

Megan did the walk and apparently she definitely wasn't a virgin. This game was invented by Year Elevens, so it must be true. I was a bit annoyed, because Megan hadn't even told me that she had lost her virginity, and I was supposed to be her best friend. She was a bit of a sly-off like that sometimes.

'She's a chicken!' Ollie laughed. 'Take-the-shame, Em! Take-the-shame!'

'Shut up, Ollie!' I snapped, and got up from the steps. I did a red-faced walk down the path, wiggling my bum in a way which I hoped resembled that of a sophisticated woman.

The vote was unanimous: *inconclusive*. They just couldn't tell. And I, of course, was keeping my mouth firmly shut because I didn't want to be known as a fridge.

The bell went and maths class came. We all spread ourselves out around the classroom – we had to sit at arm's length away from everyone, so we couldn't cheat. Megan moved closer to me until the teacher came back.

'Have you *really* done it?' she asked.

'Done what?'

'You know what I'm talking about,' she replied. 'Have you done *IT*?'

'Maybe.' I shrugged my shoulders. It's important to stay cool and aloof in these situations.

'Well, if you have, why didn't you tell *me* about it?' She seemed hurt. 'You're a bit of a sly-off like that sometimes, Em.'

'*Me?*' I was really offended. '*You're* the sly-off, Megan! Why didn't you tell me?'

'Because I haven't done anything yet, that's why!' She looked annoyed.

'Well, neither have I!'

'So you're still a virgin?' she whispered, checking that nobody could hear.

'Yes, of course I am!' I whispered back.

'But…' She was confused. 'But your bum waddled, Em.'

'So did yours,' I replied.

'That means … the game doesn't work,' said Megan.

We stared at each other, taking in this new revelation.

The Year Elevens had *lied*.

'Alright, SMELLMELINE!' Stacey Lock shouted across the class to me. She sat a couple of seats down from Ollie. The Clones followed and took their seats at her side.

'Just ignore her,' said Megan.

I turned away, glad to see that the teacher had come back.

Stacey was laughing, pleased with her little victory because I hadn't answered her back. She now called me Smellmeline each time she saw me. It really annoyed me because I knew how clean I was, but I worried that everyone else might think I was dirty.

I did my maths test. I was furiously working out mathematical equations, frustrated with myself for not being quicker, smarter and braver. Have you ever heard of 'The Wit of The Staircase'? There's a French saying for it. I think you say it as *'esprit de l'escalier'*. It's the perfect witty response that you think of *after* the conversation or argument has ended. Well, that's basically the story of my life. I have an argument with someone, and afterwards I spend all my time thinking about what I should have said. Just once, I wish I could kick someone's ass with my verbal karate and know *exactly* the right thing to say at *exactly* the right time to say it. But when I try this in real life, I'm rubbish. I just end up making a complete tit of myself.

So I spent the whole maths test scribbling answers and going over all the things in my head that would have sounded awesome if I had said them back to Stacey Lock. She was really starting to wind me up.

When I got home, Karra was outside, pacing up and down.

Big Jim was standing under the smoking shelter.

'What's the matter with you?' I asked, looking at her anxious face.

'Oh! Don't ASK!' Big Jim shouted and threw his hands in the air. 'The boyfriend hasn't phoned her for two days, and she's having a panic attack over it!'

Karra was still seeing Lucas. So far, he had turned out to be a right tool. Quinn and Little Charlie reckoned that everyone knew he was going with Sticky Vicky behind Karra's back, but Karra wouldn't hear of it.

'Shut your face, Jim!' Karra was clearly aggravated. 'I just want a missed call, that's all. Just one missed call!'

'Why do you want a *missed* call?' I asked.

She gave me an irritated look.

Jim's voice boomed from under the shelter as he laughed at her again. She threw her leg out to kick him as he lit up a cigarette for himself.

'After you, Jim?' She nodded towards the cigarette.

'You *know* I can't give you any smokes, Karra. It's against the law. You're under age – you shouldn't be smoking in the first place.'

'Oh, shut up, Jim! You always give me smokes!' she snapped at him, and he hushed her manically, looking around to make sure nobody had heard, in case he got into trouble with Auntie Sue.

'I don't get it,' I said. 'Why would you want a missed call? Why don't you want a real call?'

'Because then I'd have to answer it,' she replied.

'So?'

'Well, I don't want to *answer* it, Em. I just want to know that he's phoned, that's all. I like getting a missed call from a boy. It makes me feel in control.'

Big Jim laughed out loud. 'You kids!' He ruffled Karra's hair. 'You make my day! Honestly, you do! The nonsense you come out with! It's *buuuriful* to see, it really is.'

He nodded towards Karra as he threw half his cigarette on the bench. Looking around to make sure nobody saw, she picked it up.

He walked off and then turned back around, as if he'd remembered something. 'Emmeline, love!'

I looked over to him.

'Your social worker phoned earlier,' he said. 'Mel, is it?'

'Yeah,' I replied.

'She rang just before you got home. She wanted me to let you know that your mother is ready for visitors.'

My throat went dry. 'My *mum*?' I asked.

He nodded.

'You mean your *mam*.' Karra scowled at me.

'That's what I said.'

Big Jim went back inside the building.

'No, Em…' Karra spoke as if she was talking to a child. 'Now, come on. We've been through this, haven't we? English people say "*Mum*" and Welsh people say…' She waited for me to finish the sentence.

'*Mam*,' I said, and tried to settle my nerves.

'Good girl.' Karra smiled proudly.

I stood for a moment, slightly dazed.

Karra blew out some smoke rings and said, 'Well, at least *one* of us has had a missed-poxy-call today.'

SIXTEEN

I was sitting in the back of Mel's car.

I leant my head against the window and watched everything go by. I remembered travelling through the same streets on the very first day I arrived at the children's home.

I was as nervous now as I was back then.

We drove down the hill, and there it was, greeting me like it always did, with its beautiful white petals, like pearls. I had grown to love the white rose bush. Whenever I felt lonely or confused, I would walk to the park and sit quietly on the swings near the white roses. Just being in their presence made me feel better. The rose bush was so similar to the one we used to have at home. Even though I knew there was no way it was the same one, I liked to pretend it was.

Dad loved gardening. When he was alive, our garden was like something from one of those posh magazines. He took care of the rose bush every day to make sure it produced the most magical white roses I had ever seen. But after he died, they stopped growing. The rose bush looked how we felt inside – *empty*. Poor Mum was always asking if the roses had come back yet, and seemed devastated each time I said no. Like she thought the roses were actually a part of Dad, and if they came back, then maybe he would come back too.

When Nana Rose died a year later, Mum went to pieces. She had lost her husband and her mother within a year, and every ounce of grief showed itself in her skin. Like a disease, it spread right down to the root of her. By the time I reached fourteen, the grief was too strong for her, so she just gave up.

The rose bush disappeared from sight as we drove away, and Mel was wittering on in the front about her boyfriend. She was telling me how inadequate he was, and that I should never go for an inadequate man.

'They reckon that most people go for someone who reminds them of their parents or siblings,' she said.

'Gross.' I scrunched up my nose.

'Oh, yes, it's common knowledge!' she carried on. 'I honestly believe that's why I go for inadequate men.'

'Why?' I asked.

'Because my father's a knob.'

I laughed from the back of the car, and she winked at me in the front mirror.

'My dad was pretty cool,' I told her, and then leant my head against the window again.

'I know he was, Em.' She smiled gently at me.

We turned into the car park of the hospital.

'Here we are,' she said. 'Are you nervous?'

I shrugged my shoulders as I looked down again at the white velvet rose on my lucky cardigan.

My stomach started churning like it was full of gone-off milk.

We got out of the car and walked towards the double doors of the front entrance.

The place looked so gloomy. Concrete everywhere. I thought it was the last place you should put depressed people. If they weren't mental before they got there, they'd be mental by the time they left. How could anyone get better in a place like this?

I started getting upset, thinking how Mum must see this every day. This was her view. When she looked out of her window, this was all she saw … *grey*.

I bit my lip to stop myself crying, but my eyes filled up like a boiling kettle and I had to take a few seconds to breathe and let out the steam.

I folded my arms as I walked in. We were met by a member of staff in a blue uniform.

'Emmeline?'

I nodded and Mel shook the man's hand.

'My name is Seth.' He smiled at me. 'I'm your mum's name nurse. Your mother has been looking forward to seeing you.'

I didn't know what a name nurse was, but I nodded and smiled back at him anyway.

I could taste blood in my mouth, and I realised that my lip was bleeding from where I'd been biting it.

'How is she?' Mel asked the man.

'She's OK,' he replied. 'She's having a good day today.'

SEVENTEEN

The corridors smelt of disinfectant.

We followed Seth. I clutched the sleeves of my lucky cardigan. He had to buzz us in through the doors by tapping a code into a monitor on the wall. The doors opened automatically to let us into a bright ward with white, clinical walls.

As we walked past the patients, I tried not to stare.

A woman sat in a green chair, holding her head and whispering to herself. Next to her, another lady was holding rosary beads and praying repeatedly.

We passed the day room. There were people watching telly, reading books and playing board games. There was a man sitting at a table, who seemed to be cleaning an apple.

I looked for my mother, but there was no sign of her.

There was a little serving hatch in the wall. It was similar to the one we used in the children's home to transfer food through to the dining room. Except this one wasn't for food. There were people in pyjamas and dressing gowns queuing up outside the hatch and being served tiny cups. A nurse stood next to the queue, checking their tongues. I could hear the patients saying, '*Ahhhhh*,' with their mouths open, sticking their tongues out, like when you visit the doctor for a bad throat.

'Why are they doing that?' I asked Seth-the-name-nurse.

'We have to make sure that they're taking their medication,' he said.

'Do they not take them?'

'Well, most of them do,' he replied, 'but some patients… They like to hide them.'

'What for?'

He looked warily at Mel, and she quickly changed the subject.

We walked to the end of the ward, and I was still wondering about the medication when he announced that this was Mum's room.

'Knock, knock!' he sang as he opened the door. 'Tess, love! You have a visitor! Look! It's *Emmeline*!'

She was sitting by the side of her bed in a blue armchair.

Her blonde hair was tied into a messy ponytail, and her face was pale. She'd lost quite a bit of weight. She looked so small in the chair, like a child who couldn't quite reach the floor with her feet.

She looked up, and I don't think she realised what was going on for a second, because she had a kind of delayed reaction before she registered that it was me. As soon as she did, she jumped off the chair and threw herself at me, flinging her arms around my neck and kissing me a hundred times all over my face.

'Calm down, Mum!' I laughed and kissed her cheek. 'It's only me!'

She was crying. Big, bomping tears ran down her face. She turned away from me so I couldn't see them. Her nose was running, so I reached up my hand – still clutching the sleeve of my lucky cardigan – and I pinched her nose with my thumb and index finger to wipe it for her.

'I'm full of snot!' She laughed, her voice croaky from the tears.

'You're OK.' I hugged her tightly.

The visit was a little awkward to begin with. We hadn't seen each other since the day she was taken into hospital, and part of me resented that she didn't seem to understand the massive effect that day had on Grandma Coalman, my sister and me. I had to remind myself that Mum was unwell – she didn't do it on purpose.

We read a magazine together and did a crossword which promised a holiday to Jamaica if we won. She got a bit brighter and was chatting away to me and Mel. Her speech was a little rushed, but I think that was from the medication. She was asking about Freya and Grandma Coalman, and she kept asking if we knew when she would be allowed home. Mel said that Mum would be staying a while longer, another few weeks probably, just so the doctors could make sure that she was definitely well enough to go home.

'I can't even remember much of what happened,' Mum said, staring out of the window. 'I just remember feeling so *trapped*.' She gasped slightly. 'Can you remember it, Em?'

I didn't know whether to tell the truth or lie.

Mel must have sensed my discomfort because she started talking to Mum about something else.

I stared at the magazine page in front of me, and my mind travelled back to that day.

It was the last day of school.

I was in geography class, sitting by the window, praying for an escape before I died of boredom. If I'd known my prayers were going to be answered, I would have asked for snow. At least that way, we could have had some fun.

There was a knock on the door and the Deputy Head came in and asked if he could see me for a moment.

I was a little embarrassed. You know that feeling when a teacher wants to see you? It always feels like you're in trouble. Even if you know you haven't done anything wrong, you still panic. A bit like when you walk out of a shop and the alarm goes off. Even though you know you haven't taken anything, you still worry that they'll ask to search your bag, and somehow there'll be something stolen in it.

I got up and he told me to bring my things with me.

We walked up to his office in silence.

Awks.

The school counsellor was waiting in the office, and she told me to sit down. She explained that there had been an 'incident' at home. She didn't want me to panic, but somebody would be here shortly to pick me up from school. She said that the police had been called out to our address, and they needed my help with a situation.

'What situation?' I asked.

She said that she wasn't exactly sure what was going on, but she knew that the situation concerned my mother, and the police needed my assistance.

When I arrived at the house, there was furniture all over the front garden. Some of the front windows had been smashed and glass littered the garden path. There were police outside, and a couple of them were trying to get Mum to let them into the house, but she was having none of it.

The police asked if I would knock on the door because apparently Mum had insisted that she needed me, and *only* me.

They told me that a policewoman would come in with me to see if we could 'defuse the situation'.

As soon as I knocked on the front door, I saw Mum's face squash up against the glass to see who it was. I couldn't help but laugh. The policewoman didn't look impressed.

'Mum, it's me!' I said.

There was a couple of seconds' silence while she considered this. Her face was firmly pressed into the glass, making her look a bit distorted with a fat nose.

'Who's *Me*?' she asked.

'It's me,' I repeated. 'Emmeline. Come on, Mum. Open the door!'

She unbolted the door and opened it a tiny bit. All you could see was her eye, peering at me through the gap. Then her arm shot out like a cobra, and she grabbed me.

'*Quick!*' She was manic. '*Before they see us!*'

She pulled me straight in and tried to shut the front door, but the policewoman jammed her foot in and the door wouldn't close. Mum was banging herself against it, trying to force the door shut.

'It's OK, Mum.' I tried to control the nerves in my voice. 'She's my friend. I've brought her home for tea.'

Mum eyed me suspiciously. She knew that I never brought people back for tea.

'Why is she wearing that?' She nodded at the policewoman's uniform.

'Red Nose Day,' I replied. 'It's fancy dress. I'm putting my costume on in a minute.'

I could see she was still wary, so I smiled and said, 'I thought she could try some of your apple pie. She loves apple pie, but her mum isn't a very good cook so I said she could try yours.'

The expression on her face changed to relief.

'Ohhh!' Mum flashed her most welcoming smile. 'I am sorry! How rude of me! Come in, love. Make yourself at home!' She opened the door, and stuck her head out of it, looking quickly up and down the road, scanning for intruders.

The policewoman came into the house, and Mum was trying to be the perfect hostess – all the while checking the windows, doors, locks and telephones. She looked in the kitchen to see if she had any cooking apples, but realised there were none left.

'I'm *so* sorry.' Her eyes filled with tears. 'I don't want you to go hungry, but I've just no apples here!'

'That's fine,' said the policewoman. 'I'm not very hungry, but I'm sure your apple pie is lovely!'

'Oh, it is!' Mum looked proud. 'It's *delish*! Isn't it, Em?'

I nodded.

'I would ring my mother-in-law to pick up some

cooking apples,' said Mum. 'But I daren't use the telephone, because the government is monitoring my phone calls.'

The policewoman raised her eyebrows. 'Why do you think the government is monitoring your phone calls?'

'Because my husband wants to speak to me,' replied Mum, 'but they won't let him get through.'

This hit me like a smack in the face, and I tried to keep myself together. I hadn't realised how bad Mum was. How had I not noticed how unstable she was getting? I should have made sure that she was taking her medication properly.

'Did you know,' Mum spoke animatedly, 'if you use your mobile phone for Facebook, they're allowed to access your phone and watch you through your camera at any time they want?'

'I didn't know that,' said the policewoman.

Mum pursed her lips and nodded indignantly.

'My throat is really dry,' I said. 'I'm just going to get a drink.'

'NO!' Mum shouted at me. 'Stay … right … there. I'll get it for you. Keep an eye on that window for me!'

Mum went to make us a glass of squash. When she left the living room, the policewoman told me to just go with the flow and not to say or do anything that might freak Mum out. 'Just keep the conversation as easy as possible,' she said. 'You're doing really well, Emmeline.'

'Is that true about Facebook being able to look at you through your phone camera?' I asked her.

'God knows,' replied the policewoman. 'It wouldn't surprise me!'

When Mum came back, we all sat in the living room, talking about apple pie.

I was on the sofa, thinking how bizarre it was that the window was smashed but we were just sitting there, chatting, like it was perfectly normal.

Mum got up again and paced back and forth, constantly checking the windows.

'What's the matter, Mum?' I asked.

She appeared from behind the curtain, with wide eyes and a gossipy look.

'Don't ask!' She threw her hands in the air.

She sat back on the chair and lit a cigarette, never once taking her eyes from the window. When she thought the coast was clear, she looked at me like she had some really juicy news.

'I won't lie to you, Em…' She inhaled deeply, and blew out the smoke in a rush. 'It's your father. He Is Out-Of-*Control*! The man is *MAD*! There's no reasoning with him! Have you seen what he's done? Have you *seen* it?' She gestured to the mess that surrounded us.

Oh balls.

She'd done it this time.

Mum took another deep drag of her cigarette.

'He's a *bastard*!' she shouted, her voice getting higher. '*He* did all this, you know. He's *wrecked* the house! *Look!* Look what he's done to my good vase!'

She picked up a piece of broken glass and waved it around. 'This was an anniversary gift! It's expensive! What will I put my roses in now? Has he even brought them yet?'

'Brought what?' I asked.

'MY ROSES!' she shouted.

I stared at her.

'Mum, have you been taking your medication?' I asked.

She scoffed. 'I'm not taking that again. They think I'm stupid, Em. They're trying to drug me.'

She started laughing. 'Well, more fool them! I haven't put that filth into my system for ages! And it just proves that I don't need it, because I'm *ab-so-lute-ly fin*e.'

'Clearly.' I buried my head in my hands.

'I don't know how I'm going to sort all this out, though!' she said in a huff. 'He can pay for the damage. I know he's your father, Em, and God knows I love the man, but this! This just takes the piss!'

Her hands were shaking.

'Mum…' I started choking up a bit. 'Dad's not here. He passed away ages ago. He didn't do all this. He *couldn't* have.'

She looked at me for a second, trying to compute what I was saying. 'No,' she said.

What did she mean, no?

'No,' she repeated.

The policewoman shifted in her seat.

'NO!' She shook her head. 'NO! NO! NOOOO!' she shouted over and over again. 'He's a bastard!'

The policewoman got up and tried to calm Mum down.

I started crying. I was scared.

My mobile rang. I looked at the screen – it was Megan. She was probably phoning to see why I had to leave school early.

'WHO'S THAT?' Mum screamed at me. She looked terrified. 'Don't you answer that! Don't you *dare* answer that, Emmeline! They'll be listening!'

She dived at me, grabbed my mobile and threw it across the room. It hit the wall and broke into little pieces.

My phone! I'd only just sorted out my contacts list! I'd matched everyone's names up with their profile pictures! What was I going to do now?

She started running around the house, smashing everything and throwing things against the walls. I had never seen her like this before. It was really frightening.

'Request for backup.' The policewoman spoke into her walkie-talkie. She turned to me. 'Stay in here,' she said.

I sat on the sofa, panicking. Why was she calling for backup? What did that mean?

I got down on my hands and knees to try and pick up the pieces of my broken phone. I looked at all the bits scattered around the room, and I couldn't control my tears.

I could hear the policewoman speaking to my mother in the kitchen. 'Tess…' The policewoman tried to keep her calm. 'Why don't you put the knife down?'

I dropped the bits from my hand and I froze on the spot, unable to move.

I heard my mother crying. 'I don't want to be here,' she said quietly.

I was paralysed with fear. She wouldn't hurt herself, would she?

'Tess, you don't mean that,' said the policewoman. 'Now, why don't you just put the knife down, love? Let's make a nice cup of tea and talk about things.'

'I want to be with my husband,' Mum spoke through her sobs.

'Tess…' The policewoman's voice was shaking. 'No, Tess… TESS!'

I jumped off the sofa to run to my mother.

All of a sudden, the front door burst open. A load of people in uniforms came rushing in, and I couldn't get to my mother because they were like a swarm of bees around her.

I could see blood and I didn't know where it was coming from. Was it my mother's blood? Was it the policewoman's blood? Why was there *blood*?

I didn't know what was going on; everything happened so fast.

The paramedics were holding Mum down.

'Leave her alone!' I shouted at them. 'You're frightening her! You're *hurting* her!'

She was kicking out and trying to get them off her. She was screaming and throwing herself back and forth as hard as she could. I saw one of them take something out of a case, but I couldn't see what it was. Then he turned to face my mother, and I saw a tiny bit of liquid squirt out from the top of a syringe that he was holding.

I tried to shout again, but nothing came out. I couldn't speak.

Five people restrained her, holding her entire body down.

The paramedic jammed the needle into her leg, and she passed out on the spot ... just like that.

I heard Mel's voice calling me away from the memory, and back into the hospital room. 'Emmeline!'

I looked up from the magazine, slightly dazed.

'Wake up!' Mel clapped her hands together. 'I was just saying that when your mum is better, we should all go to the zoo. Your mum loves the zoo, doesn't she?'

'I do love the zoo, Em!' said Mum.

I tried to clear my throat so I could respond.

'We used to go all the time when Emmeline was little.'

Mum smiled. 'She was such a darling, Mel. You should have seen her when she was a baby!'

She started rummaging through her bag, taking out baby photos of me and Freya. I caught sight of a red scar on the inside of her wrist. I looked away, wincing. Mel was looking through the photos and saying how cute we were, and Mum seemed happy to be sitting there, chatting about our baby years with someone who really engaged in the conversation. I felt guilty that maybe I didn't always pay Mum enough attention. Perhaps if I had, she wouldn't have ended up in *here*. If I had just made sure that she was taking her medication every day, none of this would have happened.

Mum was looking at me, her head tilted to one side as she squinted through her half-shut eyes. She was joining her fingers together and making a square shape around her eyes, as if she was mentally fitting me inside a frame.

Mel laughed awkwardly and picked up a glass of water.

'Mum?' I frowned. 'What are you doing?'

'Just looking,' she said, squinting her eyes tightly.

'Looking at what?'

'If I look at you like this,' she said, 'you look a bit like your scan photo from when I was pregnant.'

Mel choked on her drink, snorting loudly as water shot out of her mouth and flew across the room.

Mum started giggling.

'Sorry!' Mel waved her hands. 'It just took me by

surprise, that's all.' She was getting redder and redder by the second because she was so embarrassed.

Mum found this hilarious. She was laughing so much that her nose started running. She leant over to me so I could help her.

'*Quick, Em!*' Mum shrieked with laughter. 'I'm full of snot!'

I grabbed the sleeve of my lucky cardigan. I pinched the material together with my thumb and index finger, and for the second time that day I wiped my mother's nose.

EIGHTEEN

It was the end of the week, and Jolly Clive brought me to school as usual. Every Friday, his wife gave him choc-chip muffins, so we sat in the car and ate two each while we listened to his Boyzone album. I wasn't really a big fan of Boyzone, they were a band from the olden days, but Jolly Clive seemed to really like them so I was happy to give them a chance.

I spotted Megan and Ollie getting off their bus, so I said thank you for the muffins and got out of the car as Megan walked towards me.

'You are *so* lucky to have your very own taxi driver!' She waved to Jolly Clive as he pulled off, and he beeped the horn back. 'I have to sit on that rank machine that they call a school bus, breathing in the millions of bacteria that will probably lead to my death.'

Ollie ran to catch up with us. 'Have you two done your history homework?'

'Of course we have, Ollie. It's *us.*' Megan smiled proudly.

'Good girls. I can copy some of your answers for the ones I didn't finish.' He winked at us and Megan rolled her eyes.

We walked into school, talking about all the homework that had to be finished in time for Christmas. We arrived at registration class, and the walls were lined with students. I was so involved in my conversation with Megan and Ollie that I didn't see Stacey Lock push her bag slowly out on the floor as I got closer to the registration line.

'Watch you don't trip, *Smellmeline!*' Stacey's voice was sour, and I looked up to see what was going on, but I couldn't see her mouth moving.

Just then, my foot got caught in the handle of the bag, and I did one of those weird falls where you trip over yourself and go down like a sack of spuds to the floor. My bag went flying across the ground, and as I landed, I hurt the corner of my elbow. A tingly pain went right through my arm, all the way down to my fingers. It felt like jelly. I really had to fight to stop myself crying. I was *so* embarrassed; my whole face was on fire I was blushing so much.

'Ohhh!' Stacey Lock looked down at me. '*Smellmeline!*

Look at you on the floor. I always knew you were a scrubber!' She laughed and The Clones laughed with her.

Megan picked up my bag and Ollie helped me up from the floor.

'What's your *problem*, Stace?' Ollie frowned.

Stacey looked humiliated by Ollie's telling-off.

I brushed myself down and joined the line.

'You should be more careful, Em.' She winked at me.

'Why have you got to be such a cow all the time, Stacey?' I frowned at her.

'Well, thank you very much. I'll take that as a compliment.' She smirked and walked into class.

'Did you hurt yourself, Em?' Ollie asked.

'Just my elbow, that's all.'

'Humerus?' He tried to hide his grin as he lifted my arm to see the injury.

'Oh, *ha-ha*,' I said, nursing my elbow. 'No, it wasn't humorous at all, thank you very much.'

'I'm surprised you even know what the humerus bone is,' Megan smirked at Ollie. 'Let alone how to use it in a joke. Well done, Ollie. I'm impressed.'

'I'll have you know that I'm very good at biology,' Ollie replied. 'And I also broke my humerus bone once, during a rugby match. It wasn't humorous at all for me, so I don't know why medical science insists on calling it that.'

'Will you two just shut up about the bloody *humerus*!' I

147

snapped at them as I lifted my arm up over my head to try and ease the pain in my elbow.

After that, I thought I'd heard the last of Stacey Lock for the day. *Not a chance.*

When we finished our gym lesson, I gathered my things to leave the changing room. When I turned around, I got a locker door smack-bang in my face. My nose burst straight away; blood spilling out of it like a can of cherryade that had been shaken and then popped open.

My eyes stung fiercely as the teacher sat me down on the bench with tissues for me to hold my nose.

I knew Stacey had done it on purpose, but she insisted that it was an accident. I was sent to the nurse's office. Luckily, it wasn't broken. The nurse said I was fine, but I had to take it easy for a few days because it would be sensitive. She let me stay in her office until the lunch bell went, and she gave me a lollipop. If anyone else had been there, I would have probably been too embarrassed to accept it, but as I was on my own, I just said thank you and cherished the lollipop as I sat in the office.

Lunchtime came, and I was grateful for the chance to chill out with Megan. I sat on the steps and wrapped my lucky cardigan around me to soothe the tears threatening to fall. Apart from my half hour in the nurse's office, it had been a horrible day. And, as if the universe was waiting for that perfect moment to ruin my tiny bit of peace, my nose started bleeding again just as I opened my packet of crisps.

'WHYYYYYY?' I shouted to the sky.

'Calm down, Em!' Megan panicked. 'I'll get you some tissue. Just stay still!'

A drop of blood fell onto a crisp.

I threw my head back in distress. 'MY CRIIII-ISSSSPPPPSSS!'

Megan ran quickly to the girls' toilets, and came skidding back with a load of bog-roll spilling from her hands. She threw it into my face, jumping around in alarm. I tilted my head back and covered my nose with tissue to soak up the red slime. I could taste blood in my mouth, oily, warm and metallic.

'That stupid bitch, Stacey Lock!' Megan was tamping; pacing back and forth with her hands on her hips. 'I can't believe she slammed the locker door in your face. What a low-life piece of…'

'It's fine!' My voice was squeaky from pinching my nose together. 'Don't worry about it. I'll deal with Stacey Lock in my own time.'

Megan sat down next to me on the step.

'Can't you tell those girls in the children's home? They could sort her out for you, couldn't they?' She looked at me with sad eyes.

I shook my head. 'They already think I'm a wimp. I don't want to have to call on them every time I have a problem. I want to be able to fight my own battles.'

'But that's the point, Em,' she said. 'You can't fight your

own battles, not this one anyway. Why don't you just ask them for help? Otherwise Stacey is going to keep slamming doors in your face, or tripping you up, or whatever else she can do to make you miserable, for the rest of your life!'

She had a point, but I didn't want the girls to find out about this. They would just come storming down here to give Stacey Lock a visit that she wouldn't forget. And if that happened, I could end up getting suspended from school. How would *that* look on my Record of Achievement?

Besides, Karra had been getting grumpier and grumpier over the past few weeks. You couldn't ask her what the time was, let alone ask her for a favour. That boy she'd been seeing, Lucas, had been messing her around a lot. He never rang when he said he would, it took him ages to text her back, and Quinn said it was common knowledge that he was necking Sticky Vicky behind the chip shop last weekend.

It was us that Karra took it out on. We had to tiptoe around her because if you did anything to annoy her, she would jump down your throat.

I had to think of something else. I had to take care of this by myself, and I had to do something soon because Stacey Lock was getting worse. Some days she would leave me alone, but other times it was like she'd set her eyes on me for the day, determined to make it as grim for me as possible. Today was one of those days.

So there I was, sitting on the steps in C-block, stuffing toilet roll up my nostrils like one of those stupid people who stick things up their nose because they think it makes them look like a walrus.

I couldn't go on like this. Something had to change.

Perhaps Megan was right; maybe I could just mention it to Karra.

Last class: English.

I couldn't concentrate. Usually, English was my favourite subject, but I was so irritable today I just couldn't wait to get from there. I had so much restless energy running through me I couldn't keep still. I had to keep shaking my hands, like I was trying to dry my nails, except it was to try and shake the adrenaline out of my system. What was going on? Maybe I was coming down with something.

Megan was looking at me stupid. 'What is wrong with you?'

'I'm not sure,' I answered, 'I'm just so restless. I can't focus at all.'

'Maybe you should go and see the nurse again.' Megan looked concerned. 'You might have concussion or something. You're acting *really* weird.'

I tried to concentrate on my work.

We were doing something about onomatopoeia – whatever that was.

Stacey Lock was sitting a couple of rows away, to my right; her presence irritating me like a fly that I wanted to splat with a magazine. *Bzzzzzzzz. Bzzzzzzzz.* I could hear her buzzing to The Clones about how much she hated English.

She felt too close to me, even though in reality she wasn't very near. My body pumped with frustration, just knowing that she was there.

I hugged my lucky cardigan to me, trying to ease the tension building inside.

My ear started ringing again. I would have to see a doctor about this. Auntie Sue said that it might be something called tinnitus. Usually old people suffered with it.

I pulled at the bottom of my ear, but the ringing was still there.

The teacher spoke, but I couldn't hear what he was saying. The ringing got louder, and the more I thought about it, the stronger it got. Between the noise in my head, the pain in my nose, and Stacey Lock being right *there*, I felt like I was suffocating.

I put my head into my hands.

Go away.

I pressed my thumbs into my ears, and rubbed my

forehead with my fingers to try and ease the tension. I felt like my head was going to implode. I just wanted everything to … *STOP!*

All of a sudden, everything was still.

The ringing noise had gone. I wondered where it went, and how it had disappeared so suddenly.

'What is he *talking* about?' Stacey Lock's voice made me jump.

I looked across at her, but she was facing away from me so I couldn't see properly.

'I'll just copy off someone. Whose work can I steal?' She started going through some names in the class, listing the people she could potentially copy from.

There she was, just brazenly planning her cheating methods. Out loud.

I shook my head at the cheek of it.

I heard her say Megan's name. 'Megan's smart. She always gets good marks for things. Bloody swot…'

Huh! As if Megan would even consider doing anything for her. I looked at Megan and raised my eyebrows in a *'who-the-fudge-does-she-think-she-is?'* kind of way.

Megan looked back at me in a *'what-the-fudge-are-you-talking-about?'* kind of way.

Why didn't she look annoyed at what Stacey had just said?

I heard Stacey's voice again. 'I suppose I could ask Emmeline, but she'd probably say no.'

Yeah, I thought to myself. *Too right I'd say no, you stupid muff.* Who did she think she was? I'd had enough of this. That girl needed to be told, and if nobody else had the guts to say anything to her, then maybe I should.

'I feel bad about the locker thing,' said Stacey. 'I felt a bit sorry for her. I didn't mean it to hit her that hard.'

Oh-my-life. Was she serious? Didn't mean to hit me that hard? The girl had bust my nose! I looked at Megan again to see if she was reacting at all, but there was nothing. Not even a glimmer of rage. Why was she being such a sly-off? Why didn't she care what Stacey Lock was saying?

Stacey's voice came back again, except this time it was very strange.

'I wonder what it's like in the homes. Auntie Zoe reckons Emmeline's mother is a right nutter. I bet Emmeline hasn't *really* got an en suite bathroom. That cardigan is nice. I'm going to get one the same, except mine will be better. I like her hair – it's always so *shiny.* No wonder he fancies her. No, he *doesn't* fancy her! She's probably a *man-stealer,* just like the rest of the women in her family. I wish *my* hair was like that. *Bitch.* I hope her nose is OK. *No, I don't.* I hope it's broken. *No, I don't.* I hope it's OK. Miss Baker had a right go at me. *Moany old cow.'*

What was happening? Why was she talking so fast? She was just skipping from one sentence to another. It was like her words were changing as quickly as her thoughts.

154

Who did she think fancied me? And why would she call my family *man-stealers*?

She spoke again. 'She's probably a psycho skank, just like her mother!'

WHAT?

I screwed up my face. 'Don't you *dare* speak about my mother like that!' I scowled at her across the tables. 'What's your problem? You're the SKANK, Stacey Lock!'

Everyone looked up from their books.

I was annoyed that they were all staring at me.

'Oh, yeah, that's right!' I shouted. 'She sits there, saying all that stuff. But, it's me who gets the funny looks!'

The whole class burst out laughing.

'EMMELINE ROSE!' The teacher shouted from the front of the room, 'What do you think you're playing at?'

I looked around at all the laughing faces. I looked at Stacey Lock. She was the only other person in the class who wasn't laughing. She looked like she'd seen a ghost.

The teacher tried to calm the class down. 'Alright, alright! Settle down! You've had your fun! Now, get on with your work!'

He looked across the room at me. 'Skank, indeed. Any more of that, Emmeline, and you'll be visiting the head teacher. Is that clear?'

'Sir.' I nodded my head solemnly.

Megan looked at me with wide eyes. 'What are you doing, Em?' she whispered.

I was confused. I looked across at Stacey Lock again, and she looked as shocked as me.

I turned to Megan. 'I don't know,' I whispered back.

I heard Stacey Lock's voice once again. 'What was that? What just happened?'

She sounded scared, but when I checked to see her face, she was looking down at her book. She wasn't even talking to anyone, but I could still *hear her voice*.

'Em!' Megan was staring at me, waiting for a proper answer. 'What's going on with you?'

My stomach did a somersault.

I looked back at Megan, and my nerves tingled right through my body.

'I really don't know,' was all I could manage to say.

NINETEEN

'GIRLS! THAT'S ENOUGH!' Gladys Friday waved her hands frantically.

'Keep out of it, Gladys Friday.' Karra laid the tables with a grin on her face. 'It's their beef – leave them sort it out, yeah?'

'I CAN'T, KARRA! They'll end up killing each other! I'm calling Jim.' Gladys Friday looked around for Big Jim. Her hands were on top of her head, holding little clumps of hair in them.

'Well, technically,' Karra said, 'only one of them will end up dead, because they can't kill each other at the same time, can they?'

'JIM! WHERE ARE YOU? JIIIIIIIIIIMMMMMM!' Gladys Friday screamed down the hallway.

Karra watched the girls carefully, her tongue poking the side of her mouth in concentration. 'If I had to bet on which one would end up dead, I reckon it'd be Quinn.'

Quinn and Bett were rolling around on the floor. Bett was on top of Quinn, with one hand on each side of Quinn's head, shaking it up and down. Quinn had her hand gripped to Bett's face, her fingers stuck into it like a big bowling ball that she refused to let go of. They were making the most peculiar noises I'd ever heard.

BOOM! BOOM! BOOM! The sound of Big Jim running through the corridors echoed right through the room. Everyone jumped out of the way as the giant man skidded across the floor and grabbed each girl with one hand, holding them up like coats on a hanger.

'YOU'RE LUCKY, BETTY MORRIS!' Quinn tried to wriggle free. 'IF BIG JIM WASN'T HERE, I'D WRECK YOU!'

'YOU'RE THE LUCKY ONE, QUINN DAVIES!' Bett pointed at Quinn, swinging around in Big Jim's hand.

Big Jim roared with laughter. 'HARR! HARR! HAAARRR!' He threw his head back. 'You kids make my day, you really do! Such energy in you all! Such spirit! It's *buuuriful* to see!' He grabbed them both into his chest and hugged them tightly, almost crushing their faces.

Karra put the plates on the tables, ready for teatime.

'Do you need any help, Karra?' I asked.

'Aye, go on then.' She passed me some cutlery. 'How is your nose now?'

'Not too bad,' I said.

'Only *you* could bump into a door, Em.' Karra shook her head, amused.

Yes, I'd lied about my nose. I was too embarrassed to tell the truth. It was easier to let people think I was a fool who bumped into doors than a coward who couldn't stick up for herself.

I thought about everything that had happened with Stacey Lock. I still couldn't process it all. This morning, I'd been so annoyed that she'd tripped me up outside the class. Then this afternoon, when she banged the locker into my nose, I got wound up again. I tried to forget about it through lunchtime, but the more Megan had talked about it, the more frustrated I became.

All day, I'd had this kind of pulsing energy surging through me, like I was about to explode. When we were in English class, the energy was so much stronger than I'd felt before. My ear had started ringing, and then … *I'd read her mind.*

I thought back to that last year of junior school when I used to get that running commentary going through my head when Stacey spoke. It was so long ago that I'd convinced myself it was just my imagination. So much had happened since then. Dad died. Nana Rose died. Mum lost the plot. Wales lost the rugby. We'd been in secondary school for three years now, and I hadn't experienced anything like it since. But then today… It was like that last year of junior school all over again.

It felt as if everything that happened throughout the day had all built up to that moment in English. But what did it mean? Was it real? Or was I imagining it? What if it was all in my head? What if I was mad? *What if I was like Mum?*

'Em!' Karra clicked her fingers.

I jumped, startled. 'Sorry. I was in a world of my own.'

'I can see.' She looked irritated. 'Not being funny, Em, but why don't you go and get changed or something? You're holding me up here. I want to get these tables done before Lucas rings. I'm supposed to be going out with him tonight.'

We always had fish and chips on a Friday. It was usually Karra's favourite meal, but today she just pushed her food around the plate.

'What's the matter with you, Karra?' asked Gladys Friday. 'Why are you in such a strop again?'

'Her jizz-bag of a boyfriend hasn't phoned like he promised,' Quinn said.

Little Charlie laughed at Quinn's expression.

'Is something funny, girls?' Karra gave them the evil eye.

Gladys Friday sighed. 'I know it's not nice, Karra. But try not to look so miserable. I've noticed you getting a bit moody, lately. If that boyfriend of yours is giving you grief, maybe you should finish with him. I'm sure there are plenty of other lads out there who would love to go out with you. Like our Beano over there.'

We all laughed at Beano and Karra's disgusted faces.

'Like I'd ever go out with *that*,' Karra said.

'Oi!' Beano shouted across the tables. 'In your dreams, Karra! You know you would.'

'As if, Beano!' Karra laughed.

Beano winked at her and smiled.

As I ate my fish and chips, I thought again about Stacey Lock. What an odd day. How could I hear Stacey like that?

Could I really be hearing her thoughts? Or maybe I was just losing the plot. Mental illness ran in my family, after all. So what was this? Mental illness or something else? How was I supposed to tell?

It was all exhausting. I decided I would talk to Karra about what was happening at school. She would help me. I wouldn't mention that I was '*hearing voices*'. Just saying the words sounded ridiculous! People would think I was crazy. No, I would keep that bit to myself, but I would tell her about the bullying. If there was anyone that could sort out Stacey Lock, it was Karra.

Gladys Friday was telling off Quinn and Bett, because they were giving each other stinkers across the tables.

'But Gladys!' Quinn protested. 'It's not me, it's *her*! She keeps staring at me all the time. She's winding me up!'

'It takes two to play eye-tennis, Quinn. You're both as bad as each other.' Gladys Friday pointed at the two girls.

Bett looked angry. 'Her *name* is *Gladys Friday*.'

'No, Bett,' argued Quinn. 'Her name is Gladys. You're the only one who insists on calling everyone by their full names. The rest of us are normal.'

'Shut up, Quinn Davies. I am normal!' Bett scowled.

'YOU shut up, Betty Morris. Or I'll break your *face*.' Quinn slammed her hands down on the table.

Gladys Friday started shouting something about not getting paid enough for this, and Karra sat with her face in her hands, shaking her head.

Quinn looked in Bett's direction. Her eyes blinked with shock, her mouth set in the shape of an outraged O.

I turned to Bett, who was sitting with her knife raised in the air, pointing it towards Quinn. She was silently mouthing the words, 'I. WILL. END. YOU.'

'She's threatening to kill me!' Quinn shouted.

Gladys Friday turned around just in time to catch Bett in the act.

'BETT!' She stood with her hands on her hips. 'What have I told you about threatening to kill Quinn?'

Bett looked down, ashamed that she had disappointed her cherished key worker.

Quinn stomped over to the *WHAT IS CHILD ABUSE?'* poster, and pointed to one of the illustrations. 'Gladys Friday, please take this as my official warning. If you don't report Betty Morris, then I will have to report *you* for child abuse.'

Gladys Friday looked like she was going to explode. 'WHAT?' she shouted. 'What do you mean, *child abuse*? What have I done wrong?'

'You're not listening to me,' said Quinn. 'That girl is threatening to endanger my life, and you're not doing anything about it. That means you are "*not listening*" to me.'

'Goodness gracious! Here we go!' Gladys Friday sat on her chair, defeated.

Quinn continued her rant. 'This poster clearly states that "*NOT LISTENING TO A CHILD*" is a form of child abuse. Look – it's right here, next to "*NEGLECTING A CHILD'S EDUCATIONAL NEEDS*" and "*TEASING A CHILD UNNECESSARILY.*" So I would appreciate it if my complaint was taken seriously, and you reported this to the appropriate authorities.'

There was a knock at the door.

'There's a delivery man here!' Beano shouted across the room.

'I'LL GET IT!' Bett ran for the door.

'Get out of my way, Betty Morris! It's *my* turn to answer the door!' Quinn barged past Bett.

'Get lost, Quinn Davies! It's *my* turn!' Bett pushed Quinn to the floor.

'GLADYS FRIDAY!' Quinn shouted. 'She just assaulted me in front of witnesses!'

'Will you two just … SHUT *UP*!' Gladys Friday bellowed at the girls, and walked out of the room with her fist in her mouth. She answered the door, and the delivery man looked stunned at the chaos in the background.

'Gladys Friday?' The delivery man held a pen for the package to be signed.

'Yes, I bloody *am* glad it's Friday!' She grabbed the pen and signed for the delivery. 'I can't wait to get out of this HELLHOLE for the weekend!'

After the tables were cleared, I went over to talk to Karra. Now was my opportunity to ask her for help.

She was playing with her phone.

'Alright, Karra?' I sat opposite.

'Alright, Em?' She kept her eyes on the phone. It looked like she was texting.

'Can I talk to you about something?' I asked.

'Yeah, hang on a minute.' She held up her hand for me to shut up.

After a few moments, she looked up from her phone. 'What did you say?' Her eyes flickered back to the phone as she spoke.

'I asked if I could talk to you about something.' I felt awkward, sitting there, waiting for her attention.

She sighed heavily and rolled her eyes.

I clammed up. She obviously wasn't in the mood to have a chat. Perhaps it was best to leave it for now. Although maybe she would soften a bit once I'd explained.

'Um...' I tried to talk, but the words didn't seem to come out properly. I didn't know how to bring the subject up.

Karra threw her phone on the table. 'Well?' She spread out her hands in a question. 'Spit it out then, Em. I haven't got all day.'

I was nervous. I felt so stupid, telling her that I was being bullied. Why couldn't I just handle it myself? Why was I such a *loser*?

'The thing is,' I started speaking, 'there's this girl in school...'

BRRRRRR! BRRRRRR!

Karra's phone vibrated on the table.

BRRRRRR! BRRRRRR!

She looked at the flashing screen in front of her, and jumped off the chair. '*YESSSSS!* It's Lucas. I *knew* he'd ring.'

She picked up the phone. 'Alright, Lucas?'

And then she was gone.

I sighed heavily.

'Never mind,' I said.

TWENTY

'Emmeline! Freya! What a lovely surprise!' Seth-the-name-nurse threw his hands in the air, excited.

I knew now what a name nurse was. Mel said that it was like a key worker for hospital patients.

'They've brought flowers,' said Mel. 'Just to brighten the room up a bit, if that's OK?'

'Of course it's OK!' Seth inhaled the scent of the yellow roses and breathed out happily. 'Your mum will *love* these. And yes, it will definitely brighten up the room. Lord knows it needs some colour in there! Hospital rooms are always so…'

'*Rubbish,*' Grandma Coalman answered for him.

'Well, I was going to say dreary, actually.' He frowned at Grandma Coalman and led the way to Mum's room.

Me, Freya and Mel laughed under our breath, and Grandma Coalman winked at us as we all walked down the creepy corridors of the hospital.

'My girls!' Mum hugged us tightly. 'Oh, my goodness, are these for me?' She bent down and kissed Freya's forehead, and then kissed my cheek.

Freya nodded proudly.

Mum smiled. 'They're beautiful.'

Grandma Coalman arranged them in a vase on the windowsill, and every now and again Mum would go over and admire them. When she bent down to treasure their scent, it was like she was curtseying to them because they were so special.

'I *love* roses,' she said. 'Thank you so much, girls.'

'Emmeline didn't buy them,' Freya said. 'I bought them by myself, but I put her name on the card because Grandma Coalman made me.'

'Shut up, Freya,' I said. 'You didn't even buy them. Grandma Coalman did.'

'She did not!' Freya scowled at me. 'I bought them out of my own money, actually. Grandma Coalman only put £4 towards them. I paid for the rest myself.'

'How much were they altogether?' I asked.

Grandma Coalman laughed. 'A fiver,' she said, and Freya poked her tongue out at both of us.

'I love roses,' said Mel. 'They're so … *romantic.* There's nothing quite like a nice bunch of red roses.'

'Oh, no,' said Mum. 'I much prefer white. There's something *magical* about a white rose.'

Freya threw down her colouring book in frustration. '*I knew it!*' she said. 'I knew I should have listened.'

'Listened to what, love?' Grandma Coalman asked.

'He said to get white, but I liked the yellow ones best.' Freya folded her arms and sulked. 'I should have listened and bought the white ones!'

'Who told you to buy white ones?' I asked.

'Mind your business, you.' Freya screwed her nose up at me. 'You want to know everything, don't you? I can't have anything for myself, without you sticking your nose in! If I had chickenpox, you'd want it!'

'Shut your cakeholes, the pair of you!' Grandma Coalman shouted and walked over to put the kettle on.

Mum started chatting about some art therapy classes that she'd been attending in the day room. She seemed to really enjoy them and said that it was a good way of releasing tension. I was glad that she was getting more involved in things, instead of always staying in her room. She was getting on well in her counselling sessions too. Seth-the-name-nurse said that her progress was so good, they were even considering letting her have some home visits. Mum was so much better lately. There were still glimpses of wildness, but she was gentler and more predictable, which was a great feeling for me. Freya, on the other hand, was bored by my mother's new peace of mind.

'Why don't you want to *play*?' she whined at my mother's betrayal.

'It's not that I don't want to, Freya.' Mum bent down to meet her eye. 'It's just that I'm really tired at the moment.'

'But you're never tired!' Freya scowled. 'I suppose that's what wrestling a lion does to you. You probably need plenty of rest. When you get home, we'll stay up and play games until two o'clock in the morning!'

'You can forget that idea, young lady.' Grandma Coalman gave her a no-nonsense look. 'You're in a nice routine now. Bill and Nora told me that you go to bed at eight in their house. So when your mum gets home, you can stick to the same rules.'

Freya looked at Mum, who held her hands up submissively.

'You can't tell me what to do, Gram.' Freya scowled. 'You won't even be there to check if I'm in bed or not.'

'Actually, Grandma Coalman is moving in with us,' said Mum.

'For how long?' I smiled at the prospect of having Grandma Coalman around a lot more.

'Indefinitely,' answered Mum.

'What does *indefinitely* mean?' Freya asked.

'It means *forever*,' Grandma Coalman replied with wide, threatening eyes. 'So you'd better start behaving.'

'WHAT?' Freya was outraged.

I was pleased that Grandma Coalman would be moving in to help Mum. It was the perfect solution for both of them.

Grandma Coalman was alone because she was a widow and because she was old.

Mum was alone because she was a widow and because she was crazy.

Now they could be crazy old widows together.

When I first arrived at the children's home, I couldn't wait to get back home – back to normal. But during my time there I'd started to realise that, if I was honest, I didn't *want* to go back anymore. The children's home was my home now. I wouldn't tell my mother yet, but eventually I'd have to let her know that I had made my decision – I wasn't going home.

'But why do you need to live with us?' Freya frowned at Grandma Coalman.

Mum pulled my sister to her. 'Freya, listen to me. You know how I've been feeling unwell for a while?'

Freya nodded.

'Well, it turns out that I was more unwell than I realised. The doctors say that I'll be able to go home soon, as long as I have another grown-up in the house to help me with everything.'

'Like what?' Freya asked.

'Like the housework, the cooking, making sure you get to school on time and that you have a proper packed lunch every day. Stuff like that,' said Mum.

'But Emmeline does all that. Why do you need Grandma Coalman to help if Em already does it?' Freya sulked.

Mum chewed the inside of her lip. 'Because Emmeline shouldn't be doing things like that at her age,' she said. 'Emmeline should never have been doing those things. It should be me who does your lunchbox. That's my job.'

Freya started laughing. 'Mum, do you remember the time you put Fluffy in my lunchbox?'

Mum shook her head. She didn't know what she was talking about.

Freya had a massive smile on her face. 'I opened my lunchbox at dinnertime, and there he was. He was so happy to see me! And all the other kids were soooo jealous because all they had was boring old sandwiches!'

'Who's Fluffy?' Mel asked.

'*My hamster!*' Freya squealed. 'She put my *hamster* in my lunchbox! There wasn't even any sandwiches or anything – just little old Fluffy!' Freya laughed. 'But it was OK, because my friend shared her sandwiches with me so I wasn't hungry. And we gave Fluffy a bit of her cheese for his lunch. He *loved* it.'

Panic spread across Mum's face.

Grandma Coalman got up from her chair and smoothed the invisible creases in her trousers. 'Your mum's getting forgetful in her old age, isn't she?' She smiled awkwardly.

'Maybe she's getting old-timer's disease, like you!' Freya pointed at Grandma Coalman.

Grandma Coalman winked at Freya. 'You mean *Alzheimer's* disease.'

'Same thing,' replied Freya.

Grandma Coalman laughed. 'Come on, Missy. Shall we go for a hot chocolate in the canteen?'

'YES!' Freya jumped off my mother's lap. 'Can I have a packet of crisps, too?'

'We'll see.' Grandma Coalman took Freya's hand and nodded gently to Mum as they left the room.

Mel sat in her chair, looking uncomfortable. 'Do you want a hot chocolate, Em?' she asked.

'I'm alright, thanks.' I poured some squash from the bottle on my mother's bedside cabinet. Part of me wanted to go with Freya and Grandma Coalman, but another part of me wanted to stay, to make sure Mum was OK, because I could feel her energy changing.

'Tess, do you want me to get Seth for you?' Mel could see the distress on my mother's face.

'*Her hamster?*' Mum had tears in her eyes. 'What kind of a mother am I?'

Mel looked sympathetic, but was clearly starting to panic at the change of atmosphere in the room. Mum started talking out loud to herself about Fluffy the hamster.

'I'll just go and get Seth,' said Mel as she rushed out of the room to get help.

I stood still, unsure of what to do.

Mum put her hands over her face, bowed her head and started sobbing.

TWENTY-ONE

I was studying in my room. I had a test in a couple of days, and I had to revise some grammar exercises. Karra was sitting on the floor, looking through all my notes.

'So a gerund is the *'ing'* bit of a verb that's used as a noun...' Karra focused on the grammar worksheet.

'Yes, I think so.' I looked at the paper with her.

'I don't get it,' she said.

'Neither do I.'

'How can a verb be a noun at the same time?'

'I have absolutely no idea.' I shook my head.

'That's really confusing, Em.'

'Tell me about it,' I said. 'I can't even think of an example.'

She thought for a moment and then said, *'Running is boring.'*

'I think that's right.' I flicked through the pages of my book to check. 'Can you think of a different example?' I asked.

She concentrated again. '*Swimming* is fun!' She looked hopeful. 'How about that?'

'Yeah.' I wrote the answer down. 'That's definitely correct!'

Karra grinned proudly.

'See,' she said. 'I'm not thick, am I?'

'Of course you're not thick, Karra!' I told her off. 'Why would you think that?'

She shrugged. 'It's just something my mam used to call me.'

So, that's why she was so insecure about it. Poor Karra.

'One day I'm going to The University to do a degree. *A proper one.*' Karra raised her eyebrows to show that she was serious. 'Then I can be a feminist like your friend Megan. I'll have to resit a couple of my GCSEs before I can think about anything else. I filled out my application form today.'

'That's awesome news, Karra!' I was pleased for her.

'Cheers,' she said. 'Will you look over my application to see if it's OK to send off? I don't want to mess anything up.' She looked a bit embarrassed.

'Of course I'll have a look for you,' I said. 'But it's probably fine as it is. I bet you've done a great job.'

She smiled, and we carried on studying.

I still hadn't spoken to Karra about Stacey Lock. I did

try a couple of times, but she was always so edgy these days. On the rare occasions she was in a good mood, I didn't want to spoil things. So I just kept quiet.

Things had escalated with Lucas. He had updated his relationship status on Facebook to: *'It's complicated.'* Karra wasn't amused by this. Adding insult to injury, he had also been tagged in a photo, drinking Sourz with Sticky Vicky on the big swings in the park. It wouldn't have been so bad if the photo was just on Facebook, but it was also on Instagram. Karra was *mortified.* He was making a fool of her online. It was the *ultimate* betrayal.

Since then, Karra had been more volatile than ever, and you really had to watch what you said around her because if the wrong words came out of your mouth, she was very likely to smack you in it. So when she wanted to spend some time with me, I couldn't help but feel happy. I had never known her to take an interest in anything educational before now, and I was surprised at how quickly she picked things up. I said that considering she didn't go to school or anything, I thought she was pretty smart. I think she appreciated the compliment, because she gave me half of her chocolate bar.

Speaking of school, since the incident in English class with Stacey Lock, something had switched inside me. I had started hearing her thoughts more often. It was weird. I knew I wasn't hearing her exact thoughts. It was a bit like having a bad signal when you're talking to someone on your mobile phone. You catch the odd word here and there, and it's really clear, but then it goes all crackly and you lose the connection again.

The more it happened, the more I was convinced that I wasn't imagining things. I *couldn't* be.

I didn't understand what was happening. And I didn't understand why it was happening now. I had moved to a children's home. I was being bullied. My mother was in the nuthouse. I mean, talk about rubbish timing!

The worst thing was, I didn't have anyone to talk to about it. When Nana Rose was alive, she was a good clairvoyant, and would often chat about her gift. She thrived on anything extraordinary. She told me that we were very lucky to be part of such a strong psychic line, and that we were all gifted in one way or another. But since she died, there had been no talk of such things.

Grandma Coalman was open-minded about all this. But her knowledge of psychic ability really only stretched as far as the telly.

So here I was – *hearing voices* – and I couldn't tell anybody because I knew they would think I was going crazy. I couldn't even tell Megan. What would she say? What would she think? I felt so stupid, so embarrassed. How do you explain something like this?

When Mum was younger, she had talked about her gift at school. She was ridiculed and made to feel like a freak. What if the same thing happened to me? What if I confided in somebody and then they turned on me and told everyone I was a liar or a lunatic? I didn't know if I could cope with that!

I needed to find out what was so different about me and my family. And why did Stacey Lock seem to trigger it? Would it get stronger or weaker as I got older? Would Freya go through the same thing? And why had it started happening now?

There were so many questions. And now that Nana Rose was gone, I knew that there was really only one person left who could teach me.

Mum.

TWENTY-TWO

'SHE WHAT?' Mum paced back and forth in the hospital room, eyes narrowed, ready to fight. With hindsight, maybe I should have left out the bit about Stacey Lock slamming the locker door in my face.

'Let me see.' Mum inspected my nose, lifting my nostrils up in the air.

'I'm fine, Mum. The nurse said it was OK – it isn't broken or anything.'

'THE NURSE?' she shouted, throwing her hands in the air. 'You had to go to the HOSPITAL?'

'No, no!' I tried to calm her down. 'It was just the school nurse. It was a bit swollen, but it's better now.'

'I'll break her nose!' Mum was raging. 'The little cow. I've never liked Stacey Lock. She's exactly like her Auntie

Zoe. Always has been … always will be. Three generations this has been going on for! *Three poxy generations!*

What did she mean? What had been going on for three generations?

'First, it was your Nana Rose!' Mum shouted as she circled the room. 'Zoe's mother, Stacey's grandmother, had a very turbulent relationship with Nana Rose. And then Zoe tried to bully me when we were growing up. Not that she had much luck. I gave her a good run for her money!' She smiled for a second, before remembering her rant.

'And now it's you!' she fumed. 'Now Stacey is picking on you. When will that family just *back off*?'

'But what is it about us?' I asked. 'Don't you think it's a bit odd that they keep picking on the same family?'

'Not under the circumstances,' said Mum, and then she stopped.

'What does that mean?' I looked at Mum.

'Nothing!' She rummaged angrily through the bedside cabinet.

'What are you looking for?'

'My cigs.' She pulled out a silver packet.

'But you can't smoke in here, Mum. What about the smoke alarms?'

'That's what the windows are for.' She walked across the room and lit a cigarette. She hung her arm out of the window and blew the smoke sideways so it drifted out into the cold November air.

I watched her scowl as she stared at the concrete jungle outside. The room was still, except for the opaque clouds of ghost-like smoke that crept back in and lazily danced above the furniture.

We were quiet for a moment, and I saw a tear ski down my mother's cheek. It dropped onto her neck and ran down her shoulder until it disappeared into her skin. She turned away so I couldn't see her upset.

'Why didn't you tell me?' she asked, not looking at me.

I shrugged.

'Don't shrug your shoulders. I asked you a question.'

'How did you know I shrugged my shoulders?' I asked. 'You're facing the opposite direction.'

'Mother's intuition,' she replied. 'Now, *why* didn't you tell me what was happening?'

'I don't know,' I answered. 'What was the point?'

'I'm your *mother*!' She spun around to look at me, her eyes watering fiercely. 'I have a right to know if my daughter is being *bullied*.'

She took a deep drag of her cigarette. She blew the smoke out of the window with a force, and the wind mimicked her and whistled hard, sending the smoke ricocheting back into the room and into my mother's eyes.

'Damn!' She rubbed her eyes with the palm of her hand. She flicked the cigarette so it flew outside and was hurled back towards the window, but it was already shut. Not even the wind was quick enough to catch my mother a second time.

She put her cigarettes away and washed her hands. She reached into the cupboard. 'Do you want a drink?' she asked.

I nodded.

She walked back over with a can of pop in each hand, and sat next to me. She passed one of the cans to me, and as I took it, she gently brushed my finger with her thumb.

'I'm sorry I didn't tell you what was going on,' I said.

'I'm sorry I wasn't *there* for you to tell,' she said, and I realised that she wasn't really angry with me, but with herself. 'Stacey Lock aside, I would have liked to have been there to help you with this. This is an important time in your life, Em.'

We opened our cans of pop and I felt relief as I enjoyed the first sips of the sweet, fruity drink. We finished drinking at the same time and breathed out loudly, our eyes stinging from the fizz.

I burped.

My mother smiled and held my hand. 'So…' She took another swig of her drink and looked at me, raising her eyebrows. 'You're the *Listener* in the family, eh?'

TWENTY-THREE

The Seer.

   The Sensitive.

   The Listener.

   The Channel.

These were the names given to the women in our family.

The Seer had the gift of clairvoyance – seeing things other people couldn't see.

The Sensitive had the gift of clairsentience – feeling other people's feelings.

The Listener had the gift of clairaudience – hearing other people's thoughts.

And the Channel had all these abilities combined.

Psychic bitches, say *whaaaat*? This was like something out of a film!

Mum said that our gifts went back hundreds of years, and each generation got stronger. Nobody ever knew which gift they would inherit, until it kicked in. And there was no telling when it would activate, or why. You just had to be ready to receive it. And apparently, I was ready.

I was a Listener.

'Explain to me again: what gift does a Listener have?' I asked.

'Clairaudience,' said Mum.

'What does that mean?'

'Clear-Hearing,' she answered. 'That's why you can sometimes "hear" what's going on around you, even though nobody is speaking out loud. It means that somehow, you can tune in and listen with your inner ears, so you're able to hear on a different level to normal people. Kind of like a dog.'

'Oh, thanks a lot!' I laughed.

'OK, like a dog who can read people's minds!' Mum grinned.

'O ... M ... G!' I put my hands to my face. 'Is this what's been happening to me? I'm turning into some kind of prodigy!'

'Calm down, Supergirl.' Mum rolled her eyes. 'Don't get too excited, because I don't want you blabbing about all this to your friends. Nobody can know. Do you understand me?'

I sighed and nodded my head.

Mum said that we had to keep this side of ourselves quiet because people didn't understand. But just because you didn't understand or didn't believe in something, didn't mean you should dismiss it.

Mum reached over to tidy the strands of hair that had loosened at the back of my neck. I turned around in my chair and she started plaiting my hair as we talked about Stacey Lock, and how I could hear her thoughts. I explained that when I heard her talking, it was sometimes rushed, jumbled-up speech that seemed to jump from one topic to the next in the space of a second.

'That's because you're not always hearing her actual thoughts,' said Mum. 'You're tapping into her subconscious. Her thoughts and feelings are coming through to you, but because they change from one second to the next, the information you get is changing at the same speed.'

Ahhh, that made sense. I mean, I doubt it was possible to keep count of your thoughts. But if you could, I reckoned we probably had thousands of thoughts per day! And thoughts just kind of come and go, without any real order or routine. If you see something colourful, you start thinking about it. And then it reminds you of another thing. Then you smell something, and the scent reminds you of a place or event, so your brain starts thinking about that. And then that place or event reminds you of a person. And it goes on and on and on. No wonder I couldn't always really make sense of what I was hearing.

'When it first started for me,' said Mum, 'it was difficult to catch a feeling or vibration and hold it for long enough to read it properly. It drove me mad!' She laughed, oblivious to the irony of what she was saying.

'What do you mean, *read* it properly?' I asked.

'When you read someone, you're sort of tuning into them,' she said. 'When you catch a thought or emotion that belongs to them, if you can focus on it properly, you can analyze it – or *read* it, as we say. It's a bit like reading a book or watching a film. You have to make the effort to interpret the story properly.'

I was fascinated.

She plaited the last section in the back of my hair, and then tied it together with a bobble. I turned back around to face her.

'But how do you know whether you've got it right or not?' I asked. 'How do you know if it genuinely *is* what the other person is thinking or feeling? What if it's just your imagination?'

'You won't always get it right, Em,' she said. 'There will be times when you get things wrong. But you have to learn to trust your instinct.'

'And what if I don't want this to happen to me? If I just ignore it, will it go away?'

She shook her head and patted my hand. 'When you're made like this, you can't just switch it off.'

Mum said that these things didn't have a curriculum –

you couldn't get all the answers after one lesson or one year. You never stopped learning. Which was a bit of bummer, I reckoned.

'So, if I'm a Listener, then what are you?' I asked.

'I'm a Sensitive,' she replied, rubbing her shoulders because she was getting a chill.

I looked puzzled, so she gave me an example.

'If someone has a headache, then I can feel their headache,' she said. 'If someone has something wrong with them, I feel it in my own body as though it's happening to me. I experience the same symptoms, the same feelings and emotions, and the same energy as anyone who is near me – near my aura, as I call it.'

'That's *sick*!' I said. 'So how do you protect yourself?'

'In my mind, I draw a pink circle around my body,' she answered. 'It's like a bubble of protection.'

'I'll have to learn how to do that,' I said.

'I'll teach you, soon.' She smiled.

'And Nana Rose was a Seer?' I asked.

'Yes,' answered Mum. 'Nana Rose had the gift of clairvoyance – which means clear-vision or clear-seeing. That could mean seeing spirits, it could mean seeing the past and future, or it could mean seeing what goes through people's minds. Nana Rose could see everything except spirits. She was Seer, but she wasn't a Channel.'

'What's a Channel?' I asked.

'A Channel is someone who has all the gifts of a Seer,

a Sensitive, and a Listener. And on top of that, they can also see and speak to spirits,' she said.

'Like, *dead people*?' I looked at her.

'Yes, Em.' She was amused by my tone. 'Dead people.'

'That's weird.' I shivered. 'But there's definitely no Channel in our family?'

'No,' answered Mum. 'As far as I'm aware, there never has been.'

There was a knock at the door and Seth-the-name-nurse came in to let me know that Big Jim was here to take me home. I wanted to stay longer, but Mum said that there was plenty of time to learn more when I visited her next. She walked me to the main entrance and, for the first time in ages, I didn't want to leave her.

Big Jim beeped the horn and smiled at us as he parked outside the double doors to pick me up. Tyler was in the minibus with him, stuffing his face with a chocolate bar.

'Oh! I almost forgot!' I turned to ask Mum a question. 'The other day, when I heard Stacey Lock talking...'

Mum nodded in acknowledgement.

'She said something about the women in our family being man-stealers.' I frowned. 'Do you know what she was talking about?'

Mum shook her head, but avoided eye contact. 'No idea, love. Perhaps you heard it wrong.'

She was acting suspiciously. I could tell that she was hiding something.

Beeeeeep! Beeeeeep!

The minibus horn went off again. I turned around to see Big Jim trying to wrestle Tyler's hands from the steering wheel.

There was no time left to question my mother, but I made a mental note to ask her about it another time.

I climbed into the minibus and sat in the double passenger-seat next to Tyler.

'See you in a few days!' Mum stood at the entrance doors, waving, a massive smile on her face. I knew she'd carry on waving until we had disappeared out of sight.

I waved back through the window.

'So how's your mum?' asked Big Jim.

'Much better,' I answered.

'Is she still nuts?' Tyler asked.

We caught sight of my mother, jumping up and down in the background for her last wave.

'Yep,' I said.

Big Jim laughed out loud. 'You kids are unbelievable, aye!' he shouted and shook his head. 'You just tell it as it is. Not a care in the world. It's a *buuuriful* thing!' He chuckled to himself, and we drove back home.

TWENTY-FOUR

'Graaaaaam!' Freya reached over the table to grab the colouring pencils from Grandma Coalman's hands.

Grandma Coalman laughed as she held them above her head.

'Anna! Stop teasing Freya, will you? Honestly, you're worse than any child!' Mel snapped at Grandma Coalman, and Freya smirked because she'd been given a telling-off.

'Oh, Mel…' Grandma Coalman looked bored. 'Do they ever *shut up* on your planet?'

Mel closed her eyes in frustration.

Mum looked amused. 'I've missed this,' she said. 'I'm really glad we were able to go out. It's just what I needed. Shall we order? I'm ravenous!'

Mum had been given day-out privileges by the hospital.

This was a good sign. It meant that they must think she was stable enough to leave the hospital for a few hours at a time. We made the most of the decision by going for a nice meal.

'I already know what I want!' Freya pointed at the menu. 'I'll have the chicken burger, please!'

'And I'll have sausage and mash,' said Grandma Coalman. She started digging around in her handbag for something. 'Tess, is it time for your medication, or mine?'

'Both,' said Mum. 'We need to take them with our food.'

Grandma Coalman nodded and took out two bottles of pills, along with some bubble wrap. 'This is for you,' she said to Mum.

'Why would I need bubble wrap?' Mum laughed.

'I thought it would be cheaper than therapy,' answered Grandma Coalman. 'You know what those doctors are like. They'd take your life savings, if they could. Bloody robbers, the lot of them!'

'Me and Lola watched a programme about robbers,' said Freya. 'We watched it with Bill and Nora. There was a lady on the telly, and she robbed a person in a shop!'

'Sounds serious.' Mum raised her eyebrows.

'It was serious,' agreed Freya. 'The lady was supposed to go to jail for being naughty. But instead of going to jail, she went to a special hospital because she pleaded contemporary insanity.'

'You mean *temporary insanity*,' Grandma Coalman corrected Freya.

Freya shrugged and carried on colouring her picture.

Our meals arrived and it was lovely to be able to just chat and laugh in such easy surroundings. But every now and then, I would catch a glimpse of something in Mum's eyes. She tried to relax, but there was definitely an edge to her.

'Alright, Mum?'

'Yes.' She blew her cheeks out. 'It's just the first time that I've properly been out of the hospital. I'm a little overwhelmed, that's all.'

I put my arm around her shoulders.

'Why don't we go to the play area for a while?' Mel said to Freya and Grandma Coalman. 'Let's leave Mum have twenty minutes in peace, shall we?'

'OK!' Freya jumped off her seat. 'Mum, I'll be back in exactly twenty minutes!'

'I'll keep an eye on the time!' Mum chuckled and pointed at her watch.

I got up to leave with the others.

'Em?' I felt Mum's hand on my arm. 'Would you mind staying with me? I have a couple of things that I want to chat to you about.'

'Uh-oh!' Freya laughed. 'Emmeline's in *truh-ble*.'

'You'll be in trouble, if you carry on stirring like that!' said Grandma Coalman.

They left for the play area, and Mum seemed to relax a little.

'I love spending time with you all,' she said. 'But I just need ten minutes to *breathe*. When you've spent the last six weeks in the security of a hospital, it feels strange to be out in public.'

'Yeah, it must be pretty daunting,' I agreed.

Mum nodded.

'What did you want to talk to me about?' I asked, trying to take her mind off it.

'Oh, yes!' She seemed to perk up. 'I forgot to ask you the other day. Do you get any kind of warning before you … tune in?' She looked around to make sure nobody was listening.

'What do you mean, *warning*?'

'Well, Nana Rose would get a fuzzy head before she had a vision,' said Mum. 'Do you get anything that lets you know that you're about to hear something?'

I shrugged. 'I don't think so.'

'You need to look out for the signs,' she said.

'What kind of signs?'

She thought for a second. 'Nana Rose's mother was a Listener,' she said. 'And I think she had some kind of tinnitus thing with it. It was like a little bell that went off in her ears before something happened.'

So that's what the ringing in my ears was.

Freya ran up to the table, grabbed her drink and ran back off. 'Can't stop! Soz!'

'Do you think anything like this is happening with Freya?' I asked.

Mum shook her head. 'She's too young. It won't set in until she gets older. That's how it's always happened in our family – it might be there in the background, but it usually activates when the hormones start up.'

'Why?' I asked.

'You'd be surprised how many kids experience this sort of thing when they hit puberty,' she replied. 'Their hormones are all over the place, and that makes their energy a bit wild. It can attract all sorts!'

'Like in *The Exorcist*?' I asked, wide-eyed.

She laughed. 'I don't think it's that extreme in most cases!'

She asked me had I ever heard the phone ring and just knew who it was before picking it up?

Yes, I said.

Had I ever been singing a song, and when the radio came on, the same song was playing?

Yes, I said.

Had I ever walked into a room and sensed the bad atmosphere, and just known that there had been an argument before I'd arrived?

Yes, I said.

'Well, those are all signs of this kind of gift.'

I was fascinated, but it also made me a bit nervous because I couldn't tell which parts were real and which parts were Mum's illness talking. But whether it was fact or fiction, one thing I really took notice of was the warning.

'Nobody must ever use their gift for negative purposes,' Mum warned me.

'What would happen if you did?' I asked.

'The Law of Attraction says that whatever you put out there, you get back in return,' she replied. 'If you use your gift for good, then good will come to you. But if you use your gift for bad then you'll attract negativity back.'

'It sounds like in the films,' I joked. '*With your gift comes great responsibility!*'

She looked serious. 'As cheesy as it sounds, we do have a responsibility to use our gift for good. If you abuse it, let me tell you … karma can be a real bitch.'

Oh-my-life.

'Who's a bitch?' Freya ran back to the table.

'Freya!' Mel followed her. 'I don't want to hear language like that!'

'But Mum said it!' Freya scowled at Mel.

'Sorry.' Mum shrunk in her seat, embarrassed.

'Mel, you must be super-rich to buy all that food!' Freya observed the empty plates on the table.

'The money doesn't actually come from me.' Mel shook her head. 'It comes from Social Services. I don't get paid very much, but I work 40 hours a week to be this poor!'

Freya clearly didn't get the joke, because she nodded

sympathetically and said, 'Is that why you always wear old clothes?'

Grandma Coalman laughed out loud.

Mel frowned at Grandma Coalman, and then looked back to Freya. 'My clothes are not old, Freya. They're *vintage.*'

We tried not to smile at the defensive tone in Mel's voice.

'Vintage,' said Freya. 'I've never been to that shop. I think they could do with getting some new styles, but I do like your bag.'

'This one?' Mel held up the bag to show it off. 'Yes, this is my new favourite thing. I *love* it! Look at the detail on the little white roses dotted all over it.'

We studied the bag, admiring the design.

'Mum likes white roses, don't you?' Freya grinned at Mum. 'My dad told me.'

'How do you remember Dad telling you that?' asked Mum. 'It was a long time ago.'

'What do you mean?' Freya giggled. 'It was only last week! He told me when he came to visit me at Bill and Nora's house!'

Uneasy silence sat between us like an unwanted dinner guest.

'Freya! Don't say things like that!' Mum looked shaken.

Freya's lip started wobbling.

Grandma Coalman clapped her hands together to

break the tension. 'The child's confused! She doesn't mean any harm! Come on, Freya. Let's go to the car. I'll *race* you!'

Freya and Grandma Coalman got up from the table, and Freya started running towards the entrance as Grandma Coalman chased her.

'Don't worry about Freya,' said Mel. 'It's completely natural for a child of her age to use her imagination as a way of escaping from her problems. It's probably her way of trying to stay connected to her father when she feels *dis*connected from her mother. It will pass, in time.'

Mum sighed. 'I want to go back to the hospital. I'm feeling really tired. I think my medication is kicking in.'

'Of course,' said Mel. 'I'll just get the bill.'

TWENTY-FIVE

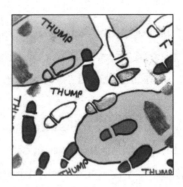

Everybody lined up outside the classroom for registration.

'This school is just *too* cold!' I complained, huddling up next to Megan, our hands on the radiator in the corner.

'I'll keep you both warm!' Ollie tried to stretch his arms around our combined waists.

'Get off me, you tit!' Megan looked at Ollie with disdain, and he released us immediately.

'I was just being gentlemanly, that's all.' Ollie protested as he stood against the wall.

'Yes, well, go and be gentlemanly elsewhere, you weirdo,' said Megan. 'You know I don't like people touching me.'

I smirked at the exchange between the two. Ollie was a genius at winding Megan up.

'Are you both free tonight?' Ollie asked. 'The athletics

team are doing a free circuits class in the park, after school. There's a bunch of us going – do you want to join in?'

'Can't, sorry.' Megan answered. 'I've got stuff to do.'

'*Stuff*?' Ollie frowned at her.

'Yes, *stuff*.'

'What *stuff*?' asked Ollie. 'Name one *stuff*.'

'I have to…' Megan tried to think of an answer as Ollie stood there, his arms folded. 'I have to go to karate,' she said.

'Whatever, Megan.' Ollie rolled his eyes. 'You don't do karate on a Friday. Your karate class is on a Tuesday – you go to the same class as my sister, remember? So, you know what you can do with your *stuff*. What about you, Em?'

'I'm going to the cinema tonight,' I said. 'It's our School Reward Night – my favourite night of the week. I *cannot* miss it!'

'Oooo! What are you going to see?' Megan clapped her hands together.

'I think we're going to see that new one with the three girls that go on holiday together, and they end up in the…'

'LAME!' Megan and Ollie said in unison, and then high-fived each other before starting to talk about a different film that had just come out.

There was a familiar ringing in my ear.

I pushed my earlobe with my thumb to ease it. I tried to listen to Megan and Ollie, but I was too distracted.

The ringing had started to come to me more often. Now that I had an idea of what it meant, I practised trying to focus so I could tap into it, like Mum had taught me.

I shut my eyes to concentrate on the sound. It kept getting higher and lower: louder and quieter. I tried to rest my mind so the ringing could find a balance.

The high-pitched noise eventually subsided and became more of a buzzing sound.

I kept still, allowing myself to focus on the energy. My senses seemed to be on red alert.

I started to hear something else. A new sound. What was it? I couldn't hear properly, but it sounded like … was that … footsteps?

I concentrated a little more.

Yes! It was! I could definitely hear footsteps!

Oh-my-life, it worked!

I had concentrated on the ringing, and then focused on the energy, just like Mum had taught me. And then I'd heard footsteps!

But whose footsteps were they?

I could just about make out the sound of somebody walking behind me, but when I turned to look, there was no one there.

Gutted.

I'd really thought I'd heard somebody walking behind me.

I must have imagined it.

I shook my head, trying to get back to normal.

Megan and Ollie stood with a group, still chatting about the new releases in the cinema. My head felt foggy and detached as I tried to integrate myself back into the conversation. It was no use. I had missed too much of what had been said. I stood back a little and tried to calm down.

The ringing came back. My ears stood to attention. I focused on the energy again, and tried to tune in.

As the shrill noise quietened down, I heard a voice.

'There they are ... *the Get-along-Gang,* having their cosy little chats, as usual.'

I'd know that voice anywhere.

Stacey Lock.

Where was she? It sounded like she was behind me, but when I looked around, I couldn't see her.

The ringing noise was still floating about in the background, but it had died down to a deep-toned buzzing sound. I tried to work with it.

I breathed deeply to calm myself.

I slowly turned my head to look behind me. And when I did, I could see shoes in the distance. I glanced as quickly as I could, and saw Stacey Lock and The Clones talking to each other as they came down the corridor.

I knew it! It was her.

She was walking towards me. The only thing I could hear was Stacey Lock's footsteps; the sound of her shoes on the corridor floor, echoing through my back.

Thump. Thump. Thump.

Like an angry rabbit.

I swallowed nervously.

The footsteps got louder and clearer.

Thump. Thump. Thump.

I focused on the energy.

'That's right, just step back a little more,' said Stacey Lock's voice.

Was she talking about *me*? I think she was. I could sense that her energy was directed at me. She was up to something. I just knew it.

My palms started getting clammy.

'Look at them, lapping it up,' she spat. '*Megan-Swot* and *Smellmeline*.' She had a real bitter tone to her. But why? What was she so annoyed about?

'I can't believe he ignored me this morning,' she said. 'I spent ages on my make-up and he didn't even *look* at me. I don't know why I bother. He's too busy flirting with those two silly cows. He probably fancies that little slapper, *Emmeline*.'

Slapper? I was no slapper! Who did she think she was?

And what boy was she talking about? Who fancied me?

'Yeah, well he won't fancy her when she's flat on her face again,' said Stacey. 'If she just steps back a teensy bit more, she'll be in the perfect position for me to...'

For her to do what?

I remembered the last time Stacey Lock tripped me up

in this very corridor. The day that I hurt my elbow. When I fell to the floor, she stood over me, laughing out loud. The same day that she bust my nose open with the locker door. She had taken real pleasure in hurting me.

Anger stirred in my belly.

'Go on, *Smellmeline*.' Stacey's voice was sly in my ear. 'Let me see you *fall*!'

She wanted to trip me up again!

What had I done to aggravate her so much? Why did she want to hurt me?

I knew that I had a choice: I could move out of the way, I could let her hurt me, or I could take control of the situation and hurt her instead. Nobody knew that I could hear her coming. As far as everybody else was concerned, I had my back to Stacey Lock – how could I possibly know that she was behind me? I could get her before she had the chance to get me, and I wouldn't get into trouble for it because I could make it look like an accident!

Thump. Thump. Thump.

The sound of her footsteps was suffocating. She was in my head, and I wanted her *out*.

I started to panic. What should I do? If I did something to harm Stacey, then I would be just as bad as her. I couldn't stoop that low. *Could I?*

But if I didn't do anything, then she would hurt me instead.

I couldn't think straight with the thud of her footsteps.

No. I wouldn't do anything. I couldn't do anything.

My shoulders slumped, defeated by my own lack of courage. Who was I trying to fool? I was a coward. I didn't have the guts to do anything to Stacey Lock.

I closed my eyes and waited for whatever was going to happen next.

Thump. Thump. Thump.

Here she was.

I braced myself for what was coming.

'Aunty Zoe reckons that they're all psychic *nuts* in that family! Casting spells to get their wicked way,' said Stacey's voice. 'It's about time my family had some justice for what her slutty grandmother did!'

What the *Donald Duck* was she talking about? Why would she call my grandmother *slutty*? What had my grandmother ever done to her family? Which grandmother was she talking about? Grandma Coalman or Nana Rose? And how did Zoe-two-doors-up know about our gifts? I had so many questions going round in my head!

'Look at her; all sweet and innocent,' said Stacey. 'She's as much of a back-stabber as her grandmother. They're man-stealing tarts, the lot of them!'

Man-stealing tarts? That made no sense! I had never stolen anyone's boyfriend. And why would she call my grandmother a back-stabber?

'The whole family are complete weirdoes,' she vented. '*Back-stabbing, slutty weirdos.*'

How dare she talk about my family like that!

I took a deep breath.

'It wouldn't surprise me if she was a mental case, just like her mother,' said Stacey. 'But a psychic? HA! Don't make me laugh! Smellmeline is nowhere near cool enough for that. She's just a useless nerd who comes from a family of *freaks*.'

She laughed and an angry heat rose up through my stomach. The sound of her breath just behind my neck let me know that she was there.

Screw it. I was going to teach this bitch a lesson!

Before she had the chance to do anything to me, I slipped my leg backwards, hooked her foot and tripped her up.

She crashed to the floor and lay in a mangled heap.

Everyone gasped.

She stared up at me in shock.

I glared at her.

Everything was silent, except for a few whispers in the corridor.

Stacey Lock got up, brushed herself off and wiped a tiny bit of blood away from her lip.

'I'm sorry, Stacey,' I said, feigning innocence. 'It was an accident.'

She looked like she wanted to kill me. 'You're an accident, you stupid *tramp*!' she shouted, red in the face, a mix of embarrassment and rage. 'I'll get you back for this!'

'Oh, come on, Stacey!' Ollie defended me. 'You heard her apologise. She didn't mean to do it. It was an accident!'

Megan was quiet.

'Yeah, right!' Stacey shouted. 'She did it on purpose! You'll be sorry, *Smellmeline*.'

'I said I was sorry, Stacey.' I made sure that I kept eye contact when I spoke to her. 'How was I supposed to know that you were behind me?'

She came closer, trying to intimidate me. I stayed where I was and tried not to show any fear. We stood like that for a moment before I leaned in and whispered, 'After all, *I'm just a useless nerd who comes from a family of freaks.*'

She blinked as the colour drained from her face. She gawked at me, astonished.

I stayed rooted to the spot – half of me enjoying the fear in her expression, the other half too afraid to move.

BBBRRRIIINNNGGG!

The bell went, and the silence was broken by the doors opening and everyone pushing and shoving their way into the classrooms. I felt like I'd been in a trance and before I had the chance to consider the consequences of what I'd just done, Stacey Lock had disappeared.

Megan, Ollie and I followed the rest of the line into registration class. Megan was looking at me strangely. I didn't meet her eye as I walked.

'How did you know she was coming behind you?' she asked.

'I didn't know she was behind me,' I replied. 'I told you, it was an accident.'

Megan raised her eyebrows to show that she didn't believe me. 'It didn't look like much of an accident to me,' she said.

I didn't say anything else. Both of us knew not to push it any further. I was grateful that she left it alone. If there was one person who had known me long enough to not be fooled, it was Megan. But I also knew that I couldn't tell her what was happening to me – I was only just beginning to figure it all out for myself. I didn't like keeping secrets from her, but this was an exception.

As for Stacey Lock, she wouldn't say anything. Would she? Well, nobody would believe her even if she did. Who in their right mind was going to believe that I was *psychic*?

I wasn't going to worry about that. I wanted to enjoy this moment and allow myself to be smug. HA! The look on her face! It felt so good to be the winner for once.

This was the first time that this clairaudience stuff had actually come in useful. I was buzzing with energy. I felt connected to myself in a way that I had never experienced before, and it felt so … so … powerful.

Only problem was, I could hear Mum's nagging voice in the back of my head, trying to spoil things.

'As cheesy as it sounds, we do have a responsibility to use our gift for good. If you abuse it, let me tell you … karma can be a real bitch.'

Well, I refused to feel bad. It was self-defence, wasn't it? The girl was going to trip me up. I just got to her first, that's all. I hadn't done anything wrong, had I?

I had got the better of Stacey Lock, and I *loved* it.

Hopefully, she would think twice before trying to hurt me again.

TWENTY-SIX

'So, have you four decided what you want to watch at the pictures?' Gladys Friday asked Bett, Little Charlie, Tyler and me.

We all spoke at once, trying to shout over each other. Little Charlie wanted to watch the same film as me, and Bett and Tyler both wanted to watch the same action film. So, it was settled – Gladys Friday would come in with Little Charlie and me, and Big Jim would go in with Bett and Tyler.

I always felt a bit bad for the others when we went to the cinema on Reward Night. The rule was that you could only go if you went to school. So the ones that didn't go to school were never allowed to come with us, and it sucked because it would have been even more fun with Karra, Quinn and Beano. But rules were rules, I suppose.

There was a lot of babble going on at the dining tables. Gladys Friday and the girls were absorbed in gossip as she laid out the knives and forks, ready for tea. I was curious to know what they were talking about, because the girls were waving their hands around like they were on a chat show and Gladys Friday kept frowning and shaking her head.

'What's going on?' I asked.

'I'll tell her!' Quinn started to explain.

'No, I'll tell her!' Little Charlie spoke over her, and they continued to squabble over who would tell me what, until Bett strolled past nonchalantly and said, 'Karra's been dumped.'

'OH, BETT!' The girls frowned and folded their arms.

'Well, you were taking *ages*,' said Bett. 'She would have been to the cinema and back by the time you two got round to breaking the news.'

'Why can't you keep your big gob shut, Betty Morris?' Quinn scowled.

'You're just jealous.' Bett folded her arms.

'Jealous of you?' Quinn laughed. 'You wish.'

'Yes. You're jealous because I was told first, instead of you and Little Charlie.'

'Karra only told you first because we weren't here,' said Quinn.

'She told me first because she likes me better.' Bett scrunched her nose up at Quinn.

'Worrevs.' Quinn put her hand up in Bett's face.

'Worrevs, back to you.' Bett shoved her own hand into Quinn's face and they both stood there with a hand blocking each other's faces, refusing to move.

'Shut up, Betty Morris. Or else I'll deck you,' said Quinn. 'Go away and play with your little friend over there.' Quinn looked over at Tyler, who was playing on the Wii.

'You shut up, Quinn Davies,' replied Bett. 'I don't want to hang around here with you, anyway. You're a boring, old trout.'

Quinn looked infuriated. '*What* did you just call me?'

'You heard,' said Bett.

Big Jim shouted at the girls. 'If I have to sort you two out again today, I won't be amused. So leave it there, or things will just get nasty. Bett, get over here – I need help with this crossword.'

Bett walked away and Quinn put two fingers up the side of each nostril and moved them up and down, pretending to scratch her nose.

I looked at the girls. 'Are you serious about Karra?' I asked.

'Yep,' Little Charlie replied. 'Lucas *dumped* her.'

Quinn shook her head with sympathy.

Poor Karra. I wondered where she was now.

'She's in her room,' said Gladys Friday, reading my mind.

'She doesn't want to talk to anybody yet. So just leave it, yeah?' Quinn warned.

'Come on, you lot!' Gladys Friday shouted to everyone. '*GRUB'S UP!*'

Karra looked absolutely miserable. She hardly ate any food, and her eyes were a little bloodshot from where she'd obviously been crying. We couldn't console her, because whenever anyone tried to show her any affection, she would scowl at them and tell them to go and fudge themselves. I suppose everyone deals with grief differently.

Bett and Tyler sat on the middle table, talking about the film they were going to watch in the cinema.

'BOOM!' Bett threw her arms in the air. 'The baddie blows the place up like that, and then Ryan Gosling comes crashing in with his top off to save the day. I saw it on the adverts. I can't *wait*.'

'Did you see the bit with the shark?' Tyler looked excited.

'YESSSS!' Bett shouted. 'Oh, Man! When the shark jumps up to attack the girl, Ryan Gosling comes running to save her with his top off … again. It's going to be AWESOME!'

Tyler didn't look so impressed. 'Why has Ryan Gosling always got his top off?'

'Because he's the King,' said Bett.

'Oh.' Tyler shrugged. 'Fair enough.'

Gladys Friday shook her head and said, 'I'm glad I'm going in with Emmeline and Little Charlie. I don't know if my blood pressure could take all that action.'

'What are you two going to watch?' Karra looked at me and Little Charlie.

'That new one that's just come out, with the three girls that go on holiday together,' said Little Charlie. 'It looks amazeballs.'

Karra sighed. 'I loved the trailer for that. Can I come too, Gladys Friday?'

'No, Karra,' said Gladys Friday. 'You know the rules. Only people who go to school have Reward Night at the end of the week.'

'But Gladys Friday,' Karra pleaded. 'I'm depressed.'

'I know you are, Karra. But I can't change the rules for one person or I'd have to change them for everyone.'

'Please, Gladys Friday?' Karra looked desperate. 'I could really do with getting out of this place for a couple of hours.'

Gladys Friday frowned. 'I'm sorry, Karra. It's not happening, love.'

'*Fine,*' said Karra, although she clearly wasn't.

Quinn was talking about the hair dye she had bought

ready for tonight. 'Why don't you stay in with me, babe?' Quinn offered Karra. 'You can help me dye my hair purple. And I've got a lovely red dye upstairs that would look lush on you.'

'I already am a redhead.' Karra rolled her eyes.

'Oh, yeah!' Quinn laughed at her own stupidity. 'It doesn't matter, though. Now you can be even redder. You'll look *fierce*.'

'Not interested.' Karra looked away.

Why did she have to be so mean all the time? OK, she wasn't feeling very good, but there was no need to be so *rude* to everyone. It annoyed me that just because *she* was in a bad mood, she had to bring everyone else down with her. I felt sorry for Karra, but it wasn't our fault that we were going to the cinema and she wasn't. If she went to school, then she would be able to go.

Beano studied Karra from the bottom table. He watched her as he put a forkful of food into his mouth.

'What happened with Lucas?' he called across the tables to Karra.

'He dumped her,' said Little Charlie.

'Like a sack of crap,' Quinn emphasised the point.

'Cheers, girls,' said Karra. 'Nice to know your friends are there to support you at times like this.'

Quinn and Little Charlie looked pleased at what they thought was a compliment.

'Why did he dump you?' Beano asked.

'Mind your own business!' Karra snapped.

'I was only asking!'

'Yeah, well, *don't.*' Karra sulked.

'Not being funny or anything, but Lucas is a tosser,' said Quinn. 'I mean, what kind of boy dumps a girl just because she won't sleep with him?'

Quinn and Little Charlie shook their heads.

Karra looked up from her plate, completely mortified. '*Oh-my-life,* Quinn! Tell the whole *world,* why don't you!'

'Sorry!' Quinn folded her arms.

'Quinn is right,' said Beano. 'If a boy really likes you, stuff like that doesn't matter. And if it does matter, then he doesn't really like you.'

Karra's face softened a little, and Beano smiled kindly at her.

'Just out of curiosity,' Little Charlie leaned in to ask Karra, 'why didn't you?'

'Why didn't I what?'

'You know…' Little Charlie raised her eyebrows and whistled.

'Because I didn't *want* to!' Karra replied in a huff. 'I know everyone thinks I'm a tart, but I'm not. I don't sleep around. Specially not with boys who have been with skanks like Sticky Vicky.'

'Good for you!' Beano shouted.

'Yeah!' said Quinn. 'And she was on the blob anyway, so

she wouldn't have been able to do anything, even if she wanted to.'

Karra looked shocked. 'QUINN!' she shouted. 'What is *wrong* with you?'

'Sorry!' Quinn put her hand over her mouth.

Karra's cheeks turned rosy.

'For future reference, just in case me and you ever get it on,' Beano called across the tables to Karra, 'I wouldn't mind waiting for you. I'd just keep having sex with you in my head.'

'BEANO!' Gladys Friday shouted at him.

'EWWW!' All the girls echoed each other.

Big Jim clipped Beano around the ear. 'I don't want to hear things like that coming from your mouth again, boy!' he told Beano off. 'You're better than that. Have some respect, will you?'

'*Ouch!*' Beano rubbed his ear. 'Sorry! I was just *joking.*'

Gladys Friday and Big Jim started clearing the plates from the tables. Everyone made our excuses not to help, and then we made a run for it as fast as we could.

Tyler and Bett were the only ones left behind, still finishing their meals.

'This place has gone really downhill,' said Bett. 'All this talk about … sex.'

'I know,' Tyler agreed. '*Filth.*'

I ran some lipgloss over my lips, put on my shoes and grabbed my lucky cardigan, ready to run downstairs.

As I went along the corridor, I could hear Bett's thundering jogging footsteps coming from the opposite direction. I braced myself and stood still, knowing any moment now, she would come skidding around the corner.

'BOOM!' She threw her arms up in the air and shouted as she raced past me, her big backside covered in bright blue velour trackie-bottoms.

'You look smart!' I complimented her as she stopped by the mirror.

'Thanks, Emmeline Rose. You look nice, too. I would have lent you something a bit more glamorous, but you have to be a certain type to be able to pull off a look like this.' She proudly ran her hands down her body.

'I know,' I replied. 'Thanks, anyway. You look lovely.'

She smiled and shyly adjusted her T-shirt. It had *Don't Touch What You Can't Afford* written on the front.

I put my lucky cardigan over the back of the chair in the dining area and checked that I had everything I needed in my bag.

Quinn and Karra came over to talk to us.

'Are you looking forward to your film?' Quinn was

examining the box of hair dye that she'd bought. 'Save me some popcorn, will you? And just so you know, I'm probably going to have purple hair by the time you get back.'

'I can't wait,' said Little Charlie, with a big smile on her face.

'For what?' asked Quinn. 'The film or my epic purple hair?'

'Both!' Little Charlie beamed.

'Alright, alright,' said Karra. 'Don't rub it in, you knob-cheese.'

'OK, Karra.' I frowned a little. 'Leave her alone. She didn't mean anything by it. She's just excited, that's all.'

'*Shut up*, Em,' Karra hissed at me.

Usually, I wouldn't say anything, but today had been a great day for me and I was annoyed that she was trying to spoil my good mood. Well, I had already dealt with one bully today, so I was sure that I could deal with another.

'Why don't *you* shut up, Karra?' I snapped.

The other girls looked up at me, surprised at the confrontation.

'Oh, *here we go*.' Karra rolled her eyes. 'Little Miss Perfect has finally found her balls. Well, I suggest you go and slap them in somebody else's face, because I'm not in the mood for it, OK?'

'Only *you* could defend yourself by talking about balls, Karra.' I shook my head and laughed.

'And what's that supposed to mean?' She folded her arms.

'Well, it's probably the only thing you know anything about,' I replied.

Karra got up from her chair and walked closer.

I won't lie to you: I pooped my pants.

'You calling me a slag?'

'No,' I answered. 'I didn't say that, did I?'

'But you implied it,' she said.

I stayed still, unsure of what to say next.

'You *really* think you're something special, don't you?' She had a warning tone to her voice. 'Walking around, thinking you're better than everyone else, with your fancy words and your stupid *cinema trips*.'

'Leave it there, Karra,' said Quinn. She tried to touch her arm, but Karra shook her off.

Gladys Friday came over and stood in front of Karra.

'Get out of my way, Gladys Friday!'

'Karra, I know you've had a bad day, but this isn't the way to deal with it, love,' said Gladys Friday.

'Yeah, that's right – stick up for *her*!' Karra scowled. 'You automatically assume it's my fault. That's discrimination, that is! I could report you for that!'

'Oh, for goodness' sakes, Karra!' Gladys Friday rubbed her eyes with the stress.

'She's right, actually.' Quinn walked over to the *'WHAT IS CHILD ABUSE?'* poster.

'QUINN!' Gladys Friday shouted. 'Not *now*!'

'But she's *right*, Gladys Friday!' Quinn pointed at the poster. 'Look! It says here: "*DISCRIMINATING AGAINST A CHILD BECAUSE OF RACIAL, CULTURAL, SOCIAL, OR ACADEMIC DIFFERENCES*".'

Gladys Friday blew her cheeks out, trying to control her frustration.

Quinn pointed to an illustration of a little boy covering his willy with both hands and said, '*See*! It's right next to: "*TOUCHING A CHILD WHERE OR WHEN HE OR SHE DOESN'T WANT TO BE TOUCHED*".'

'Ha!' Karra snorted. 'I told you! DISCRIMINATION.'

'But I'm not discriminating against you, Karra!' Gladys Friday was struggling to keep calm. 'And I'm not touching you where you don't want to be touched either!'

'Break it up now, girls!' Big Jim called over. 'Emmeline, get your cardigan and let's go. Karra, go and cool off on the sofa for a minute.'

I went to get my lucky cardigan off the back of the chair, but Karra grabbed it and ran to the back of the table.

'Give me my cardigan,' I said, irritated that she was being so childish.

'Oh, I'll give you your *lucky cardigan* … when I've wiped my arse on it!' She pretended to wipe herself with the cardigan, and if I wasn't so angry, it would have been hilarious.

'Just give me my cardigan!'

'Or what?' Defiance crossed her face, and she wrapped her fingers around the delicate white velvet rose, getting ready to rip it off the blue cardigan.

Panic spread through me as I stared at the rose, desperately holding on to it in my mind.

I didn't argue with her. We both knew that I wouldn't … couldn't do anything about it. Not just because I wouldn't stand a chance against someone like Karra, but because … *she was my friend.*

What was I doing? I didn't want to fight with her. We were mates. This was just stupid.

Karra looked at me with a mixture of anger and sadness in her eyes. *Was she thinking the same as me?* I tried to focus so I could tap into her thoughts and hear what was going on, but it was no use. For some strange reason, whenever I tried to tune into other people's thoughts, I couldn't do it. Yet whenever Stacey Lock was around, I automatically heard what was going on in her mind. I couldn't shut off from the girl, even if I wanted to!

'Some friend *you* are, Emmeline!' Karra spat her words at me.

'ME?' I shouted. 'What about you? You've been stomping around here for weeks, grunting at everyone and picking on us all. You haven't had time for any of us! You haven't had time for your *friends*! You haven't had time for…'

I was sad all of a sudden. All these weeks, we were both

going through a tough time – Karra with Lucas, and me with Stacey Lock. But we hadn't been there to help each other. I had tried to talk to her about what was going on with Stacey, but she wouldn't listen.

'Time for what, Em? Time for you?' Karra smirked. 'You are such an attention-seeking cow. You think that just because you come from a *nice house*, and you have a *nice family*, and you go to a *nice school*, you deserve to have special treatment. Well, I'm not falling for it because I don't give a *flying…*'

'You're wrong!' I snapped. I wasn't an attention seeker. Why would she say that?

'Oh!' Karra threw her hands in the air. 'Yet again, everyone else is wrong, and Little Miss *Perfect* is right, as always!'

I didn't want to argue with her, but she was just *so…*

'You're INFURIATING!' I shouted. 'You think you're the only one who's had a tough time of it lately? You think that nobody else has problems? You walk around as if you own the place; shouting and swearing at us all, just because you can. We're supposed to be your friends. Your family.'

She looked away.

'And all because of what, Karra?' I asked. 'Because your boyfriend is a jizz-bag who cheated on you with Sticky Vicky? Well, just because he treated you like rubbish, that doesn't give you the right to treat us like rubbish, too!'

Guilt spread across her face.

Quinn interrupted us. 'Actually, Em … he's now her *ex-boyfriend*.'

'*SHUT UP*, QUINN!' Karra and I both shouted at the same time, and Quinn stepped back.

'What problems?' Karra asked.

She caught me off guard and I stuttered because I didn't know what to say.

'What problems have you had?' She waited for an answer.

I felt the colour rise in my cheeks. I wanted to tell her about Stacey Lock, but I couldn't just blurt it out here, in front of everyone.

'Nothing,' I said. 'I wasn't talking about anything specific, I just meant…'

'Whatever.' She turned her back on me. 'Just go to the cinema, Em. Watch your wonderful film and enjoy your little *school reward*.'

'You could go to the cinema, too, if you just went to school,' I replied.

'Don't lecture me, Emmeline. It's none of your business, OK? We can't all be perfect like you.'

'I'm not perfect,' I said. 'I'm just normal.'

'OH!' Karra shouted again. 'And I'm not? I don't go to school out of choice, alright? Because school can't handle me. They can't handle *this*.' She clicked her fingers with attitude.

'Karra…' I was losing my patience with her. 'It's not a

joke. If you went to school, then you could come to the cinema with us. If you went to school, then you would know that there is more than one university in the world. *The University?* I mean, c*ome on!*'

As soon as I'd said it, I knew I was in the wrong. I knew I'd gone too far.

Karra stared at me.

I wished I could take it back.

'*Harsh,*' she said, her voice breaking.

'I'm sorry,' I replied. 'I didn't mean it.'

'Yes, you did.' Karra looked at me with sad eyes. Then her expression turned to one of anger. She curled her fingers around the little white velvet rose on the front of my lucky cardigan ... and ripped it off.

TWENTY-SEVEN

'Morning, Seth.' We smiled at Mum's name nurse.

'Morning, lovies!' Seth smiled back at Mel, Freya, Grandma Coalman and me.

We walked through the ward, past the lady with the rosary beads. She was praying, as always. There was another woman who kept wetting herself in the reception area. Freya and I thought she was hilarious, but Mel told us off if we laughed at her.

It was weird to think of Mum as one of these people, because she really wasn't like them. Or at least to us, she wasn't. Mum may have suffered a breakdown, but she wasn't completely off her tree, like some of the characters in this place. I was fed up of coming here now. Although it was good to see my mother, these Saturday-morning visits were starting to get on my nerves. And after yesterday's episode with Stacey Lock, and last night's argument with Karra, the last place I wanted to be was in a psychiatric ward! I wanted to be back in the children's home, snuggled up in bed, reading a magazine and eating peanut-butter ice cream. But instead, I was stuck here watching crazy people literally peeing their pants.

'Mum!' Freya's voice echoed through the clinical walls. She ran to my mother and wrapped her arms around her neck.

'Hello, my girl!' Mum grinned widely. 'You've grown since last week!'

'That's because I've been eating all my vegetables,' said Freya, matter-of-factly. 'Bill and Nora give me and Lola gold stars if we eat them!'

'Well, aren't you lucky?' Mum smiled. 'Maybe we should do a star chart when I get home. If it helps you to stay healthy, then it's worth a go!'

Freya nodded enthusiastically. 'Perhaps we could do one for you, too. You can have a star for each time you take your tablets.'

'That's a marvellous idea,' said Mum. 'That can be our first activity as soon as I come home.'

'When will you be allowed to come back?' asked Freya.

'Not long to wait, my darling.' Mum showed a calendar to Freya. 'It's now the second week of December, so we have another week to go. I'll be home very soon!'

Freya leaned in close to my mother and looked sneakily in Grandma Coalman's direction. 'Does *she* still have to live with us?'

Mum leaned in close to Freya. 'Yes,' she answered. 'I'm afraid she does.'

Freya folded her arms in a huff.

'Everything alright, love?' Grandma Coalman winked at her.

'Yep,' Freya replied through gritted teeth. 'Everything is just perfect.'

'Good.' Grandma Coalman laughed craftily. 'We're going to have *such* fun when we live together! It'll be like living in the Big Brother house. I'll be able to keep an eye on you at *all* times.'

Mum and I tried to hide our smiles as Freya sulked dramatically in the corner.

'Freya, shall we go for a hot chocolate, so Emmeline can have some time with your mum?' asked Mel.

Freya got up from her chair and ignored us all.

'Come on, *Roomey*!' Grandma Coalman teased. 'I'll treat you to a packet of sweets in the canteen.'

They left the room, and Mum walked over to the kettle and filled it with water before switching it on.

'Cup of tea?' she offered.

'Yes, please.'

I watched her take out two mugs, standing them next to each other on the unit. She turned around as the kettle boiled.

'Has anything else happened since I last saw you?' asked Mum.

'Not really,' I replied.

'You're lying,' said Mum.

How did she know?

'Stacey giving you grief, is she? Have you done anything to sort it out?' Mum studied me from across the room, and I tried to avoid eye contact.

What did she mean by that? Did she know that I'd tripped Stacey up? What if she could sense what I did? Was she just waiting for me to confess? Should I confess? Or should I just keep quiet? No, I'll keep quiet. It's not lying; it's just … being selective with the truth.

She poured water into the mugs and let the teabags settle.

'I haven't even heard from Stacey Lock. I think she's got bored of me now,' I said.

I hadn't told her what had happened in the school corridor, because I knew that she would tell me off. She had specifically warned me not to use my gift negatively, and that's exactly what I'd done.

'Well, *something* has happened,' she said. 'I can feel it. I can sense your guilt.'

She made her way over to me with the two steaming mugs.

'Guilt?' I swallowed. 'I have nothing to feel guilty about.'

'So, what's bothering you then?' she asked.

'Nothing, Mum. Just leave it, will you?'

She rolled her eyes and sat on the chair opposite me. 'You're very grumpy today,' she said. 'I just want to know what's going on in my daughter's life. Is that such a bad thing?'

'No.' I sighed. 'I've just got a lot on my mind.'

'Like what?' I could see that she was worried.

I told her what happened with Karra, and how rotten I'd felt ever since. I told her how Karra had slept in Quinn's room last night, because she couldn't stand to look at me after the argument we had. And how Karra had broken my lucky cardigan, and how I'd cried because it was my favourite item of clothing in the world.

'Ed Sheeran touched that cardigan.' I put my hand over my face, trying to control the wobble in my voice. 'Karra *knew* it was special to me, and she *wrecked* it!'

'I'm sure the cardigan can be fixed.' Mum patted my back for comfort. 'Why don't you bring it to me? I'll see if I can mend it for you.'

'That's not the point, Mum!' I argued. 'She knew how important my cardigan was to me, and she *broke* it ... *on purpose.*'

'She may feel the same way about you.' Mum raised her eyebrows at me.

I knew what she was getting at. I had betrayed Karra when I embarrassed her in front of everyone by mocking what she'd said about *The University*. I wished I'd never said it, and I felt really guilty about hurting her feelings like that.

I looked away from Mum. She was irritating the life out of me with her self-righteous crap. Since when did *she* become the voice of reason? This was the same woman who was taken into the *nuthouse* for smashing up the family home! And here she was, eight weeks later, acting like Mary-frigging-Poppins!

'It will all come out in the wash, Em. You'll see.' She winked at me. 'Things like this have a habit of sorting their selves out. You'll be friends again in no time.'

She didn't understand. How could she? She didn't have a clue what was going on with me in the children's home.

'So, how are your exercises coming along?' she asked.

'I haven't done them,' I answered.

'Why not?' She frowned. 'I told you, it's important to do them.'

'I haven't had *time*. I've been studying for my tests.'

Last time I'd been there, she had given me three exercises to do to help control my energy.

The first was to ground myself when I was feeling fuzzy-headed or when the ringing sound was distracting me. I put both feet firmly on the floor, and I had to imagine tree roots coming from my feet and going deep into the ground. Apparently, this was where the saying 'down to earth' came from. In the olden days, gifted people used to ground themselves so they could stay 'down-to-earth' and not get carried away by their abilities.

The second exercise was for protection. I had to draw an imaginary pink circle around myself each night before I went to sleep. The protective circle would keep me safe from other people's intrusive thoughts, so I could stay focused.

It was the third exercise that I struggled with. I had to sit for ten minutes a day and just *breathe*. I mean, how boring was that? Mum said that it would discipline my mind – whatever that meant.

'Em, you have to do them,' said Mum. 'It's not a game. You can't just pick and choose when you want to play with your gift.'

'Oh, Mum! Give it a rest!' I snapped. 'I don't want to do the stupid exercises – they're *boring*.'

Why was she hassling me?

'Well, I'm sorry they're so *boring*,' she replied. 'But this is a part of who you are, Em. It will always be there, whether you like it or not. You have to learn to control it and work with it. Trust me, I know. If you ignore it, it won't go away; it will just get stronger and stronger until you acknowledge it. And if you don't learn to manage it, you could lose control and end up...' She looked panicked.

'Like you?' I asked.

'Yes, Em.' Her shoulders slumped. 'Like *me*.'

We sat quietly for a moment.

'*You* stopped doing your exercises when Dad died,' I said.

'I don't want to talk about that,' replied Mum.

'Why not?'

'Because I *don't*!' She walked over to the cabinet drawer to get her cigarettes. She lit one straight away and rushed over to the window.

'OK, OK.' I rolled my eyes at her. 'Keep your knickers on.'

'Never mind,' she said. 'It won't be long now. I'll be allowed home in another week, and we can all spend Christmas together. You and Freya can move back home with me and Grandma Coalman. Everything will be fine. Everything will be perfect.'

Was she *serious*? Surely she wasn't really expecting me to go home next week? I'd settled into the children's home now. I had a new room, new friends, and a new routine. She couldn't just take me away from all that!

'Mum…' I frowned, but I had to get it over with. 'I'm not coming home. I'll have overnight visits, but I'm not moving back properly – I've settled nicely into the children's home. I've been there for two months. I like it there.'

She took a long drag of her cigarette, and kept the smoke in her mouth for what seemed like ages. And then she blew it out slowly, purposefully.

'Freya's coming home,' said Mum. 'She's moving back

home, but she'll still be staying at Bill and Nora's house on the weekends.'

'I know,' I mumbled.

'Then why can't you do that? Why can't you just stay at the children's home on the weekends?'

'Because I don't *want* to, Mum.'

'Is it the cleaning?' she asked. 'You don't have to do the cleaning anymore. We've got a special lady coming to help me keep up with the housework. She's going to help me with the shopping and the bills as well!'

'A nurse?' I asked.

'No, she's not a nurse. She's a *care co-ordinator*,' Mum replied in a posh voice.

'That'll be nice for you,' I said.

'It'll be nice for us *all*.' She looked out the window. 'It's going to be much easier this time round, Em. It'll be much more fun ... I promise.'

Why wasn't she listening to me?

'Mum, I'm really not moving back home,' I said.

She exhaled some cigarette smoke out of the window again.

'And I said that you *are* moving back home, Emmeline Rose,' she emphasised her warning by using my full name.

'*No, Mum...*' I mirrored her slow, deliberate tone. '*I'm not.*'

'*Yes, Em...*' She took a final drag of her cigarette, and her voice was croaky. '*You are.*'

'*Not,*' I said.

'*Are,*' she replied.

'I'm *not.*'

'You *are.*'

'I'm not.'

'YOU AAARRREEE!' she bellowed, and turned around to glare at me.

I sat in silence.

She finished her cigarette and flicked it out of the window. 'Do you know, Em?' Her voice was restrained. 'I'm not sure I *like* you very much sometimes. You can be a real *brat* when you want to be.'

'Well, that makes two of us,' I replied.

'Don't you speak to me like that!' she shouted at me. 'How dare you come in here, with this bloody mood you're in, and start causing drama!'

'You're the one who's throwing a hissy fit, Mum!' I shouted back. 'What makes you think that you can just tell me what do after two months of not being around? I've been in that children's home for two months. You can't just order me to leave! I've settled in. I like it there! I don't want to come home!'

She frowned.

'And what about poor Freya?' I was so angry now. 'She's been living with Bill and Nora for the last two months! She has a *foster sister,* for goodness' sakes! She has a *routine.* She has regular meals on the table, and she bakes cakes on the weekends, and she has a lunchbox with *actual* sandwiches inside it, instead of FLUFFY-THE-FLUFFING-*HAMSTER!* Are you just going to take her away from all that?'

Mum looked ashamed.

'We didn't choose this, Mum!' I cried with temper. 'You chose this. You did this!'

'Do you seriously think that I choose to be this way?' Mum laughed bitterly. 'It's a *DISEASE*! I don't *choose* to be unwell. Nobody *chooses* to have mental illness, you ignorant little cow!'

Hot tears flowed from my eyes.

'I watched them put a needle in you, Mum!' I sobbed. 'You were bleeding, because you had hurt yourself! The paramedics held you down and jammed a needle in your thigh, and I couldn't do anything to help you because the policewoman was holding me back. And you just passed out! Just like that! You just … passed out. Right in front of me! How am I supposed to forget something like that? I can't get the image out of my head – it's stuck there. You did that to me!'

Her hands flew to her mouth. Pain was etched all over her face as she remembered.

'I thought…' Her voice was shaky. 'I thought I had dreamt that.'

'No,' I said. 'It wasn't a dream, Mum. It was a real-life *nightmare.*'

She started crying. 'I'm sorry, Em. *I'm so, so sorry.*'

She wiped the tears from her face and walked cautiously over to me.

I looked down at the floor.

I felt her arms around me, hugging me tight. Even though I didn't want to hug her back, I couldn't help myself. I responded automatically – two months of loneliness and confusion, needing to be comforted. I sobbed into my mother's shoulder, letting all the pain and resentment melt back into the person who had caused it.

We stayed like that for a while, and then I swallowed the last of my tears.

'I'm not coming home,' I said quietly. 'Please don't try and make me.'

'Are you sure that's what you want?' asked Mum.

I nodded.

'In that case…' She sighed and gave up the struggle. 'We'll just have to work something out.'

TWENTY-EIGHT

We dropped Grandma Coalman home, and then I sat in the back of Mel's car with my little sister and we shared the packet of sweets that Grandma Coalman had bought her. It was comforting to sit close to each other. We hadn't really had much chance to connect properly over the past two months, and a small distance had grown between us. She had become more attached to Bill, Nora and Lola. I had become more attached to life at the children's home. And we'd become more detached from each other. I was looking forward to the day that we could spend time at home with Mum and Grandma Coalman, watching cartoons together again. It would be nice to have comfortable time together, instead of rushed visits in a mental hospital. But at this very moment, we were sitting next to each other, sharing sweets. We looked at one another and smiled.

'I've missed you,' I said to her.

'I've missed you too,' replied Freya.

She took out a sweet and aimed it at my mouth. I opened my mouth to catch it as she threw it in the air.

'Well done!' Freya clapped her hands and then opened her mouth to catch one that I threw.

'*OHHHH!*' I shouted. 'What a catch!'

'You can't really miss *your* mouths.' Mel laughed from the front of the car. 'They're big enough!'

'Shut up, Mel!' I chuckled and opened my mouth for the sweet that Freya was about to throw.

The car pulled up outside Bill and Nora's house. Freya opened the car door to get out. Bill and Nora came to greet her, and Lola came running out with two tennis racquets in her hands.

'Freya!' she called my sister. 'Look what Bill and Nora have bought us! They're taking us to a tennis court this afternoon! And then we're going to buy a Christmas tree!'

Freya and Lola squealed with excitement, held hands and jumped up and down.

I watched them skip around the garden, happy together. A part of me still felt a little jealous of the bond that my sister had formed with her new foster sister, but I had kind of made my peace with it. Eventually, Freya and I would get back to how we used to be. I knew that it wouldn't be easy, but we'd get there in the end.

I kissed Freya on the forehead and said goodbye. 'The next time I see you will be back at home!' I smiled.

'I know! I can't wait!' Freya grinned widely.

'Is your mum allowed home from the hospital yet?' asked Lola.

'The doctor says that she can go home in *one* week,' answered Freya.

'And did they manage to get that lion to go back in the zoo?' Lola looked concerned. 'We don't want him turning up at your house again – especially now that it's all been fixed.'

The two little girls looked up at me for reassurance.

'The lion is firmly back in the zoo. He won't be coming to the house again, I promise.' I hugged Freya.

'*Ooof!* That's a relief!' Freya breathed out, puffing up her cheeks.

'Your dad must have been right when he said that everything would be OK!' Lola handed a tennis racquet to Freya.

'*Yep!*' Freya hit the tennis ball over the other side of the garden. 'Now, let's play tennis!'

Bill, Nora, Mel and I watched the two girls with baffled expressions. Bill raised his eyebrows. 'Kids!' he said, and chuckled to himself.

'Come on, Em.' Mel got in the car and started the engine. 'Let's get you back.'

I got in the car and put on my seat belt. Something caught my eye in Mel's bag.

'Your phone is flashing,' I said.

'My phone can bugger off,' she replied. 'I've had enough of the thing. It's probably another missed call from the children's home. They rang me twice while we were in the hospital, but I missed the calls.'

'What did they ring you for?' I asked.

'How am *I* supposed to know?' Mel laughed. 'They were *missed* calls. They were probably just ringing to see what time I was bringing you back. You know how fussy they get. If somebody is half an hour late, they ring the police. I mean … *paranoid, much?*'

'Yeah,' I agreed. 'But I suppose they're only doing their job.'

'I know.' Mel sighed. 'Don't take any notice of me. I'm just grumpy because I'm tired. I'll be fine when I get home. I'm going to put on my pyjamas, lie on the sofa, catch up with *X-Factor* and spend some quality time with my two favourite men.'

'Simon and Louis?' I asked.

'No,' she answered. 'Ben and Jerry.'

We both laughed and did a high-five as we pulled into the car park of the children's home.

Mel wasn't the only one looking forward to chilling out for the rest of the day. I couldn't wait to have a shower, put on my onesie and watch some telly. I was *knackered* from all the recent drama. In the last twenty-four hours, I had tripped-up Stacey Lock, had a big argument with Karra, and had an even bigger argument with my mother. My head felt as if was going to explode!

I closed the car door and waved goodbye to Mel as she drove away.

'EMMELINE ROSE!' Bett ran towards me, panicking.

'Hi, Bett. What are you looking so flustered about?'

'Haven't you heard?' she asked. 'I thought one of the staff would have let you know.'

'Let me know what?'

'They did try to phone your social worker, but they've just been so busy with the search party,' she said.

'Search party?'

'They didn't realise that anything was wrong until breakfast time. Everyone thought that she had slept in Quinn Davies' room,' said Bett.

'What are you talking about?' I asked.

'But then Quinn Davies said that she hadn't seen her since yesterday.' Bett shook her head sadly.

A nasty, uneasy feeling started rising in my stomach.

'Bett, slow down and tell me *exactly* what's happened.'

She was quiet for a moment while she composed herself.

'Karra Lewis has *absconded*,' she said.

'What does that mean?' I asked.

'It means,' Bett looked worried, 'she's gone *missing*.'

'OK, PEOPLE!' Gladys Friday blew loudly on a whistle hanging on a blue string around her neck.

We all gathered around the staff, ready for Operation Find Karra.

'Gladys Friday will be taking Bett and Tyler with her,' said Aunty Sue. 'They will be searching all the parks in the area.'

'Yes!' Gladys Friday nodded. 'Aunty Sue will be taking Quinn and Little Charlie with her. They will be searching around the chip shops and the rugby stands.'

'Emmeline and Beano will be coming with me,' said Big Jim. 'And we'll be searching around the streets, roads and bus stops.'

'Don't worry,' Beano reassured everyone. 'We'll find her. I won't stop looking until we do.'

Big Jim wiped a tear from his eye. 'That's *buuuriful*, that is. Good boy, Beano.'

'*RIGHT!*' Gladys Friday bellowed. 'LET'S *MOVE! GO! GO! GO!*'

Everybody split into our teams and went with our mentors to look for Karra. We searched, trying to spot any flashes of red hair walking around the streets. But it was no use. The staff kept in contact with each other the entire time, but no group managed to track her down.

Where could she be?

'This is my fault,' I said. 'If I hadn't argued with her, she wouldn't have left.'

'Don't blame yourself, love.' Big Jim patted my shoulder. 'Karra's had a lot on her mind lately. The argument with you was just the straw that broke the camel's back.'

'What are these ridiculous sayings that you oldies come out with?' Beano laughed. 'How the Donald Duck can a *straw* break a camel's back?'

'Shut up, boy!' Big Jim chuckled to himself. 'Don't talk to me about ridiculous sayings. At least I don't go around *hashtagging* everything. *Hashtag*YOLO, *Hashtag-*Amazeballs…' He stood in the middle of the street, crossing his four fingers to make a Hashtag sign as he mocked us.

Beano and I laughed out loud.

'Big Jim is right,' said Beano. 'It wasn't your fault that Karra went missing. She's just had enough of that dickhead Lucas. I think he sent her over the edge. You know he did a Snapchat story with Sticky Vicky, don't you?'

I nodded. 'Quinn told me,' I said. 'The boy is so disrespectful, it's unreal.'

'Maybe we should split up.' Big Jim looked at all the bus stops surrounding us. 'There are about fifty bus stops in this area, and she could be sitting in any one of them. It's probably best if we all look individually for her, but keep in touch by text. If anyone gets any progress, be sure to let the rest of us know, OK?'

We agreed with Big Jim.

I walked the streets, searching for Karra. My legs had started to ache by now, but I wouldn't give up. I felt so bad about what happened. I needed to find my friend and tell her that I was sorry.

Why didn't I just check Quinn's room last night?

I really thought that Karra hadn't come to bed in our own room because she was still angry with me, so I just assumed that she went to sleep in Quinn's room instead. It wouldn't have been the first time she'd slept there, so I had no reason to think she would be elsewhere. And poor Quinn felt terrible because she had just thought that Karra was sleeping in her own room with me. But if she wasn't in our room, and she wasn't in Quinn's room, then where could she have been? Where did she sleep?

Think, Em.

Focus.

I just had to listen to my instinct, that's all. I was sure that if I listened to my gut, it would lead me in the right direction. I just had to … *listen.*

OMG! I could try to see if I could hear Karra's voice in my mind!

I slowed my walking pace down to a stroll.

I breathed in and out, purposefully listening to my breath. I strained my ears.

But I couldn't hear any trace of Karra's voice.

Come on, I tried to encourage myself.

I tried visualising Karra in my imagination, and I directed all my energy on the image.

Still nothing.

WTF?! How come when Stacey-Stupid-Lock was around, I had the hearing ability of a superhero? But when it really mattered – when I actually *needed* my gift to work – it was completely absent? That wasn't fair!

I decided to try a different tactic. Perhaps if I focused on the sounds going on around me, then it would help.

As I walked, I took notice of all the little noises I could hear in the background.

The rustling of trees in the wind.

Cars driving in the distance.

Birds tweeting.

Children playing in the back gardens of the terraced houses I passed.

But it was no use. Nothing happened.

I was *so* frustrated!

Why wouldn't it work? My friend was missing, and I needed to find her! If there was any time when I needed my gift to be active, it was now!

Concentrate, Em.

I was startled by a sudden piercing noise in my ear.

Ouch! That stung! My body automatically responded to the familiar pain. My hand shot up to protect my ear.

I breathed slowly, allowing the soreness to subside.

I closed my eyes and pictured Karra in my mind, trying to tap into her energy.

The shrill sound hit me again, but it wasn't so harsh the second time. I tried to control my emotion so it didn't distract me.

Where are you, Karra? I sent out my plea to her.

The ringing came back, and it must have been third time lucky because it wasn't too painful. I nursed my aching ear as I let the ringing noise lead the way. I carried on walking and I focused all my attention on finding Karra. I didn't really know where I was going.

I approached the end of the street and realised I had come full circle on the search route. I had ended up at the bottom of the hill near the children's home.

I looked across to the park at the bottom of the hill.

The ringing noise seemed to increase, as if to direct me to the park.

The gate was open.

I felt drawn to the comfort of the rose bush. If I could sit by the white roses for just a few minutes, I was *certain* it would help.

I walked towards the park, looking forward to resting for five minutes while I gathered my thoughts and planned where I would start searching next.

As I got closer, a familiar voice spoke in my head. And for once, it wasn't Stacey Lock.

'She had *better* not come in here!' Karra's voice sounded annoyed.

I looked across the park. I could see somebody sitting on the big swings. I walked slowly, trying to judge the situation before going any further.

'Has she seen me?' Karra asked herself. 'No, I don't think she has.'

I sat on the pavement, pretending to tie my shoelaces.

'I don't want to see her stupid face after what she did to me!' Karra vented. 'I can't believe she brought up that thing that I said about *The University*! I mean, how was I supposed to know that there was more than one university in the world? I was never taught anything like that! It's not as if my mother was ever going to teach me about how many universities there are; she's off her tits half the time! Besides, she always said that I was too thick to do anything good in life, so why would I ever need to learn about university stuff?'

I sighed guiltily. I knew she was right. I should *never* have said it. I took something private that Karra had said to me, and I used it against her as ammunition. And I especially shouldn't have said it in front of the others. I felt terrible that I'd embarrassed her like that. I really wished that I could take it back.

Would she ever forgive me? There was only one way to find out.

I got up from the pavement and walked to the park.

The beautiful white roses glistened in the damp winter air. I touched them as I walked past, for reassurance.

I approached the swings.

Karra ignored me.

I perched on the swing next to her.

The swings swayed gently in unison as we sat side by side.

'Alright?' I greeted her.

'Alright?' she replied, but didn't look at me.

'I'm *so* sorry about what I said.' My voice broke as a tear caught in my throat. 'There's no excuse for it. I was a really bad friend to you.'

'You screwed me over, Em,' she said. 'In front of *everyone.*'

'I know,' I replied. 'And I swear to you, if I could take it back, I would.'

'You know that I'm insecure because I'm not very brainy.' She made eye contact with me for the first time, and I could see that she was trying not to cry. 'And you took that insecurity, and used it to humiliate me. I would never do that to you. I might be a lot of things, but disloyal isn't one of them. I don't screw my mates over like that, because screwing your mates over is not cool.'

I nodded my head. 'I would never deliberately hurt you. Since I've been at the children's home, you've been my best friend.'

'HA!' Karra pointed at me, triumphantly. '"*SCREWING*

252

your mates over is *not* cool!" *See!* You're not the only one who knows what a stupid *GERUND* is! So you can stick your fancy grammar up your *arse!*'

I stared at her for a moment, not knowing how to respond. And then we both fell into fits of giggles.

'I'm sorry!' She threw her head back, laughing. 'I just remembered what a gerund was! I got excited, that's all!'

'Well, at least you've learned your grammar!' I grinned. 'That's the best example of a gerund that I've heard.'

'Come on.' Karra got off the swing. 'We'd better get back. The others will be wondering where we are.'

'Don't you know about the search party?' I asked.

'Search party?' She looked shocked. 'What search party?'

'The search party for you.'

'Why would they organise a search party for me?'

'*Uhhh…* Maybe because you *ran away*,' I replied.

Karra looked puzzled. 'What are you talking about, Em?'

'You didn't sleep in our bedroom last night,' I said. 'You didn't sleep in Quinn's room, either. And you weren't at breakfast this morning. Everyone thought you had run away!'

Realisation dawned on her. 'I fell asleep in the pool room! When I woke up, there was nobody around so I went to town to grab a breakfast roll. After that, I went back home and there was still nobody there, so I just came here for a while.'

'Oh,' I said. 'We'd better let everyone know, so they can call off Operation Find Karra.'

'Operation Find Karra!' She laughed out loud. '*Operation Epic Fail,* more like!'

TWENTY-NINE

The whole school was standing in the yard, freezing our bums off in the December air while the fire alarm screamed through the buildings. Megan and I had been in the middle of an unfortunate game of netball outside, so we were grateful when the fire alarm mercifully saved us. The downside was that we were now standing in a fire drill line wearing our P.E. kit and jumping lightly from foot to foot, because we were so cold. The P.E. teacher told us that if we kept moving, it would keep us warm. And even though it's a well-known fact that teachers lie, we followed her advice out of desperation.

Ollie made his way over, mocking us as he hopped dramatically across the yard.

'You two are a right pair of nerds!' he laughed.

'*Shut up*, Ollie,' said Megan. 'I wish this bloody fire drill would hurry up. I don't understand why they insist on having a fire drill outside in the middle of December. Actually, I don't understand why they insist on having anything outside in the middle of December! Haven't they ever heard of influenza? They'll have a school full of people suffering from it, if they carry on.'

'What's influenza?' Ollie asked.

Megan rolled her eyes. 'It's the proper term for flu.'

'Why don't you just say flu?'

'Because she likes things to be done proper,' I said.

'Proper*ly*,' Megan corrected me. 'I like things to be done proper-*ly*.'

The fire alarm had been going off for ages and the noise was starting to hurt my ears. I pressed my freezing hands against them, but the whistling pain in my eardrum wouldn't go away.

'That's so loud!' I frowned.

Megan and Ollie looked at each other and then back at me.

'Em,' said Megan. 'The fire drill has already finished. It stopped about a minute ago.'

'I must still have some leftover ringing in my ears.' I shrugged. 'It'll probably wear off when I get used to the quiet again.'

'Maybe you have something wrong with your ears,' said Ollie. 'What's that condition called? My grandfather gets it – like a ringing in your ears… Oh, what's the name of it?'

'Yes!' Megan held her forehead, trying to think of the word. 'I know what you mean! It begins with T. What's it called? What's it called?'

I shook my ear out with my little finger.

I had a feeling to look around. Stacey Lock was standing two rows down, giving me stinkers across the yard. *Oh, boy.* She looked in a *real* grim mood.

'Tinnitus!' Megan and Ollie shouted the answer together.

Stacey said something to The Clones. Then all three of them looked in my direction.

'What's her problem, today?' Megan had seen the three girls casting menacing glances my way.

'I don't know,' I replied. 'But I don't have a good feeling about it.'

'OK!' The P.E. teacher yelled across the yard. 'My class – back to your netball positions! The rest of the school, make your way back to your classes in a timely, orderly manner!'

The lines started to move towards the school entrance.

The ringing noise was still in the background of my mind, and I was starting to get a headache.

Megan walked back to her side of the netball pitch and I headed for mine. As we parted ways, a force hit me from behind.

'Sorry, *Smellmeline.*' Stacey Lock smirked. 'I must have bumped into you by accident.'

The *Rudeness!* Why was she such a knob? What had I done this morning to wind her up? *Nothing whatsoever!* Yet she still felt the need to hassle me. The girl had issues.

I ignored her and carried on to my position as the game picked up where it left off. As usual, I was Goal Shoot because I was rubbish at everything else so it was safer to keep me in the circle by myself, where I couldn't injure or embarrass anyone else.

On the bright side, I was never lonely because if I needed someone to cheer me up, all I had to do was look across to the circle at the other end of the pitch and I could see Megan. We may be on opposing teams, but we played the same position because we were both as rubbish as each other.

I waved to her and smiled.

She gave me the thumbs up.

'FOUL!' The teacher blew her whistle. I looked across to see who had done what and I could see Stacey Lock pushing another girl. She was a right grump today.

'Go!' The teacher blew her whistle again.

It was so loud. What was with all the noise? My headache was getting worse.

I closed my eyes because the ringing was still there – a constant high-pitched buzzing in my mind. I rubbed my forehead with both hands, but it just wouldn't ease up at all. It seemed to be getting louder; it was like someone scraping a fork down a china plate inside my head. Everything around me had faded into a haze of muffled voices. I couldn't focus on anything, because the piercing sound was so dominating.

I closed my eyes again and breathed out slowly. *Ground yourself, Em.*

I pressed my feet firmly on the floor and I imagined tree roots coming from them, like Mum had taught me.

The ringing noise started to settle a little.

It was working.

I allowed my eyelids go heavy.

I just needed a minute to relax.

'EM!' I heard Megan shout my name. The shock made me jump. I opened my eyes and...

SMACK!

I sat in the nurse's office, holding a tissue to my nose. *Again.*

'We should have a bed with your name on it, Emmeline.' The nurse winked at me.

I smiled politely.

'I'm just popping to the staffroom for a minute. Will you be OK in here with Megan?'

259

I nodded.

As soon as she left, Megan started kicking off. 'I'm telling you now, Em. She did it on *purpose*! You should have seen her face. The girl is messed *up*.'

I knew that Stacey had deliberately thrown the netball at me. But I couldn't understand *why*. I had to figure out what I had done to wind her up again.

'Please tell those girls at the children's home,' Megan pleaded. 'They would sort her out in a second.'

'*Exactly*,' I said. 'I don't want that. I have to learn to fight for myself. Besides, I've only just made up with Karra. I don't want to risk cocking things up with her again.'

'Fair enough.' Megan sat next to me. 'But if anything else happens with Stacey Lock, I'm warning you … if you don't tell those girls, then *I will*.'

I groaned as I held the tissue to my nose for the second time that term. 'It HURTS!' I whined.

'You wait, Em…' Megan paced up and down the room. 'When I've got my black belt, Stacey Lock will be sooo sorry.'

I nodded to show my gratitude.

'I think I'm a natural at martial arts,' she said. 'I even make up my own moves.' She started lowering herself to the floor and leaning forward in a weird position. 'This is called *Crouching Tiger*,' she announced.

'That's very…' I took a moment to think of the right word. '*Impressive*.'

She bent over with her arms waving at the sides. 'And this one is called … *Octopus Death.*'

I tried not to laugh. 'How long have you been going to karate now, Megan?' I asked.

'Two years,' she said.

'I didn't realise you'd been going so long. What belt are you now?'

'White,' she replied.

Lunchtime came around.

Ollie joined me and Megan in the dinner queue.

'*Ooof!*' He cringed at the sight of my nose. 'What happened to *you?*'

'Stacey Lock happened,' I replied.

'WHAT?' Ollie was outraged. 'Has she done something to you again? What the hell is that girl's problem?'

The three of us waited for our curry and chips, and the ringing in my ears started up again. I was really frustrated with it now. It had stopped when I managed to ground myself, but then I was smacked in the face with the flipping netball. Where's the justice in that? Every time Stacey Lock was anywhere near me today, my ears started playing up terribly. Maybe it was because she was in such a bad mood. Perhaps my ears responded to the energy she was vibrating and that was why they were hurting me so much.

We paid for our food at the till, and walked to a table near the ketchup stand. We had to pass Stacey Lock again. She was sitting with The Clones. They all smiled sweetly at Ollie.

As we walked past them, I heard Stacey's voice. '*Stupid skanks!*' She spat her words out. 'Why does he spend so much time with them? It's doing my head in, watching him flirt with *Smellmeline.* All the effort I make, and he doesn't even notice that I'm here.'

She'd been bumping her gums about some boy flirting with me the last time she had tried to trip me up, but I hadn't realised who she was talking about.

'Well,' she said, 'whatever floats your boat, Ollie. If you want to get off with some weirdo, then be my guest. It's your loss, not mine.'

AH-HA! Stacey Lock fancied Ollie Hart! And she was jealous because he always bothered with us, instead of her! *That's* why she tried to trip me up in the hallway the other day – because Ollie was talking to me at the time. And that must have been why she was so angry this morning – because Ollie was chatting to me and Megan during the fire drill.

Oh-My-Donald-Duck! Ollie Hart was of no interest to me. I was no threat to Stacey. Where Ollie was concerned, Stacey was her own worst enemy. Ollie Hart liked nice girls, not nasty ones who threw netballs at people's faces.

Why hadn't I figured this out earlier? It was *so* obvious!

Well, at least now I understood what the trigger was for Stacey's bullying. Should I have a chat with her? I suppose I could reassure her that she didn't need to worry about me getting in her way if she liked him. Maybe then, she'd back off and leave me alone.

Then again, after today's antics during the netball game, I could play some dirty tactics of my own. Why should I show any mercy to Stacey Lock? She certainly never showed any mercy to me.

What should I do?

I felt like I had two different sides to myself. Two different heads.

One was nice.

One was naughty.

One was telling me to be kind.

The other was telling me to be cruel.

One was telling me to let it go.

The other was telling me to make the most of this situation.

Either way, whichever side of myself I listened to, I knew that this new information meant two things:

1 – I now understood what Stacey Lock's problem was.

2 – This was a *great* opportunity for revenge.

THIRTY

'Oh, *Ollie*! You're *so* funny! Ha-Ha-HAAA!' I laughed and brushed against Ollie's arm. I glanced over to Stacey Lock and she looked like she wanted to murder me, so the plan was working.

Yes, that's right. I listened to my naughty side. I knew deep down that it was wrong, but Stacey had annoyed me so much today, and I won't lie to you: revenge was *sweet*.

Megan and Ollie looked at each other and raised their eyebrows.

'Em?' Megan half-grinned. 'What are you *doing*?'

'Nothing, why? I'm just saying. He's a funny guy, isn't he?' I smiled at Megan and then looked back to Ollie. 'You're a funny guy, Ollie.'

He looked confused. 'Thanks. *I suppose*. I didn't do anything funny though, Em. I just ate my chips.'

'*HA-HA-HAAAAA!*' I saw that Stacey was giving me the evil eye and I threw my head back laughing. 'That's awesome! *You just ate your chips!* You're *so…*' I made sure that Stacey could see me as I sat close to Ollie and rubbed his shoulder. 'You're so … *smexy.*'

Megan started giggling.

I frowned at her.

Ollie looked a bit frightened.

I could hear Stacey's voice, but I couldn't make out what she was saying because of all the noise in the cafeteria.

I looked adoringly at Ollie.

Megan laughed again. 'Are you trying to *flirt* with Ollie?'

'No,' I said. 'Of course not!'

'You are! You're trying to flirt with Ollie Hart!' she teased, little squeals of delight coming out of her mouth through the giggles.

Ollie cast his eyes in every direction, except mine.

My face turned the colour of a cherry tomato.

Super Awks.

'I'm sorry, Em,' said Ollie. 'I'm not really comfortable with you touching me up and stuff. I've known you since I was three years old. I don't like you in that way. No offence.'

Megan screamed out loud, laughing and jumping a little bit in her seat. She was making sounds that could only be described as *monkey noises.*

I was mortified. I didn't even fancy Ollie. I just wanted to make Stacey Lock jealous, that's all. It had obviously worked, because she could have turned me to stone with her eyes. But I'd made a fool of myself in the process, and I'd also embarrassed Ollie. Was there no end to my stupidity?

'I'm sorry, Ollie. I didn't mean to touch you up or make you feel uncomfortable,' I said.

'Ooo! Ooo! Oooo!' Megan pursed her lips together and laughed wildly, still making her monkey noises. She clearly enjoyed the sight of her best friend squirming.

'I know you don't think of me in that way,' I said. 'I don't think of you in that way, either. I was just…'

Stacey Lock started walking in my direction, with The Clones at her side. Stacey had a cup of pop in her hand, and she sipped it as she weaved through the tables. She frowned at me over the top of the cup.

Oh, no.

What was she going to do?

She got closer to me and I pretended I didn't see her, while I tried to plan my escape. *You utter pleb, Emmeline!* I taunted myself. *What do you think you're playing at? Now look what you've done!*

Megan was still laughing. 'You are the worst flirt *ever*!' She started making an impression of me. 'Oh, Ollie… You're soooo…' She did her best seductive voice and copied what I had said to Ollie. 'You're so … *smexy*.'

'Shut up, Megan!' I snapped at her.

'SMEXY!' She screamed with joy. 'Who in the world says SMEXY?'

I kept a subtle eye on Stacey as she moved closer to our table. I felt really uneasy. I had to get away, before Stacey got to me.

'I need the toilet!' I declared.

I got up from my seat, but Ollie stopped me.

'Don't be embarrassed.' He gently sat me back down. 'It's OK, honestly. There's no need to leave. Let's just forget that it happened.'

'Ooo! Ooo! Ooo!' Tears of laughter filled Megan's eyes. 'This is too good!'

Stacey Lock was behind me. I panicked and jumped up from my seat, accidentally sending my chair flying backwards into Stacey. The cup that she was carrying went shooting all over her and The Clones.

All three of them gasped in shock as the drink hit their faces.

Megan covered her mouth with both hands, and you could just about make out the muffled sounds of a chimpanzee.

I looked at the three girls. 'I'm *so sorry!*' I said. 'It was an accident, I swear! I was just getting up to go to the toilet.'

Stacey was furious. 'Accident!' she shouted. 'You did it on purpose – I *know* you did!'

'Don't be ridiculous!' said Ollie. 'How could she possibly

have done it on purpose? She had no way of knowing that you were walking past at that exact moment. What is she? Psychic?' Ollie laughed and passed Stacey and The Clones some serviettes.

Stacey wiped her face and looked suspiciously at Megan, Ollie and me.

'Oh, I get it!' She scowled at us. 'You're *all* in on it, are you? I should have known! My Auntie Zoe was right about you, *Smellmeline*. You *are* a freak. Just like your *psycho* mother!'

'Don't you talk about my mother like that!' I snapped. 'I said I was sorry. It really was an accident.'

Ollie stepped in. 'That's well out of order, Stacey,' he scolded her. 'You can't speak about people's mothers like that. Have some respect!'

'Yeah, well, her mother is a psycho!' Stacey folded her arms. 'The whole family are psychos. Walking around, thinking they can see the future? Speaking to dead people! You're *freaks*, the lot of you! Your mother is in the right place, if you ask me. She belongs in the nuthouse! I only wish you would join her there!'

The canteen went silent.

Everyone fixed their eyes on me, and I felt my face heat up to the colour of hot ash.

Megan had stopped laughing. 'You've got a real cheek,' she said, glaring at Stacey Lock.

Stacey scoffed at her.

'You walk around this school as if you *own* it.' Megan's eyes burned. I'd never seen her look so annoyed. 'You think it's OK to bully people on a daily basis, even though nobody has done anything to deserve it.'

'So?' Stacey smirked, but I could see her faltering.

'So, that's the reason why you haven't got any friends,' said Megan. 'Even your two little sidekicks are only friends with you because they're too frightened to leave. Nobody else in this school can stand the sight of you because you're just a *troll*, Stacey Lock. You're a mean, pathetic, *disgusting* little troll.'

My mouth literally dropped open. It wasn't like Megan to say such things. She was usually so reserved. She hated confrontation, but she still defended me. Her loyalty made my heart ache with thanks.

Stacey wiped her face down one last time and then chucked the serviette at us.

'This is *NOT* over,' she warned me. '*You. Just. Wait.*'

And this time she was definitely talking out loud, because everyone around us had gone eerily quiet.

'I can't believe you did it!' I shouted at Megan. 'You called Stacey Lock a troll! It was *epic*.' I laughed as I replayed the moment in my head for the fiftieth time.

'Oh, stop!' Megan lapped up the attention. 'You're making me blush!'

Ollie had gone to play football with the boys. Megan and I sat on the steps of C-Block, drinking our pop.

'Em…' Megan looked at me.

'Yeah?'

'What's going on with you lately?'

'What do you mean?' I asked, but I knew what she was getting at.

'Come on, Em,' she said. 'Don't play dumb with me. I've known you practically my whole life. I can tell when you're hiding something from me.'

I thought for a moment. I could pretend that I didn't know what she was talking about, but what good would that do? Was I really going to go the rest of my life without telling my *best friend* that me and my family were – I didn't even know what to call it. The word *'psychic'* was too cheesy. How was I supposed to explain all this to her?

What would she think of me when I told her? Would she think I was lying? Would she think I was a freak? What if she thought I was *nuts*?

I took a deep breath.

'Do you remember my Nana Rose?'

She nodded. 'Of course I do.'

'Well, when she was alive, she was a bit different to everyone else. She was what you would call a…' I stuttered, not being able to find the right words.

'A psychic,' Megan said matter-of-factly.

I looked at her, surprised. 'Yes,' I said. 'How did you know that?'

'Everyone said so,' she replied. 'My mother and my auntie used to have readings from her. They were devastated when she died, because they had nobody to do their cards for them!'

'Oh,' I said. 'I didn't know that.'

'But what has that got to do with this?' she asked. 'Why have you been acting so strange?'

'The thing is,' I said, 'I've started to realise that I'm quite a lot like my Nana Rose.'

She scrunched her nose up in confusion. 'What do you mean?'

I looked at her, waiting for her to catch on to what I was saying.

'Em, answer me.'

I stayed silent and smiled. Any minute now, she would guess how the two stories were connected, and...

'O ... M ... G.' She snapped her eyes open, pronouncing each letter slowly and deliberately. 'Are you *serious*?' She put her hands to her face, because she didn't know what else to do with them.

I nodded.

'YOU'RE PSYCHIC?' she shouted.

'Well, not a *psychic* exactly,' I said. 'I'm a Listener. It's complicated – I won't bore you with the details. But yes, it's kind of the same thing.'

'You *will* bore me with the details!' She smiled widely. 'You will bore me with ALL the details – *every single one of them*!'

I started to explain what had been happening to me. Megan absorbed each word, desperate to know everything. I didn't have the chance to explain it all, because the bell rang for us to go back to class, but I promised to tell her more later. We walked back into the main building, and I felt about a stone lighter. A weight had been lifted off my shoulders – the burden of not being able to tell anyone was obviously heavier than I realised. I felt much better now that I didn't have to keep secrets from my best friend anymore.

As we lined up outside the classroom, Megan looked at me and said, 'What am I thinking now?'

I laughed. 'It doesn't work like that!'

'OK.' She thought again. 'What colour am I thinking of?'

'I don't know, Megan. I said it doesn't work like that.' I rolled my eyes at her, and we made our way into class.

'Well, how does it work then?'

'I'm not completely sure,' I said. 'I've only just started learning about it. I haven't figured everything out yet.'

'Fair enough,' she replied. 'I won't mention it again until you want to talk about it.'

'Thanks,' I said. 'I appreciate that.'

We took our seats at a table by the window.

The teacher shouted at everyone to be quiet so she could start the lesson.

I opened my book, ready to work. Megan leaned across and whispered to me. 'I'm thinking of a number between one and ten. *What number is it?*

The last bell rang and everyone made their way into the yard to wait for the school buses. I could see Jolly Clive waiting at the end of the street in the taxi.

My ear started ringing again.

I was saying goodbye to Megan, when something started happening behind us. A crowd had gathered and was heading in our direction.

The ringing sound intensified and I winced as it screeched through me.

What was going on?

I closed my eyes tight and pushed my ears to make it stop.

When I opened my eyes, I saw Megan's face and I just knew there was trouble.

'It's Stacey Lock,' Megan gulped.

Oh balls.

The crowd reached us.

'*Smellmeline.*' She greeted me with a nod of her head.

'Stacey.' I nodded back.

'Let's not mess around; I'm just going to get straight to the point. *I don't like you one little bit* – I think I've made that clear by now,' she said.

'You have,' I agreed.

'And I know that you don't like me either.'

'Well, I wouldn't say I don't *like* you, Stacey,' I tried to reason with her. 'It's just…'

'Save it for Jeremy Kyle,' she interrupted me. 'I'm not interested. Here's what's going to happen: tomorrow, straight after the lunch bell, you and me will meet on the hockey pitch, behind the school. We'll sort it out there.'

'Wh—What for?' I asked, even though I knew the answer.

'So we can join hands and sing Kumba-fudging-ya. Why do you think?' Stacey folded her arms.

I stood still, not knowing how to respond. I'd never had a fight before. Not a proper one.

'And if you don't turn up,' Stacey continued, 'everyone in school will see what a chicken you *really* are.'

O.

M.

G.

'OK,' I replied, trying not to show my fear.

'Good.' She smirked. 'See you there.'

THIRTY-ONE

'Do you want a cup of tea?' Mum asked.

I nodded, and she put the kettle on.

'Listen, Mum. I want to apologise about the other day.'

'*Shush*, now.' Mum shook her head. 'There really is no need.'

'Yes, there is,' I replied. 'I was horrible to you. I didn't even mean half of the stuff I said, and I've felt terrible ever since. I've just had a lot on my mind. I argued with Karra, I had tests in school, and then there's all this stuff with Stacey Lock.'

I blew hot air out of my mouth, slowly. I gazed at the floor, trying to compose myself.

I felt Mum's hand on my shoulder.

I burst into tears.

'Oh, Mum,' I covered my face. 'Everything's gone wrong. *I don't know what to do!*'

Mum sat down next to me and passed me my cup of tea. 'Drink that,' she said. 'And tell me what's going on.'

I sipped my tea and explained everything about the Stacey Lock situation. Mum listened and didn't interrupt. I spent the next half an hour, crying and telling her the whole story.

After I'd finished, we sat quietly for a few moments before Mum finally spoke. '*Heavy stuff*,' she said.

'Tell me about it.' My shoulders slumped. 'The worst thing is, I don't even understand why Stacey Lock hates me so much. Is it just because of Ollie? And it's not just me, either – she seems to hate our whole family! Talk about being obsessed!'

Mum shifted uncomfortably in her chair.

I carried on. 'And why is Stacey Lock the one person who really triggers the clairaudience in me? What is it about that girl that sets me off?'

'Em…' Mum started speaking, but I interrupted her.

'And why does she think that I fancy Ollie Hart anyway?' I jumped up and paced the room, waving my arms around like a maniac. 'I've seen the boy pee in a sandpit! As if I could ever fancy him after that!'

'Em…' Mum tried again, but I carried on with my rant.

'And now she wants to fight me! She wants to take my

head, squeeze it in her hands, and drain me of all my brain juice until I DIE!'

'Em…' Mum rubbed her forehead with the stress.

'She wants to kill me, Mum. She wants to KILL ME!'

'EMMELINE!' Mum shouted at me. '*SHUT UP!*'

I snapped out of my hysteria.

'Sit down,' she said. 'There's something I need to tell you.'

I couldn't believe what I was hearing.

'Back in the day, Nana Rose had a client list of people she would give readings to. She made no secret of the fact that she was clairvoyant.'

I nodded, remembering what Megan had told me about Nana Rose giving tarot readings to Megan's mother and auntie.

'Nana Rose was good friends with a woman called Sylvia Lock,' said Mum. 'Sylvia was Stacey Lock's grandmother.'

'What?' I was shocked. 'Nana Rose was friends with Stacey Lock's grandmother!'

Mum nodded. 'They were close friends when they were younger. Sylvia Lock used to help your Nana Rose with her readings. Sylvia wasn't psychic, but she loved going with your Nana Rose and taking notes for the people who were having a reading.'

I was intrigued.

'They had a great friendship, until…' Mum trailed off, lost in an old story.

'Until what?'

Mum sighed. 'Nana Rose took a shine to Sylvia Lock's husband.'

'What do you mean?'

'Nana Rose fell in love with him,' she said. 'And they had an *affair*.'

'Nooooo!'

'Yes.' Mum nodded. 'It was quite the scandal. The two women had a big fall out over it. Sylvia became incredibly bitter towards Nana Rose. She started spreading rumours saying that Nana Rose was a fake, that she wasn't clairvoyant at all – she was just a fraud. Nana Rose couldn't go anywhere without being picked on by Sylvia's friends and family.'

I was taken aback.

'The friendship ended very sourly,' said Mum.

'What happened to the man?' I asked.

'He died from a heart attack, not long after the whole thing came out in the open,' replied Mum. 'When he was on his death bed, Sylvia was by his side, and…'

Mum put her hand over her face.

'What?' I asked. 'What happened?'

'*He asked for Nana Rose,*' answered Mum.

I gasped.

'You can imagine what that did to Sylvia Lock.' Mum shook her head. 'She never got over it. The poor woman was crushed. She cried for months. She spent the rest of her life hating Nana Rose and hating this family. She trained her girls to feel the same way about us, and now the bitterness has been passed down to Stacey.'

'So that's why they've always picked on us.'

'Exactly,' said Mum. 'Sylvia Lock's daughter, Zoe, bullied me when we were kids. It was like she had been programmed to despise me as soon as she met me.'

'Do you mean Zoe-two-doors-up?' I asked.

Mum nodded. 'And when we were about seventeen, I started going out with your father. She *really* didn't like *that.* Zoe and her two stupid sidekicks would taunt me whenever they saw me, and Zoe told everyone that I was a *witch.*'

'But why?' I asked.

'Because she was jealous,' replied Mum. 'Zoe had a massive crush on your dad. So when I started going out with him... Well, you can *imagine.* In Zoe and Sylvia Lock's eyes, two women from the same family had *stolen* their men.'

'Man-stealers,' I said to myself.

'Well, I wouldn't put it like *that,* Em.' Mum was offended. 'It wasn't my fault. I didn't even know that she had a crush on your father. I didn't find out until after I had started going out with him, so I wouldn't exactly call me a *man-stealer*!'

'No, no!' I laughed. 'I wasn't calling you anything. It's just that I've heard Stacey Lock saying those words about our family. She keeps calling us man-stealers.'

Mum rolled her eyes. 'I understand that it must have been terrible for poor Sylvia to know that her husband was in love with Nana Rose. But ever since, the women in that family have made our lives miserable!'

'That still doesn't explain why it's Stacey Lock that triggers this Listening stuff,' I said.

'I'm sorry, Em.' Mum got up from her chair to put the kettle back on. 'It seems that you're the one taking the brunt of all this. All that bitterness and resentment, all stored up in one family. Imagine the energy there.' Mum whistled theatrically. '*You*, my lovely girl, are tapping into *all* that energy. And your main connection to that energy is … Stacey Lock.'

THIRTY-TWO

The next morning, I felt sick all the way to school. I almost chickened out and pretended I was ill, but I knew that if I did that, I would never live it down. If I didn't go through with this fight, I would be the laughing stock of the whole school.

I was wearing my lucky cardigan for comfort. Karra had apologised for ripping the white velvet rose off the front. While I was visiting Mum, Karra had taken the cardigan from my drawer and given it to Auntie Sue to mend. Now it was as good as new! I didn't usually wear it to school, but today was definitely a lucky cardigan kind of day. I needed all the help I could get. My tummy churned as we drove down the hill, and I looked out of the taxi window at the white rose bush. When I saw the lovely white petals, I felt calm for a second.

'Them roses are stunning, aren't they, pet?' Jolly Clive smiled.

I took in their beauty again, for probably the hundredth time since I'd moved to the children's home.

'Funny how they seem to blossom all the time, isn't it?' he said.

'What do you mean?' I asked. 'Are they not supposed to?'

'Well, not in the winter!' He laughed. 'It's December. They should have died out long before now. It must be a sign!'

'A sign of what?' I asked.

But he'd already started singing to his Boyzone CD, so he didn't answer.

'Breathe…' Megan shoved the paper bag in front of my face. 'Just *breeeathe.*'

'I'm going to die. I'm actually going to DIE!' I was having a panic attack, I *knew* it. I had watched a documentary with Peter Andre a while back, and he said that he used to suffer with panic attacks. He said that some of the symptoms were palpitations, sweaty palms, not being able to think straight, and trouble breathing.

I had all of the above.

'You're not going to die, Em. I promise.' Megan squeezed the paper bag to help me breathe properly.

'I'm having a panic attack!'

'You're not having a panic attack, Em. You're just nervous, that's all. It is your first proper fight, after all.'

'But I don't want to fight anyone!' I shouted, my voice ten octaves higher than usual. 'I don't like fighting! I don't even like watching other people fight. Not even on the telly. It makes me feel sick. *Oh God,* I'm going to be sick.'

'Just calm down, Em. You have to think. What can we do?'

I blew ferociously into the paper bag.

'Did you tell your friends at the home about today?' she asked.

I shook my head.

'WHY NOT?' she bellowed at me.

'Because I went to visit my mother last night, that's why,' I said. 'So I didn't have time to say anything to them. And besides, I've only just made up with Karra. I don't want to ruin things by asking her to do something that could get her into trouble.'

'But Em!' Megan was frustrated. 'She's your friend. You know that she would help you.'

'Please don't shout at me,' I pleaded.

'Soz,' she replied. 'You're just silly sometimes.'

'I know.' I nodded. 'I thought about not coming to school today, but if I back out of this, Stacey Lock will *never* leave me alone. And then I'll be known as *Emmeline-Chicken* for the rest of my *life.'*

Megan sat down next to me.

'Can't you use your woo-woo stuff to get inside her head and make her change her mind?' she asked.

I massaged my forehead to try and ease the stress. 'No, I've told you before – it doesn't work like that.'

We folded our arms around our knees.

Megan shot back up. 'We could move schools!'

'We're not moving schools,' I replied.

'Then what are you going to do?'

I wrapped my lucky cardigan around me, and blew again into the paper bag.

BRRRRRING! BRRRRRING!

The sound made us jump.

The lunch bell.

'There's only one thing for it,' I said. 'I have to fight.'

THIRTY-THREE

I walked to the hockey pitch with Megan, dragging my legs up the hill. My body felt as if it was simultaneously made of bricks and feathers. In one way, I felt *so* heavy – every step was an effort. But in another way, I felt like I was floating.

This must be how people feel, just before they die.

We arrived at the pitch and she was already there.

The crowd was *massive*. There were loads of people waiting to witness my final moments. I had no idea I was so popular.

'You'll be OK,' said Megan. But the expression on her face wasn't as confident as the words from her mouth.

Megan and Ollie had been panicking all morning. Ollie had even threatened to go to the head teacher so he could put a stop to the fight, but I had convinced him not to. Even though I was terrified, I knew that if I didn't do this, I would always live in fear of Stacey Lock.

'Em, this is stupid,' said Ollie, trying to control his worry. 'Please don't go through with it. What if you get hurt?'

'I have to go through with it, Ollie.'

He ran over to Stacey Lock. 'Stacey, come on…' he pleaded with her. 'Hasn't this gone far enough?'

'Sorry, Ollie.' She shook her head. 'It's done.'

I took a deep breath. I was shaking all over. The fear gripped me like a seatbelt stuck tightly around my neck. I was too frightened to cry. That was a good thing, I reckoned. It made me look less scared than I actually was.

I took off my lucky cardigan and handed it to Megan.

'If anything happens to me … I want you to have this.'

'No, Em!' said Megan. 'Not your lucky cardigan.'

'Yes. Take it.'

I started walking towards Stacey Lock.

I had never really noticed how stocky she was until now. She glared at me across the pitch.

The fear stopped me in my tracks. My legs turned to jelly.

I started reciting The Lord's Prayer in English.

Our Father, who art in Heaven…

I looked at Stacey. She was rolling up her sleeves.

I started reciting The Lord's Prayer in Welsh.

Ein Tad, yr hwn wyt yn y nefoedd…

She scowled at me and spat on the ground.

She was going to destroy me.

I started reciting The Lord's Prayer in French – just to be on the safe side.

Notre Père, qui es aux cieux…

Stacey Lock walked slowly towards me, like a lion about to eat its prey.

I recited The Lord's Prayer one final time in Spanish.

Padre nuestro que estás en los cielos…

'SMELLMELIIINEEE!' she roared. 'LET'S *DO* THIS!'

Oh balls!

Balls, balls, balls, balls, BALLS!

I tried to think of all the things that made me angry, so I could get into the zone. It was the only thing I could think of to bring out my fighting spirit. That's if I had any.

I thought about Mum and all the stupid stuff she'd done. I mean, who smashes their kids' home up? What kind of mother puts their kids through something like *that*?

I thought how Freya and I had been separated. My little sister had gone to foster parents and I had been taken into a children's home. *Pathetic.*

But then I thought how Mum was trying her best to get better, and how difficult it must be for her to be away from us and stuck in that horrible hospital, all by herself.

I thought about how much she and Grandma Coalman loved me and Freya. We may be a slightly dysfunctional family, but we really did care about each other.

I thought about how happy Freya was with Bill and Nora, and how she had a little foster sister there with her making the experience fun. If I was honest, it had been more of a positive experience for her than a negative one.

It wasn't working. The anger for my mum had gone. How odd… When did that happen?

I tried to think about something else instead.

I thought about my argument with Karra and all the mean things we'd said to each other. She had called me an attention seeker. But then again, I had embarrassed her in front of everyone, so we were both in the wrong.

I thought about all the times she'd been in a mood over Lucas. I mean, you just can't go around treating your friends like dirt, because some boy is giving you a hard time. Whatever happened to *Sisters before Misters* and *Fries before Guys*?

Then again, it must have been horrible for her to be with someone who cheated and made her feel like crap.

And then I thought about how much I had missed Karra when we weren't speaking.

I thought about all the laughing we had done over the last couple of months. About how much easier she had made my time in the children's home and how she'd lent me her lovely hot-water bottle during my first night there.

Nope.

I still couldn't get angry.

I had to try something different.

I looked at Stacey Lock. She was standing opposite me with The Clones at her side. They seemed to find the whole thing quite amusing. Stacey looked like she had done this a *hundred* times before. She was probably a pro at ripping people's heads off.

I thought about all the things that Stacey had done to me.

Tripping me up in the corridor.

Slamming the locker door into my nose.

Throwing the netball at my face.

Calling my mother a psycho.

Calling me '*Smellmeline*' all the time.

I washed, *damn it*. I washed every day! How could she call me smelly? And how could she be so nasty as to make fun of my mother for being in the hospital?

But, it occurred to me, if it wasn't for Stacey Lock being so mean to me and triggering the Listening, I would never have understood it. I would never have learnt that I was a Listener. I would never have gone to my mother for help. And my mother would never have taught me about all this new stuff – a whole world of real-life awesomeness that I wouldn't have had a clue about. And because of that, Mum and I had somehow managed to repair the wounds that had gaped between us like a rip in a pair of tights.

I couldn't even be too angry with Stacey Lock. In the end, she had actually done me a favour.

For every reason I came up with to be angry, there was an even better reason *not* to be.

It suddenly dawned on me that my life was actually … OK.

And for the first time that day, I smiled.

CRUNCH!

I was jolted out of my lovely epiphany as I hit the floor, landing on top of my schoolbag.

'What are you smiling about, you *freak*?' Stacey Lock stood over me.

I got up, glancing at the crowd that surrounded me.

'I can't look!' Megan covered her eyes.

I could do this – I had to do this. It was now or never.

I tried to motivate myself.

Think like a bull, Em. Think like a bull.

I don't know why I imagined a bull, but it seemed to work. I thought like a bull and charged at her, as fast and as hard as I could. I knocked her down onto the hockey pitch.

She was shocked.

I was shocked.

Megan clapped.

Ollie fist-pumped the air.

Please, God. Don't let me die. Don't let me die.

Stacey stood back up. Giving me daggers, she got ready for her next move.

What was I supposed to do now? I had never hit anyone properly in my life. I didn't know how to fight.

She came closer.

I closed my eyes and braced myself for the next impact.

I waited...

And waited...

I heard footsteps.

'I think you'd best step away from my friend,' a familiar voice warned.

I opened my eyes.

Karra.

But how did she know where I was? How did she know about the fight?

Quinn, Bett, Little Charlie and Karra walked in unison onto the hockey pitch, like a slow-motion scene from a blockbuster film. It was epic.

Karra stepped forward. There wasn't even a hint of fear in her face. The girl was solid.

'If you want to pick on someone,' she said to Stacey, 'then pick on me, you grim little skank.'

Stacey looked unsettled. 'This is between me and *Smellmeline.*'

'Between you and *who?*' Karra asked.

'*Smellmeline.*'

Bett came and stood next to me. 'Why do you call her that?'

'Because she smells, obvs.' Stacey laughed at Bett.

293

'Emmeline Rose doesn't smell,' said Bett. 'She showers every day. She's one of the nicest-smelling people I know. She smells like raspberries.'

Stacey smirked at Bett.

Karra grabbed her by the jumper. 'You find my friend funny, do you?' She was nose-to-nose with Stacey Lock. 'Well, you won't find her so amusing when you haven't got any teeth left to smile with!'

My ear started ringing again. Oh, come *on, not now*!

The noise scraped through me. I winced and covered my ears. I couldn't hear anything that Karra was saying, but I knew she was still talking because I could see her mouth moving.

The high-pitched sound eventually settled down, and the pain started to subside.

I heard someone *crying*.

I looked around me. Everyone seemed fine. So, where was the crying coming from?

'This girl is crazy.' I heard Stacey Lock's voice, and I realised that the crying sound was coming from her. 'I can't fight her,' said Stacey. 'She'll slaughter me!' She sounded genuinely scared.

Karra was pretty intimidating when she wanted to be. I could see that she was ready to deliver the smack-down of the century to Stacey. And I could also see that Stacey was terrified of Karra. I knew how it felt to be that scared of a person. I had always felt so frightened of Stacey Lock.

But looking at her now, I could see that even *she* was frightened sometimes. And that made her seem less scary.

I couldn't let Karra beat her up. If I did, then I would be just as bad as Stacey. I was the only person who could hear how frightened she really was. I felt a tiny bit of responsibility to help her.

This was a chance to put things right.

'Karra, leave it there,' I said.

Karra turned to me. 'What? Are you mad?'

'Please?'

She huffed loudly. 'Are you *sure*? Because I'll deck her if you want me to. You know I will.'

'It's fine, honestly,' I replied. 'Let's just go.'

Karra let go of Stacey Lock's jumper.

'You're lucky,' she said to Stacey. 'But I'm warning you … if you mess with my friend again, I'll break your face, alright?'

Stacey nodded.

Megan and Ollie picked up my schoolbag and we started to walk away.

Bett turned back to face Stacey Lock.

'You're a really mean girl,' said Bett. 'You're just a bully.'

Stacey snarled at Bett. 'Piss off back to special school, *Chubs.*'

I gasped in shock.

I looked across to Bett. Her bottom lip wobbled and she had tears in her eyes.

'Woah, woah, WOOOAH!' Quinn's eyes widened and she had a look on her face that I'd never seen before. 'BACK ... THE TRUCK ... *UP.*'

She walked over to Stacey Lock and stood in front of her.

Stacey looked at her with attitude. 'What do *you* want?'

Quinn slowly lifted her arm up high, bringing it as far back as she could. Then she brought her fist down sharply and...

SMACK!

She punched Stacey Lock right in the face!

Everyone cheered as Stacey fell backwards and held her nose.

Quinn shouted at her, 'NOBODY speaks to Betty Morris like that – except ME!'

Stacey grabbed her bag and staggered away from the hockey pitch as fast as she could.

Bett was beaming. 'Quinn Davies! I can't believe you just did that. *For me!*' She threw her arms around Quinn.

'Yeah, yeah.' Quinn hugged her quickly. 'Don't milk it.'

'Thank you for sticking up for me,' said Bett.

'You're welcome,' replied Quinn. 'I know we have our arguments, but I won't stand by and watch someone treat you badly. You may be a massive turd, but you're my massive turd.'

Little Charlie jogged in front, doing boxing impressions of Quinn's victory punch. Bett ran to join her, fist-pumping the air.

Megan handed my lucky cardigan to me. 'You'll probably want this back.'

I gratefully put it back on and felt the comfort wrapping around my shoulders, making me feel safe once again.

I looked at Karra. 'But how did you know about all this?'

'Your friend phoned the home earlier and filled us in on all the goss,' Karra answered and pointed at Megan, who shrugged her shoulders.

'I *did* warn you that if you didn't tell them, I would tell them myself,' said Megan.

I put my arm around Megan's shoulders and kissed her cheek.

She smiled.

Then I put my arm around Karra's shoulders and kissed her cheek, too.

'You're welcome,' said Karra. 'Now get off me, you lezzer.'

THIRTY-FOUR

Mum sang happily to Christmas songs as she and Freya danced around with tinsel on their heads.

Grandma Coalman was sitting on the sofa, fiddling with some string on one of the tree baubles. She'd been trying to tie it for about ten minutes, but kept losing the string at the very last second.

'Here, Gram…' I took the bauble away before she lost her temper. 'Let me do it. You can do these ones instead.' I passed her the hanging reindeer to put on the tree.

It was going to be an epic Christmas. Mum was home and the house was all fixed up lovely. Grandma Coalman had done a wonderful job with organising everything.

Freya now had my old room and she *loved* it. Grandma Coalman had moved into Freya's old bedroom and Mum's room had been done out in lilac – just like she had always wanted.

The living room was great, too. We had a nice new telly because Mum had smashed the last one up when she thought the government was using it to spy on us.

Mum seemed really happy now that she was at home again. She and Grandma Coalman bickered a little, but they would soon get used to living with each other.

Freya was also back at home, but she was still going to visit Bill and Nora every weekend for respite care and to see Lola. They had become firm friends and Mel had organised a care plan to make sure that they all saw each other regularly.

Grandma Coalman still had her bungalow if she wanted to go back up there for some space, but I think she liked being around to look after Mum and argue with Freya.

Mum was taking her medication every day, so her moods had stabilised. She had a lady who called round to make sure everything was running smoothly. Mum seemed so different since she was home, much more settled. And she was cooking again. She hadn't cooked in a long time, but now her and Grandma Coalman had started watching Jamie Oliver on the telly and spent loads of time making his posh thirty-minute meals, which really took two hours.

And me? I hadn't moved back home, no. I gave my

room to Freya and moved my stuff to the attic bedroom. I came for overnight stays on Tuesdays, Thursdays and Sundays. Mum would have preferred me to be at home more than that, but we had come to a nice compromise and I was grateful that she didn't pressure me.

Mum sang as she strung a set of white lights around the tree and Grandma Coalman joined in, throwing the silver tinsel over the branches.

Freya and I helped by hanging the last of the tree decorations up and eating most of the little chocolates.

'What time is your party, Em?' asked Mum.

'It starts at seven, so Mel's picking me up at half six,' I answered.

She stuffed a chocolate into her mouth. 'I've ironed your clothes ready. They're on your bed, OK?'

'Cheers, Mum.'

Grandma Coalman pinched one of Freya's chocolates.

'Oi!' Freya folded her arms. 'Give that back!'

'Or *what*?' Grandma Coalman teased.

You'd think that living together would have mellowed them out a bit, but no. They still squabbled about twenty times a day.

'*Childish!*' Freya shouted at Grandma Coalman.

'*Brat!*' Grandma Coalman shouted back.

'Gram…' Freya looked at her. 'Have you always been like this?'

'Like what?'

'So offensive,' replied Freya.

'Oh, yes.' Grandma Coalman looked proud. 'It's how I was raised. My brothers and I were brought up on insults – it's how we showed our love.'

'That's messed up, Gram,' I laughed.

'It's true!' she said. 'It's how my mother used to put us to sleep at night. She'd shout up the stairs to us, 'Now get to sleep, you little bastards!'

I raised my eyebrows.

'*Ahhh*, those were the days.' She smiled nostalgically.

Freya picked up a bauble with a picture of a white rose on it.

'Here you go, Mum.' Freya passed the bauble to my mother. 'Look, it's a white one for you!'

'Cheers, my little angel.' Mum was busy adjusting the lights on the tree, so she took the bauble from Freya without looking at it.

Freya frowned and then stuffed another chocolate into her mouth.

'Did you know,' said Grandma Coalman, 'that the word Angel literally translates to the word Messenger?'

'Does it?' Mum shouted from behind the tree.

'That's what I am!' Freya clapped her hands.

'What? An angel?' Mum shouted again, with tinsel dangling from her head.

'No, not an angel!' Freya laughed. 'A mess…'

'Too right, you're not a flipping angel!' Grandma

Coalman interrupted her. 'More like a little monster!' She tickled Freya.

Mum put the last piece of tinsel on the tree. 'Almost finished! Is everyone ready for the lights?'

We cheered and Mum switched on the Christmas tree lights. They twinkled prettily in the corner of the room.

After Freya put the star on top of the Christmas tree, I went upstairs to finish getting ready. The children's home was having a Christmas party and I was really looking forward to it.

'You look lovely, Em!' Mum smiled as she stumbled into my room with a big pile of clean washing. 'Will you just help me with these for a few minutes?'

I took the stack of washing and put it on my bed.

'Well, you might not live at home anymore, but you'd never know it with all this washing that I'm still doing for you,' said Mum, winking at me.

Mum seemed to really enjoy doing the washing since she'd been home. She enjoyed the routine of it. She thrived on doing the laundry tasks every day and looked for any excuse to get out the fabric freshener. This made me laugh, but Grandma Coalman said that it was an important part of Mum's progress.

I had stayed over a few times since Mum came home. The care co-ordinator said that it would be best for her to have familiar faces around her. So Grandma Coalman, Freya and I spent a lot of time helping her to settle in again. We played board games and watched Christmas films. I could see how shaky Mum was at first – getting overwhelmed by the tiniest things. But gradually, as the days went by, she started to relax.

Mum sat on my bed, separating the knickers and socks. 'Are you excited about the Christmas party?' she asked.

I nodded as I put on some lipgloss.

'We should have a Christmas party of our own next year,' she said. 'Maybe you and Freya could invite some of your friends over. We could play games and pull crackers. Grandma Coalman and I could even make cupcakes!'

I smiled and sat down on the bed to help her with the washing.

'Do you like staying in the attic room?' she asked.

'I love it,' I answered. 'At night, I feel like I'm up in the sky. The stars seem so bright and so close. I can hardly tell where I end and where they begin.'

'That sounds lovely,' replied Mum.

'It is,' I said. 'And Freya much prefers it in my old room.'

Mum nodded and started folding the socks. She looked a bit sad.

'I'm sorry, Em.'

'What for?' I asked.

'For *everything*,' she replied. 'I love you and Freya *so* much. I would never hurt you for the world. But, I know that I messed up … I messed up *big time*.'

'Everyone messes up sometimes,' I said. 'We mess up,

we put things right, and then we learn how to be better people from it.'

She grinned at me. 'You're so much like your father. He always knew the right thing to say.'

'Mum…' I said cautiously.

She looked up from the socks.

'I know you don't like talking about it, but why did you stop using your gift when Dad died?'

'All my life,' she said, 'I tried to be like Nana Rose, helping people who needed us. I never used my gift for selfish reasons; I always treated it with respect. But we were never allowed to tell anyone, because people just don't understand things like that. Then I met your father. He was different from everyone else. He didn't judge me in any way. He accepted me for all that I was. He just … *let me be.* He was such a wonderful man.'

I could see that she was starting to get emotional, so I held her hand.

'I had always been a bit of a loner,' she continued, 'and having these abilities was a pain in the backside, to be honest. I mean, what's the point in having a gift that you're not allowed to open? That's not fair, is it? But when I met your father, I just knew that I could trust him. So I told him everything. Good and bad. Of course, he didn't always understand it all, but he never rejected it. He never rejected me.'

She got up from the bed, walked to the skylight

window and stared outside for a moment, before speaking again. 'We always promised each other that if something happened to any of us – if one of us passed away without the other – then the one who had passed would come back to visit.'

She took a deep breath and started to cry, her face creased with pain.

'For months and months, I waited for him,' she said. 'I prayed for him to come – just to let me know that he was OK … that I would be OK … that we all would be OK. I just wanted to know that he was with me.'

She wiped the tears from her face. 'But he never came.' She shook her head.

I could see that the pain was still raw, even after all this time.

'Maybe he *did* come back, but you just couldn't see him,' I tried to console her. 'You said yourself that there were no Channels in our family. I thought you said that only a Channel could speak to people who had passed?'

'I know.' She sniffed. 'I just hoped that I had enough strength to somehow reach him. But I think I knew deep down that it wasn't in me. Channels are a rare find, Em. They're like precious jewels – pure and filled with light.'

She sat back down on the bed and started folding socks again.

'We had a secret.' She laughed to herself. 'We made a pact that if one of us was left behind, then the one who had passed away would come back and give the other one a special sign to prove that we were really there.'

I smiled. What a lovely thought.

'But I've never had the sign,' she said. 'It doesn't matter, I suppose. Just knowing that he's there would be enough. But if it happened, it would mean the *world* to me. Silly, isn't it?'

'Not at all,' I replied.

She looked so young, with her red nose swollen from crying. I could see how much it had affected her when Dad died. No wonder she had gone so loopy – she had lost *the love of her life.* And everything she'd been taught, growing up, about her gift, about life, about death … it must have all seemed like a big, fat *lie.*

The only thing that would restore Mum's faith again would be if she could have the sign that she had been waiting for. But what *was* it?

'Mum, what was the sign that you and Dad had talked about?'

She blushed. 'Do you mind if I keep it to myself, love? It's just that it's *our* sign. The only way I'll know that it's definitely him is if nobody else knows it.'

'Fair enough,' I said. 'I just hope that it comes for you – whatever it is.'

'Me, too.' She sighed. 'Me, too.'

Mel beeped the car horn.

I grabbed my bag to leave for the Christmas party.

'Don't do anything I wouldn't do,' said Grandma Coalman. 'But, then again … don't do anything I would do, either.'

'Gram!' I cringed. 'I'm *fourteen*!'

'I don't think it makes any difference these days, does it?' Grandma Coalman rolled her eyes. 'I saw this programme on the telly, the other day. There was a girl on there – sixteen years old with ten children.'

'That doesn't make any sense, Gram,' I said. 'That would mean she had been getting pregnant since she was *five*.'

'I know,' she replied. '*Disgusting,* isn't it?'

'But that's not possible, Gram!' I shook my head. I could see why Freya got so frustrated with her. 'There's no way she could be pregnant all that time. What programme were you watching?'

'Can't remember.' She waved her hand dismissively.

'Are you making it up?'

Grandma Coalman folded her arms. 'That's all you do is moan, moan, moan. Nag, nag, nag. I'm just repeating what they said on the telly, that's all!'

'Just go!' Mum ushered me out of the house. 'Have a good time and ring me tomorrow!'

I could hear Grandma Coalman and Mum arguing as I walked up the garden path.

'These kids are winding me up!' Grandma Coalman shouted.

'Anna!' Mum shouted back at her. '*Nobody* can have ten children by the time they're sixteen!'

Mel started the engine.

I was just about to get into the car, when I saw Stacey Lock coming out of Zoe-two-doors-up's house.

'Can I have another couple of minutes?' I asked Mel.

'Yeah, of course,' she said. 'I'm reading my gossip magazine, anyway. I need my weekly bitch-fix. Take as long as you need.'

I called to Stacey.

She looked warily at me.

We started walking towards each other, meeting halfway.

'Alright?' I greeted her.

She ignored me.

Awks.

'Listen, Stacey. I know all this business with our families has been going on for years, but don't you think it's about time we just … *let it go?*'

'That depends,' she said.

'On what?'

'On whether you think it's OK to be a *back-stabbing tart* who steals other people's men?' She tapped her foot irritably.

'I'm sorry for what my Nana Rose did to your grandmother,' I said. 'It was wrong of her to have an affair with your grandfather. It must have been really difficult for your family.'

Stacey frowned. 'It was,' she replied. 'My grandmother was devastated. Her husband asked for another woman when he was on his deathbed. Not just any other woman – your Nana Rose, my grandmother's so-called best friend. It makes me *sick*. If that's how friends treat each other, then I'm glad I haven't got many!'

It was horrible to hear somebody speaking about my Nana Rose like that. But I could see why Stacey and her family were so bitter.

'I understand,' I said. 'If someone hurt my Grandma Coalman, I would want to scratch their eyes out. So I can see why you're so protective of your grandmother. I'm genuinely sorry for what happened.'

'And what about your mother?' she snapped at me. 'She stole my Auntie Zoe's boyfriend as well. I mean, what is it with the women in your family?'

'Mum didn't even know that your Auntie Zoe had a crush on my dad until after Mum had started going out with him,' I replied. 'But your Auntie Zoe had never actually been out with him. She just fancied him. So, in fairness, my mother didn't do anything wrong.'

'Oh.' Stacey almost looked embarrassed. 'Auntie Zoe said that she was his girlfriend when your mother came along.'

'No.' I shook my head. 'He never went out with your Aunty Zoe. He always loved my mum.'

We stood for a moment, struggling to move forward with the conversation.

'And as for Ollie Hart…' I said.

'What are you bringing up Ollie Hart for?' She instantly got defensive. 'He's got nothing to do with this.'

'Stacey.' I looked at her. 'I *know* that you fancy Ollie.'

'How do you know?' Her tone was sarcastic, and then she realised what I meant. '*Oh*. So, it's true then – about the psychic stuff in your family?'

'Yes, although you've probably heard a more exaggerated version of it all.'

She smiled a little. 'Auntie Zoe *does* tell a few fibs.'

'Anyway,' I carried on. 'Just so you know, I have absolutely *no* interest in Ollie. I've known him since I was three years old. I've seen him pee in the sandpit. It was … disturbing.'

She laughed.

'If you want, I can give you his number. Maybe you can text him,' I said.

She looked surprised. 'Why would you do that, after everything that's happened? Is this a joke?'

'No! I just thought…' I tried to find the right words. 'I just thought that if you liked him, then you could let him know.'

Her face softened. 'Thanks for that,' she said. 'But to be

honest, I'm not fussed anymore. There's a new boy that's just moved into my street – he's *well* fit. So Ollie Hart is old news.'

Mel beeped the horn for me to get a move on.

'I've got to go,' I said. 'But good luck with the new boy!'

'Cheers,' she replied, and waved to me as I walked away.

I was filled with a strange sense of relief.

I wasn't sure if I had made a big enough difference to heal a grudge that had lasted so long, but at least it was a start. And I didn't get the ringing noise in my ear when I saw Stacey this time, so surely that was a good sign!

Yes. There was definitely a change in the air. I couldn't quite tell what it was or what it meant, but it moved like a whisper in the wind.

And for the first time in ages, I felt free.

THIRTY-FIVE

'Alright, Posh?' Beano passed me a drink. 'Have you tried my special fruit-cocktail punch?'

'It's *lush*,' said Karra, and she took a sip out of her plastic cup.

'What's in it?' I asked.

Auntie Sue wobbled over to us. 'Fruit juice and berries,' she slurred. 'Beano was very helpful with the preparation for the Christmas party, weren't you, Beano?'

'Cheers, Auntie Sue,' said Beano, and he winked at me and Karra. He took out a small bottle of vodka from his jeans pocket and waved it around behind Auntie Sue's back to show that he'd snuck it into the punch.

'It's delicious, Emmeline!' Auntie Sue smiled. 'Gladys Friday and I can't get enough of the stuff! It's just so yummy.'

Gladys Friday sauntered over to us and started dancing with Auntie Sue.

'Can I sneak a cheeky kiss under the mistletoe with you two lovely ladies?' Beano held a piece of mistletoe over their heads and puckered up his lips, playfully.

'Oh! You little devil!' Gladys Friday blushed. 'You're a charmer, you are! Isn't he a charmer, Auntie Sue?'

Auntie Sue hiccupped. 'Could charm the robins from their nests,' she slurred, and gave Beano a big sloppy kiss on the cheek. 'But as we all know, Gladys Friday, Beano only has eyes for our Karra.'

'Shut up, Auntie Sue! In her *dreams,* maybe!' Beano laughed and his face flushed beetroot red.

'Now, come on, Beano!' Gladys Friday joined in. 'Tell Karra what you told us earlier. What did you say she looked like tonight?'

'I can't remember,' Beano said. 'Let's get you another drink, ladies. Your glasses are nearly empty.'

'He said you looked *STONKING!*' Gladys Friday pointed at Karra. 'Didn't he, Auntie Sue? Didn't he say that Karra looked *stonking?*'

Auntie Sue nodded her head enthusiastically. 'He did, indeed! He said that you looked *stonking*. Didn't he, Gladys Friday?'

Gladys Friday nodded back and they both stood there, grinning tipsily at Beano and Karra.

Beano looked like he was going to pass out.

'Oh, well,' said Auntie Sue. 'Come on, Gladys Friday. Let's get some more of that lovely punch and leave these two luuurve birds alone.'

'What love birds?' Big Jim danced behind the women. He was wearing a paper Christmas hat.

Aunty Sue and Gladys Friday both winked theatrically in Beano and Karra's direction.

'WHO?' Big Jim shouted. 'BEANO AND KARRA?'

The two women smiled.

Big Jim grabbed Beano and Karra. He pulled them both close and wrapped his arms around them. '*BUUURIFUL!*' He kissed their foreheads. 'That's just *buuuriful,* that is! You two kids make a *buuuriful* couple!'

Aunty Sue and Gladys Friday looked at me and moved their eyebrows up and down in a way that they thought was inconspicuous.

'Emmeline.' Auntie Sue nodded her head towards the exit. 'Go and refill the ice bucket, will you, love?'

'We haven't got an ice bucket,' I said.

'Noooo!' She rolled her eyes at me. 'GO … and FILL … the ICE BUCKET.'

'HAHAHAAAA!' Big Jim threw his head back and laughed joyfully. 'She's trying to tell you to go away and give Beano and Karra some space! Young Love is a *buuuriful* thing, isn't it?'

The three members of staff grinned merrily at their matchmaking skills, then linked arms with each other and walked over to the cocktail jugs, dancing from side to side as they wandered through the room.

'*Stonking*, eh?' Karra winked at Beano.

'They're steaming, ain't they?' Beano blushed. 'They don't know what they're talking about!'

'Worrevs,' said Karra. 'I think I'm going to grab another one of them cocktails before they're all gone. Do you want one?'

'Yeah, I think I *need* one,' replied Beano.

'Are you coming to get a cocktail, Em?' asked Karra.

'In a minute,' I said. 'I'm just going to get my cardigan. I'm a bit cold. I won't be long.'

I got my lucky cardigan from my bedroom, and as I walked back through the hallway to rejoin the party, I heard the familiar thunder of running footsteps in the corridor.

'COMING THROUGH!' Bett shouted at the top of her voice as she skidded past me. She was wearing her new Christmas tracksuit and a hairband with reindeer antlers sticking out of the top.

'Do you like my new tracksuit, Emmeline Rose?' She did a twirl for me and when she turned around, I saw that the tracksuit bottoms had *Naughty List* written on the bum.

'It's gorgeous, Bett!' I couldn't help but laugh.

'And my nice new reindeer hairband that Gladys Friday bought for me?' She put her hands up to her hair and switched on a button. The antlers came to life with flashing lights.

'Yes.' I smiled widely. 'They're very festive!'

She admired herself in the mirror. 'What do you think I look like?' she asked.

'You look like…' I tried to find the right words as she stared at me, waiting for a good response. 'You look like a *Christmas Miracle!*'

Bett was delighted. '*A Christmas Miracle!*' She sighed happily. 'Thank you, Emmeline Rose. That's exactly how I feel.'

We walked out of the front door to join the Christmas party in the gym hall. Quinn, Tyler and Little Charlie were standing outside. All three of them looked taken aback when they saw Bett.

'I've got a new tracksuit, Quinn Davies!' Bett showed off her outfit.

'I can see,' replied Quinn. 'It's quality, innit?'

Bett smiled and nodded, before something caught her eye over by the gym hall.

'Who's that skinny boy?' Bett squinted to try and get a better look.

'*Oh–My–Donald–Duck!*' Quinn's eyes widened. 'It's *Lucas.*'

We all rushed over.

'Alright, Lucas?' Quinn and Little Charlie said at the same time.

'Alright, girls?' He winked at them. 'Is Karra here, by any chance?'

I went inside to get Karra.

'You have a visitor.' I nodded my head towards the door.

Karra's eyes followed mine, and they narrowed when she saw who was waiting for her.

She went outside to see Lucas, but told us we weren't allowed to go with her. As soon as she left, we crept behind the door and lined up perfectly by the gap in the corner, so we could see what was going on. Karra must have heard us shuffling, because she turned around to see a set of five heads stacked up, one on top of the other, staring at her through the side of the door.

'What do you want, Lucas?' asked Karra.

He moved closer to try and kiss her, but she put her hand up to block her face.

'Babycakes, *you* are looking *fiiit*!' Lucas wolf whistled at Karra. 'Why are you rejecting Lucas's kisses? Give Lucas some sugar, yeah?' He tried to put his arms around her, but she moved away.

Karra frowned at the boy. 'I'm not being funny or anything, but what are you doing here? I haven't seen you for *weeks*. Sticky Vicky dumped you, has she? Well, if you think I'm going to settle for that *skank's* sloppy seconds, you can think again.'

'*WOAH!*' Lucas threw his hands in the air to show how offended he was. 'First of all, let's get one thing straight, yeah? Sticky Vicky did *not* dump Lucas. The girl is high maintenance, and Lucas don't *do* high maintenance. I got to concentrate on my music and stuff, haven't I? I can't afford to have distractions like that.'

'So why are you here?' Karra folded her arms.

'To see *you*, innit? Come on, Karra…' He tried to kiss her again. 'You *know* you've missed me.'

Ew. This boy was a real muff, wasn't he?

'What's going on?' Beano saw us hiding. 'Why are you all lined up like *Mission-Frigging-Impossible*, spying behind the door, you freaks?'

'*SHHHH!*' I put my index finger to my mouth.

Beano joined us behind the door, just in time to see Karra pulling away from Lucas and telling him to leave her alone.

Lucas stepped forward aggressively. 'What's your *problem*?' He waved his hands around. 'You think you're too good for Lucas, do you?'

Karra looked uncertain.

Lucas started laughing. '*Oh-my-life!* You *DO!*' He gave her a stinking look. 'This is *too* funny, Karra! Come on, babe. You *know* you won't get no better than Lucas. You ain't exactly Ariana Grande, innit?'

Karra looked down at the floor.

'It's not like you've got the brains to make up for it either!' He smirked. 'And to top it all off, you're a *fridge*! Why do you think I had to keep going back to Sticky Vicky all the time?'

We all gasped in shock from behind the door. Did he really just say those things?

'OMG,' whispered Quinn. 'That's like … *totes inappropes.*'

What a pig. I didn't know what Karra had ever seen in that boy. No wonder she was always so on edge when she was going out with him. He probably made her feel like *crap*! I couldn't just stand there and watch him speak to my friend like that.

I walked outside.

'*Oi.*' I stood next to Karra and gave Lucas the evil eye.

He looked me up and down. 'You didn't tell me you had such *hot* friends, Karra.' He winked.

'Excuse me,' I said. 'Please don't speak about me like that. I don't appreciate it.'

'Ooooo!' Lucas mocked me. 'Feisty, much? Lucas luuurrrves me some feisty laydeees!'

He swung his hips from side to side and fist-pumped the air at the same time.

'*Come on*, Karra,' he pleaded with her. 'Lucas been working on my personal growth.' He bit his lip in a way that he thought was seductive. 'Maybe you can bring your feisty friend out with us, and the two of you together can help me '*grow*' as a man … *if you know what I mean.*'

He looked down to his trousers and moved his eyebrows up and down.

If I wasn't so mortified, I would have laughed. Who was this kid? And what *planet* was he from?

I scowled at him and poked my finger into his chest to tell him off. 'Now, *you* listen to me, you son of a motherless GOAT!'

He staggered back.

'Firstly…' I prodded his jacket as I scolded him. 'I don't know why you've come here, but Karra clearly isn't interested in you. Probably because she's realised what a complete and utter *cock* you are!'

He gawked at me.

'Secondly…' I continued my rant. 'Stop referring to yourself in the third person, because it's really annoying and just plain *stupid*!'

Karra started giggling and Lucas looked puzzled because he didn't have a clue what I meant.

'And thirdly…' I narrowed my eyes at him. 'An erection does not … I repeat, NOT count as *personal growth*!'

We heard sniggering from behind the gym-hall door.

Karra laughed out loud and put her arm around my shoulder.

'What she chattin' about?' Lucas raised an eyebrow to Karra. 'Is she drunk or what?'

'No,' replied Karra. 'She's just too smart for the likes of you. And while we're at it, so am I.'

'You're *what*?' asked Lucas.

'Way too smart for boys like you,' said Karra.

Just then, Beano came out of the gym hall and put his arms around Karra's waist.

Karra looked surprised, but Beano winked at her on the sly, so she went along with it.

'*Oh-my-life,*' said Beano. 'You are *lushness* personified. *Oooft!* You're mint! I want to smash the pasty off you!'

Lucas blinked in shock.

'Ariana Grande ain't got nothing on you!' Beano nuzzled Karra's neck and she looked a bit embarrassed.

Lucas's eyes nearly popped out of his head.

'Oh, yes…' said Beano. 'I'm going to train that Va-dragon like a pro!'

'OK, Beano!' I cringed. 'I think we get the picture.'

'Too far?' asked Beano.

I nodded.

'Sorry,' he said to Karra. 'I would never disrespect you. You're far too good for that.' He tried to redeem himself. 'It won't happen again.'

Karra chuckled at his backward attempt of sticking up for her.

Lucas nodded towards Beano. 'Who's this?'

'My name's Beano.' He tilted his hat to greet Lucas. 'I'm Karra's *boyfriend.* Who are *you?*'

'He's…' Karra looked at Lucas for the last time. 'He's *nobody.*'

Lucas looked thoroughly put in his place.

Beano took her hand. 'Come on, Karra. Let's go back into the party.'

Lucas walked away, looking rejected and embarrassed.

He would never be able to make Karra feel bad about herself again.

Inside, the girls were squealing at the drama that had just unfolded right before their eyes. Even if it *was* from behind a door.

Beano and Karra let go of each other's hand.

'You *do* know that was just pretend, yeah?' Beano said to Karra.

'Yeah, like I'd ever really get it on with you.' Karra pulled her most disgusted face.

'I don't want you coming on to me all the time now – making things all uncomfortable and stuff.' Beano grinned at her.

'*Don't worry,*' Karra replied sarcastically. 'I'll try my best to *resist* you.'

They smiled awkwardly at each other.

'Cheers, Beano.' Karra hugged him. 'What you did, out there … it was really nice of you.'

'You're my friend,' he replied. 'I'll always support you.'

'I know,' said Karra. 'And Lucas's face was classic! Did you see how annoyed he looked when he thought you were my boyfriend?'

'Yeah, well, he deserved it.' Beano coughed nervously. 'If I was your boyfriend, I would never treat you the way he did. You should treat a lady with respect.'

Karra blushed. 'You think I'm a *lady*?'

'Yeah, of course you are.' His face went bright red. 'I think you're an *epic lady*.'

'Cheers,' said Karra.

'You're welcome,' replied Beano. 'Now, come on. Let's get smashed on them cocktails!'

THIRTY-SIX

It was a gloomy day. Everything felt slightly ominous. I tried to breathe, but I was puffed out. My dad was walking in front of me, and he was walking too fast for me to catch up. The faster I tried to walk, the slower and heavier my legs felt.

I called out to him, but he couldn't hear me.

Hurry up, Em, my subconscious told me off. *You're going to miss him if you don't get a move on.*

He started walking up a hill. I struggled to run after him. Everything was in slow-motion. My brain was telling my legs to run, but my body wasn't responding.

At the bottom of the hill, there was a little park with a wonderful white rose bush by the gate. It was the same rose bush that had grown in our garden for years.

We stood at the top and bottom of the hill. The rain was drizzling and just the thought of having to walk up that hill to see him made my legs ache.

I looked at Dad and everything felt so … familiar. And yet something seemed out of place.

I tried to work it out, but my mind was fuzzy.

Think, Em, think.

I searched around me to see what the time was. Usually, I had a good instinct for the time when there were no clocks in sight. But here, I couldn't even tell whether it was day or night. I knew that it was New Year's Eve, but that was the only solid fact I was certain of.

The air seemed different somehow. I felt so connected to it. There was no separation between me and … anything. What a strange feeling.

Something cold hit my face. I looked up and saw tiny snowflakes starting to fall around me.

It was *snowing*! *Yessss!*

Within seconds, the entire place was covered in a blanket of pure white snow that seemed to be studded with diamonds. The beauty of it took my breath away. And then out of nowhere, something *amazing* happened.

The sun came out, and the whole place *lit up*. It was so bright that it hurt my eyes at first, but then it settled a bit, so I could see properly.

Dad was here – with his arms around me. I stood there for ages, enjoying the familiar, comforting, clean smell of the washing powder on his jumper. Something in my head told me to cherish this moment. I couldn't remember why it was so important, but I instinctively squeezed my dad tight; that wonderful hug that I'd missed so much.

I looked at him closely. 'There's something different about you,' I said.

He laughed. 'What do you mean?'

'I'm not sure,' I replied. 'But there's a glow about you.'

'That's because I'm healthy again,' he said.

I studied his face and thought how perfect his skin looked. It almost sparkled. And his eyes … I'd never seen them so healthy and *alive*.

He turned to look at the rose bush by the gate. It was coated with shimmering snowflakes that were tinged with a pink blush by the sun. One of the beautiful white roses loosened from the bush and floated through the air to my dad.

He handed the stunning rose to me. 'Will you give this to your mother, please? Tell her it's a special gift from me. She'll understand.'

'Of course I will.'

I smelt the rose. It was intoxicating and wonderful. I wished that I could have one for myself.

He must have read my mind, because he cast his eyes back to the rose bush and another three white roses came floating over to him.

He handed one of them to me. 'This one is for you, Em.

Keep it with you, in your heart. Trust in yourself and know that Nana Rose and I are always taking care of you.'

'Thank you,' I said, inhaling the scent of the white petals.

He handed me another one. 'This one is for my little angel, Freya. As the roses grow, so will her strength. I hope to see her a lot more as she gets older.'

'She'll love it,' I said.

I didn't have a *clue* what he was talking about, but for some reason, I didn't care. Everything he was saying made total sense, even if I didn't understand any of it.

He handed me a final white rose. 'And this one is for Grandma Coalman,' he said. 'Please tell her that I will always be grateful for all that she did for me, and that she really is a wonderful mother.'

I nodded and took the rose carefully from him. I held all four roses in my hands.

He looked over to the white rose bush and said, 'I've been growing them special. I know that it's taken a little while, but now they're ready for you all.'

I smiled.

He waved his hand towards the rose bush, like a magician. White petals moved gently from the branches and danced through the crisp air, taking on a life of their own. They floated all around us, mingling happily with the snowflakes in the bright blue sky. They waltzed together in harmony, and I laughed at the dazzling show.

I held out my arms to catch some in my hands, and I looked down at my feet, fascinated by the carpet of white petals and snow on the ground.

When I looked back up, Dad was gone.

And then I woke up.

THIRTY-SEVEN

It was New Year's Day and I was sitting in the back of Mel's car.

I started thinking about the night before.

The dream.

It had felt so vivid, so real. I could have sworn that it was more than just a dream, but how could that be?

I was probably reading too much into it. I was really hyper when I went to bed the night before, so maybe my sleeping pattern had been messed up.

Perhaps it was common for strange dreams to occur on New Year's Eve.

Should I speak to Mum about it? She would be able to interpret the dream. She was clever like that. But was she strong enough? Would it upset her? I wasn't sure. Maybe it was best to just forget the whole thing.

'So, what are you all doing for New Year's Day?' Mel interrupted my thoughts.

'We're going to that new Italian place that's just opened in The Bay,' I answered.

'That'll be nice.' Mel smiled and then beeped her horn at the car in front because it had stopped suddenly at the bottom of the hill.

I stared out of the window, lost in a world of my own.

A single snowflake landed on the window, right by my nose.

'Mel!' I got excited. 'Look! It's *snowing*!'

She beeped again at the car in front.

I opened the window and stuck my hand out in the cold air to feel the slushy white snowflakes fall onto my hand. I couln't believe it was snowing. Just like my dream!

I looked across to the park at the bottom of the hill.

The park looked different, somehow.

BEEP! BEEP!

'COME ON! I HAVEN'T GOT ALL DAY!' Mel shouted at the car.

I studied the park, trying to figure out what was different about it. Why did I feel like there was something missing?

The man in front stuck his middle finger up. Mel looked outraged and returned the gesture furiously.

'MEN!' she shouted. 'They think they're so much better than us, don't they?'

I nodded to keep her happy.

'They're all the same,' she said. 'You'd swear their poop smelt of roses, the way they carry on.'

Roses!

That was it! There were no roses in the park!

The rose bush was missing.

I looked around, but I couldn't see it anywhere.

How could it just not be there?

'Thank you very much, you idiot!' Mel waved at the man in front, pulling faces at him as she drove away.

I looked through the back window of the car, staring at the place where the lovely white rose bush used to be.

It was just … *gone.*

Mel dropped me off at Mum's house.

I was still thinking about the white rose bush as I walked in to find Grandma Coalman decorating a cake.

'That looks delish, Gram!' I ran my finger through the buttercream.

'Get lost!' She smacked my hand. 'This is a work of art! I got the recipe off the interweb.'

'You're getting really good at doing things online, aren't you?'

'That's because my friends help me,' she replied.

'What friends?' I looked suspiciously at her. 'Have you been chatting to strangers on the internet? That can be dangerous, Gram!'

'Yes, but these people are my friends. They help me with everything!'

'Well, who are they?' I asked.

'I don't know their names, but they work at a company called Google,' she answered. 'I tell you what, Em ... the service is *fantastic*! I type my query into the question box, and they answer me *straight away*! Sometimes they get the answers wrong, but they always try their best. They've been a tremendous support for me.'

I smiled and put the kettle on to make everyone a cup of tea.

'Hello, love!' Mum came into the kitchen.

'Hi, Mum. Are you having a nice New Year?'

'It's nicer now that we're all together,' she replied. 'Did you have a good night with your friends?'

I nodded as I reached for the milk out of the fridge.

'Where's Freya?' Mum asked Grandma Coalman.

'Outside,' Grandma Coalman replied.

Mum frowned a little. 'It's a bit chilly to be playing outside, isn't it? Have you seen that snow?'

'Leave her to it,' said Grandma Coalman. 'She's wearing a coat, and she's quiet. That's good enough for me!'

I was still thinking about the rose bush as the kettle boiled. Jolly Clive had told me that it was very rare to find roses in the winter. Perhaps they weren't able survive in the cold, and so they'd perished over New Year.

I took the tea bags out of the jar.

'Make mine a strong one.' Grandma Coalman nodded to the mugs. 'I like my tea the way I like my men: *strong and sweet!*' She chuckled at her own joke.

I stirred the tea and carried the mugs over to the kitchen table.

Grandma Coalman put her cake in the middle of the table and called Freya to come in and join us.

'CLOSE YOUR EYES!' Freya shouted to us from outside the door. 'I have a special gift for Mum.'

'*Oooo!* That's exciting!' Mum clapped her hands together.

We closed our eyes. I heard Freya walk into the kitchen.

A wonderful scent filled the room. I breathed in deeply, enjoying the perfumed air.

'OK,' said Freya. 'You can open them now.'

We opened our eyes.

Freya stood next to Mum, holding a bunch of beautiful white roses.

Mum threw her hands over her mouth. 'Where did you get those, Freya?' she asked. 'They're absolutely *gorgeous!*'

Mum turned to me and Grandma Coalman for an explanation, but neither of us knew.

'I picked them from the garden!' Freya looked very pleased with herself. 'They grew back last night.'

'What do you mean, they grew back last night? It's the middle of winter! Roses can't grow in this weather!' Mum got up from her chair and ran out the back door.

There, in the corner of the garden, was our lovely white rose bush. The one which hadn't grown since my dad passed away, but was now in full bloom for the first time in years.

The sun broke through the clouds, lighting up the crisp winter's day and highlighting the rose bush in all its pure white glory.

The white rose bush had left the park and come to us!

That must have been what Dad meant in my dream, when he said that the roses were ready for us. Maybe the dream wasn't just a dream, after all.

But how could it grow back in one night? Was that even possible?

I gave up trying to work it all out. If I had learned anything over the last couple of months, it was that some things are just meant to be accepted as they are. Human beings want to put an explanation to everything, but the truth is that every day, we are surrounded by thousands of little synchronicities that we are mostly unaware of. Some of them, we can see, hear, smell, taste and touch. And some, we can only feel with our hearts – if we blink, we miss them. Sometimes, we just have to have faith.

I looked across at Mum. She had the biggest smile on her face. 'I can't *believe* it!' She started giggling.

'They're from Dad,' said Freya.

We turned to her.

'I've tried to tell you before.' Freya stood with her hands on her hips. 'But you *never* listen to me! When I brought those roses to you in the hospital, Dad told me to get them for you. He told me to get white ones, but I liked the yellow ones best. Sorry about that!'

Mum, Grandma Coalman and I tried to take in what she was saying.

Freya continued. 'When we all went out to dinner, Mel had little white roses on her bag. I tried to tell you then that Dad had visited me the week before and told me that you like white roses. But you shouted at me for saying it!'

We all stared at her.

'And when we put the Christmas tree up, I gave you that bauble with the white rose on it, but you didn't take any notice of me!' Freya sulked. 'I've tried loads of times to give you something from Dad. He so wanted you to have a white rose. But you *just … never … listen.*'

'What do you mean, Dad tells you?' Grandma Coalman asked.

Freya looked at Grandma Coalman as if she was stupid. 'He tells me. He speaks to me. You think these two are the only ones in this family who are psycho?'

'Psychic,' Grandma Coalman corrected her.

'Yeah, that's what I said.' Freya waved her hand dismissively. 'Nana Rose could see stuff, Mum can feel stuff, and Emmeline can hear stuff. But *I* can do *all three*!'

We gawked at her, our mouths open.

'I did try to tell you ages ago,' Freya said to Grandma Coalman. 'You said that the word angel means messenger, remember?'

Grandma Coalman nodded at the memory from Christmas.

'Well, I'm a messenger!' Freya grinned proudly. 'That's how I can do everything that Nana Rose, Mum and Emmeline can do – because I have to be extra strong to be a messenger. And I'm the *first* one in our family to *ever* be one.'

I was stunned. This meant that Freya was a…

'A Channel,' said Mum.

Grandma Coalman looked like she was going to faint.

I turned to Mum. She was holding the bunch of white roses that Freya had given her. She started crying quietly. Not sad tears, but happy tears.

'Dad said that they're important because they're like our name,' Freya said to Mum.

Mum looked up and nodded. '*Rose,*' she said. 'It was a joke between us, because I wouldn't change my name to Coalman when we got married.'

Grandma Coalman wrinkled her nose in disapproval.

Mum smiled at me. '*A white rose,*' she said.

I knew in that moment that this was the sign Mum had been waiting for, all this time.

We stood with the fresh winter's chill on our cheeks.

The glow of the New Year sun pushed its way through the clouds. The sky was glittery from the snow.

I admired the beautiful rose bush that had once again blossomed in our garden, and my heart was filled with a sense of magic, as the white petals sparkled and shone like velvet in the sunlight.

CHAPTER HEADINGS

We held a competition for the drawings for the chapter headings for artists aged 11-18. It has been a joy to see the wonderful work sent to us. The selected shortlist worked with the author, Maria, to produce a piece that would fit each chapter. Our congratulations to the artists selected, listed here, we really appreciate the excellent work you've put into this, and our great thanks to everyone who entered.

Chapter 1: Saima Ali – Coleg y Cymoedd, Nantgarw.

Chapter 2: Kristopher Ware – Coleg y Cymoedd, Nantgarw.

Chapter 3: Seren Fowler – Ysgol Gyfun Garth Olwg, Pontypridd.

Chapter 4: Aerun Edwards – Coleg y Cymoedd, Nantgarw.

Chapter 5: Morghann Linnett-Richardson – St Edwards College, Liverpool.

Chapter 6: Brandon Wangiel – Coleg y Cymoedd, Nantgarw.

Chapter 7: Lily Beer-Doblon – Ysgol Penglais School, Aberystwyth.

Chapter 8: Marion Williams – Willows High School, Cardiff.

Chapter 9: Lauren Mogford – Ysgol Gyfun Garth Olwg, Pontypridd.

Chapter 26: Marion Williams – Willows High School, Cardiff.

Chapter 27: Stella Marie Sheppard – Coleg y Cymoedd, Nantgarw.

Chapter 28: Petra Silva – Coleg y Cymoedd, Nantgarw.

Chapter 29: Jess Evans-Equeall – Coleg y Cymoedd, Nantgarw.

Chapter 30: Rosie Phillips – North Walsham High School, Norfolk.

Chapter 31: Lowri Keane – Radyr Comprehensive School, Cardiff.

Chapter 32: Bibiana Viazzani – St. Clare's School, Porthcawl.

Chapter 33: McCory Harris – Coleg y Cymoedd, Nantgarw.

Chapter 34: Lucy Buckland – Coleg y Cymoedd, Nantgarw.

Chapter 35: Brandon Wangiel – Coleg y Cymoedd, Nantgarw.

Chapter 36: Lily Beer-Doblon – Ysgol Penglais School, Aberystwyth.

Chapter 37: Charla Marie Grace – Ysgol Gyfun Garth Olwg, Pontypridd.

Scene break rose: Jamie Smith, Pontypridd.

AUTHOR'S ACKNOWLEDGEMENTS

I would like to express my gratitude to the many people who have been with me over the course of the years, and I ask forgiveness of all those whose names I have failed to mention. Whether it was yesterday, or when I first started the book, whether it was one time, or a hundred, thank you. You all know who you are.

Janet Thomas & Penny Thomas at Firefly Press: thank you for seeing the diamond in the rough.

Beth Reekles, Rhian Elizabeth & Philip Gross: thank you both for your time and your quotes!

Paul Lavagna, Nantgarw Students & Staff: thank you for the time and effort you put into the *White Petals* project.

White Petals Illustrators: thank you so much for your time, effort and creativity. I'm so proud to have your illustrations in the book.

Gav & Lou: thank you for always letting me stay at your flat when I was working on the book in London.

Kelly Cairns: thank you for giving Megan a name. Thanks for Steps & for S-S-Samuel.

Jan Delbridge, Jan Clunn, Sherry Evans & Yvonne White: thank you for the support, the Friday nights, and for teaching me so much.

Rhondda Cynon Taff & Caerphilly Borough Council: thank you to all the social workers, mental health professionals and young people in care. Your input really helped me to write the novel as authentically as possible.

Rob Middlehurst: thank you for always *getting it, and* for being the best dissertation tutor that I could have asked for.

Philip Gross: thank you for teaching me how to write for the reader, instead of myself.

Gemma Starling, Rebecca O'Sullivan, Danielle Bowen, Gunita Sapa, Rosalie Jones & Glamorgan Classmates: heartfelt thanks for the workshops & feedback, the friendship & support, the faith & guidance.

Karina Gregory & Dewi Mitchell: thank you for always getting excited with me, and helping me with story ideas!

Gareth Jacob: thank you for the guidance, the dinners, the first laptop, and for being my best best mate.

Anna Davis: thank you for helping me to be objective with the story, and for the ongoing support.

Curtis Brown Creative (2011): *Anna, Jake, Emily, Chris, Barney, Bob, Jessie, Dan, Jo, Catherine L, Catherine B, Gill, Nan, Amy, Liesel and Antonia:* warmest thanks for the Captain's Cabin, the encouragement, and all the workshops. Also, thank you for making me keep the lucky cardigan!

Family:

My lovely family: Mam, Gav, Kaylee, Auntie Tina & Nanny: thank you for the family dinners, afternoon tea, the support, guidance, laughs & loyalty. I am truly grateful to have you all in my life. If I could choose again, I'd still choose you lot – *every time*.

My extended family: thank you for the dinners, the laughs and all the alcohol! Both sides of the family are pretty awesome and I feel lucky to have you all in my life.

Charla: thank you for always championing me, even though it is *you* who is the real champion. You make me laugh every day, and you really arc my sunshine.

Jamie: thank you for the endless support, for listening to countless chapters ovcr countless cups of tea, and for being a wonderful companion.

Bella: thank you for your goofy doggy smile, and for keeping me company every day when I write. You're a better listener than most!

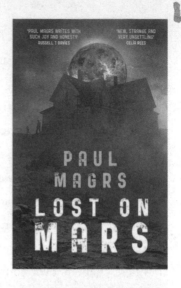

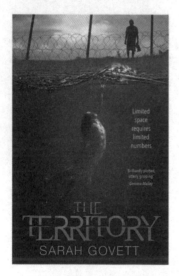

'truly unputdownable', '*so* good', 'strange and satisfying', 'NOTHING like I expected ... but EVERYTHING you would look for...'

Unforgettable YA fiction from Firefly Press
www.fireflypress.co.uk
@FireflyPress